# Glyndŵr's Daughter

# Glyndŵr's Daughter

## JOHN·HUGHES

yLolfa

First impression: 2012
Second impression: 2013

Cover photograph: Natalia Ciobanu

ISBN: 978 1 84771 331 5

Published and printed in Wales
on paper from well maintained forests by
Y Lolfa Cyf., Talybont, Ceredigion SY24 5HE
*e-mail* ylolfa@ylolfa.com
*website* www.ylolfa.com
*tel* 01970 832 304
*fax* 832 782

Gwenllian was Owain Glyndŵr's daughter.
Her life was tied to the ebb and flow of her father's war.

A story inspired by poems written by
Lewis Glyn Cothi, Llawdden and Ieuan Gyfannedd.

Verses from an elegy to Gwenllian, Owain Glyndŵr's
daughter and the wife of Philip ap Rhys of Cenarth, written
by Lewis Glyn Cothi.

Penillion o farwnad Gwenllian, merch Owain Glyndŵr a
gwraig Philip ap Rhys o Genarth, gan Lewis Glyn Cothi.

Y wraig a oedd aur ei gwallt,
O ryw hyddod y Rhuddallt;
Llawen vu Wenllian verch
Owain hen, Duw'n ei hanerch.

Y iaith, er ban aeth i'r bedd,
O'i thir a aeth i orwedd;
Diogach bellach i'r barth,
Y daw gweiniaid i Genarth.

Nid oedd Wenllian annoeth,
A Gwen oedd dda ac yn ddoeth.
A'i thad oedd D'wysawg cadarn,
A holl Gymmru vu'n ei varn;

Duw a ethol y doethion,
Minnau sydd val briwydd bron.
A Iesu vo cynnwyswr
I Luned wen o Lyn Dwr!

# Chapter 1

**23 June 1401**

THE ARROW WAS through his throat before anyone knew that there was an ambush in the making. The noise of the impact drew everyone's attention and with blood spraying in all directions they knew that he would be dead in minutes. The two oxen drawing the cart instantly became aware that there was an incident and stopped in their tracks.

"Where did it come from?" Gwenllian shouted in fear, not so much for herself but for her child.

She shouted to Rhys, her seven-year-old son, in the cart behind her, "Keep down on the floor of the cart."

But talking to Rhys was a waste of effort: he was fast asleep and was not disturbed by the noise of the arrow or its effect.

Philip was already off his horse with an arrow set in his bow ready to fire. He called to Gwenllian, "Get off your horse."

Three men were running at them across the river armed with swords and spears, but not for long. The lead attacker was struck squarely in the chest by Philip's arrow. When he fell in the river the other two slowed and stumbled momentarily, giving Philip time, from his crouched position, to fire another arrow into the man on the right, the larger of the two, bringing him to his knees in the river.

The third attacker, uninjured, stopped and went to the stricken man's assistance, helping him back from the middle of the river as quickly as he could. He half dragged and half carried the wounded man to the far bank, where he left him and ran beyond the riverbank up the hill opposite in full retreat and total panic. Philip did not fire his third arrow: he saw no point in killing or injuring anyone unnecessarily.

It was all over. Perfect peace reigned again in this beautiful valley at the Rhyd-y-groes ford on the river Ystwyth.

It was a beautiful June day, two days after the longest day of the year, with many of the wild flowers in full bloom. The buttercups were particularly prevalent and their colour did not fade following the deaths. The rooks at the nearby rookery were finishing feeding their last brood of young rooks for the year but still had the need and the energy to make their endless croaking, oblivious of the violence that had taken place so near their home.

The river was shallow at the ford but fast moving and the current had carried the dead man's spear away, but his body had been wedged, face downward against two protruding stones. The river was crystal clear but the water flowing downstream of the dead man was coloured red by the blood streaming from his lifeless body. Minutes after the violent encounter, which had left two men dead, the ford area was again tranquil, quiet and safe to cross.

Gwenllian ran to check that Rhys, her eldest son, was uninjured in the cart. After the initial shock of finding him lifeless she realised that he was asleep, but checked his body thoroughly for any injuries. Only after completing the check was she satisfied that he was unharmed.

As her nerves calmed she realised that she could hear, faintly above the sound of the river, the groans of the injured man on the opposite bank. Philip walked across the river sword in hand, ignoring the body in the river. He disarmed the injured man of his sword without difficulty and realised quickly that he posed no immediate threat.

"Is Rhys safe?" Philip called to Gwenllian anxiously.

"He's fine. He slept through it," she replied.

"Take the sword from the cart and stay on guard," Philip called back as he climbed higher up the bank and found another two injured young men lying on their backs and hidden from view of anyone crossing the ford. They had no swords or any other weapon and were incapable of putting up any resistance. He returned to the river and dragged the body from the water on to the bank, placing him near his injured comrade.

Gwenllian was keeping an eye on the soldier who had run from the area. She could see him about half a mile away running as fast as he could uphill and away from the river.

Still with his sword in his hand Philip shouted across the river, "All is well. There is no danger here."

Relieved, Gwenllian turned her attention to the dead cart driver, a valued and trusted farm hand, but realising that there was nothing she could do for him, she mounted her horse and crossed the river. She did not have to tell Philip that Hywel was dead: he knew that the arrow had severed the main artery as it passed through his throat.

Philip told her that there were two other badly injured men higher up the bank just out of her sight and returned to the wounded man brought from the river. Holding the point of his sword to his throat Philip asked him, "Who are you?"

"Jenkin," the man replied quietly while trying to raise himself on to one elbow.

"Where are you from?" asked Philip maintaining the slight pressure with the point of his sword.

"Pembroke," he replied slumping back flat on his back.

"What are you doing here?"

"All of us have been in a battle in the Hyddgen valley on the side of Pumlumon with Glyndŵr's rebels and our army was beaten. Hundreds of us have been killed," said Jenkin with difficulty, partly because of the sword at his throat.

Philip and Gwenllian looked at each other in shock. They knew that Glyndŵr's men were active in the north and had heard in recent weeks that there had been an occasional skirmish involving the rebels and groups loyal to the king but they had no idea that there had been a battle pending, never mind fought and won by Glyndŵr.

"When was this battle?" asked Philip.

Jenkin replied, "Yesterday afternoon."

"Were the other two up there also wounded in the battle?" asked Philip taking his sword away from Jenkin's throat to point up the river bank.

"Yes," said Jenkin. "We managed to get them this far and we wanted your cart to take them south and home. We were exhausted. It's been a disaster."

"Tell us exactly what happened," ordered Philip as he glanced at Gwenllian, who was listening with great interest.

Jenkin, slowly at first, described how an army of about one thousand five hundred soldiers was raised in south-west Wales and made up, in the main, of Flemish settlers who were determined to sort out the Glyndŵr rebels once and for all. They intended to stop any further raids on their area from the north and at the same time show that they supported the king in his effort to sort out the rebels.

"We marched up through Ceredigion along the coast in very good spirits, confident in the knowledge that we were going to surprise the rebels and teach them a lesson. We were going to capture Glyndŵr and put an end to his destructive and unlawful behaviour," Jenkin said with a mixture of sadness and cynicism in his voice.

Jenkin, gaining confidence that he was not going to be

killed immediately, continued, "Our army moved into the mountains around Pumlumon and advanced up the narrow Hyddgen valley where our commanders were confident the rebels were hiding. Our spies had told our leaders that the rebels were weak and drunk most of the time and would be easily defeated."

"Do you want a mouthful of water from the river?" Gwenllian asked.

"Yes, desperately," the wounded man replied and Gwenllian quickly obliged raising a handful of water to Jenkin's mouth.

Jenkin continued, "When we reached the Hyddgen area there was no sign of the rebels but there was quite a thick mist on the higher slopes. Some of us were tired from the uphill march and we sat down near some white rocks. All was peaceful, tranquil and silent except for the cat-like call of a buzzard high above us – quite an eerie sound in the mountains. But we were in high spirits and confident."

With a painful look on his face, caused either by the pain he was in from the wound or from the actions that he was recalling, he said, "Without any warning the rebels descended on us with great speed and force. The air was suddenly full of arrows, swinging swords and sharp spears. The noise was deafening. Some of my friends said they had seen the golden dragon banner unfold but I saw nothing. Nothing, but blood. I was struck in the face by a hand sliced off with a sword."

He could not carry on immediately and Gwenllian offered him more water which he accepted.

"There weren't many of them," he said. "But they were fierce and desperate looking. There was a fury and determination about them that we could not match. At first they forced us back slowly but we were soon running away from them. They kept coming after us and it was then that many of my friends were killed. If they tripped or slowed for any reason the rebels were on them and killing them with their swords and spears."

"It was horrendous," Jenkin added, shaking his head in disbelief.

Jenkin was now in a state where he wanted to talk about what had happened. He wanted to get it off his chest, he wanted people to know and share his disappointment, despair and guilt. "I had to leave my friends. I had to allow them to be killed. I couldn't do anything, could I?" he queried hopefully but his appeal to be absolved of blame through his tears drew no comment from Philip or Gwenllian.

"One of my friends was only twelve years old but they showed no mercy to anyone. They behaved like wild animals, killing and screaming with success," he continued.

To steer the subject away from the killing Gwenllian asked him, "How did you get here?"

"A group of five of us had come together to help each other," said Jenkin. "I knew one of the injured men: the one with the sword cut on his thigh. We are from the same village near Pembroke. I came across him a mile or two from the battle site and helped him to reach the river ford at Rhyd-y-groes. The others arrived a few hours later and we decided that they would never be able to complete the journey home on foot. We did not wish to leave anyone behind to perish or be slaughtered by the rebels." Jenkin's fear again overwhelmed him.

"Are they here?" he asked. "They are hunting for me and my friends."

Gwenllian said to Philip "I think he's hallucinating."

"He's frightened," he said to Gwenllian. Turning to

Jenkin, he tried to reassure him, "There is nothing to worry about now. You will be cared for and they won't pursue you this far."

Jenkin recovered a little after Philip's reassurance and confessed, "When we came to this ford we had decided to wait until a cart came. We did not trust anyone and we decided to attack the driver of the first cart that arrived at the ford, take the cart and use it to get all of us to Pembroke. Foolishly we did not expect you to fight back."

Gwenllian felt sorry for all the injured soldiers, particularly Jenkin who was only a young man, barely in his twenties, and she was thinking of her own boys being in the same predicament when they would be older. She said to Philip, "There is nothing to be gained from more bloodshed. I know that they have killed Hywel but I think that we should help them as much as possible to get home." Then added, "That is, without putting our own lives at risk."

Philip agreed that there was nothing to be gained from letting these young men perish. Gwenllian examined Jenkin's wound and found that the arrow had entered just below his left shoulder. He had managed to remove it himself but had lost a lot of blood. She collected some dock leaves and told him to hold them tight on the wound. She had a strong faith in the healing power of the dock leaf. She made much wider use of them than the treatment of nettle stings on her boys.

Meanwhile, Philip had gone to see to the other two wounded soldiers, who had sword and spear cuts to their arms and legs. They were also very young and not much more than boys. Some of the cuts were deep and there had been a substantial loss of blood. One soldier was obviously in more pain than the other and was quiet except when he occasionally sobbed and asked for his mother.

Again, Gwenllian applied large dock leaves to all the wounds and advised them to hold them tight on the wounds. Though they had tried to kill her and Philip she felt sympathetic towards them and hoped that they would survive and somehow get home safely. She was thankful that Rhys and Philip were unharmed.

Alone with Philip she asked him, "Can we believe what Jenkin said?"

"I think so," replied Philip.

"What can we do to help these young men and boys?" she asked.

"We've done what we can, Gwenllian. It's up to them now. We had better be on our way home."

"I'm not happy about leaving them here and we passed a Knights Hospitaller of St John about a mile back. Could we not take them there?" Gwenllian asked.

Philip was not so sympathetic and told her that he was more concerned with getting Rhys home safely. This worked on her and she agreed to leave the wounded at the ford. Someone was bound to stop and help them, she thought.

While they were arranging Hywel's body in the cart and preparing to continue their journey, an oxen-drawn cart driven by two monks came down the road towards them from the direction of Cwm Ystwyth. When the monks reached the ford they stopped and looked on in amazement at the sight by the river.

Philip, assisted by Gwenllian, explained to the monks what had happened by the ford and told them that there had been a battle in the mountains a few miles to the north between an army from the south-west and Glyndŵr's men.

The monks explained that they had travelled from the abbey at Cwm Hir that morning and were on their way to the abbey of Ystrad Fflur. They had not heard any news of any battle.

Gwenllian asked the monks if they could take the injured men to the Knights Hospitaller of St John about a mile along their way at Ysbyty Ystwyth. If they found the hospital inundated with injured soldiers and unable to accept additional patients, could they take them on to the abbey at Ystrad Fflur?

The monks, very obligingly, agreed immediately and the three injured soldiers and their dead friend were placed in the monks' cart and they departed uphill towards Ysbyty Ystwyth. Gwenllian was relieved to see them on their way and felt sure that they would be cared for at the hospital and their wounds treated properly.

Philip, who was pleased to get started again, mounted his horse quickly and waved the small convoy on. Gwenllian took the reins of the cart and with her horse tied to the back they crossed the river and left Rhyd-y-groes to begin their journey through the Cwm Ystwyth valley. Thankfully, Rhys was still sleeping as they climbed into the mountains, initially on a track following the north bank of the river and proceeded as quickly as the oxen would allow.

Hywel was not married but had family on the north side of Rhayader and they decided to take his body to those relatives.

Philip, Gwenllian, Rhys and Hywel had crossed the Cambrian mountains and passed through Cwm Ystwyth on their journey to Philip's home in Glyn Aeron five days earlier to attend Philip's father's funeral.

On the way to Glyn Aeron they had crossed the mountains

with a group of horse riders and some others driving carts, but on the way back they had to do so on their own. At the start of the journey they were not particularly concerned to be on their own because Philip and Hywel were well armed and were skilled bowmen.

Naturally, they were more concerned about traversing this mountainous area than the hills of Ceredigion, and as a group they were one armed man down on this return journey. The attack had left them shocked and grieving for Hywel who had been a faithful and hard-working servant for many years at their Cenarth farmstead, situated a few miles south of Llanidloes. It is not surprising that they were alert and a little nervous as they plodded their way slowly into the mountains. The worry about their safety was paramount in Gwenllian's mind and the grief for the death of Hywel took second place. She regretted having taken Rhys with them.

The sides of the mountains were steep in the Cwm Ystwyth Manor, farmed by the monks of Ystrad Fflur. They cultivated the land on the valley floor, tended their sheep on the surrounding hills and mined copper and lead on the slopes.

Though there were many signs of human activity surrounding them in the valley, Gwenllian was unsure of their safety in Cwm Ystwyth and found the narrow valley threatening. Driving the cart on an unfamiliar track was also stressful.

After a period of silence broken only by the sound of the hooves on the gravel and the wheels grinding and slipping on some of the larger stones, she called to Philip on his horse just ahead of her, "I don't see any of the birds that were here when we came through a few days ago. Where have the ravens, the buzzards and the kites gone?"

Philip had also noticed their absence and had already guessed the reason and called back to her, "They have all gone to Hyddgen to pick at the flesh of the dead soldiers. There is plenty of food for them up in those mountains now and the birds know where to go for a feast."

The answer served to increase her unease, "I liked the sound of the buzzards mewing above us despite the fact that it was an eerie sound. I wish they were here now because the silence is even more unnerving."

Philip made no reply but called at the oxen to encourage them on their way to the river Ystwyth again, but this time higher up the valley where the river was much narrower than at Rhyd-y-groes. Gwenllian was glad that they had not left Hywel's body at Rhyd-y-groes to be eaten by the birds and the wild animals.

"Do you think Jenkin was telling the truth when he said that the rebels were running wildly about killing young men?" Gwenllian asked.

She often asked questions if there was something that unsettled her or that she did not fully understand and it was clear to Philip that she was concerned about something now. He also knew that she would pursue the issue until she would be satisfied with the answers.

Patiently he assured her, "In a battle no side can afford to show mercy until they are sure they have won the battle decisively. Remember that the men in a battle know that they could be killed themselves at any instant and in the heat of the moment they do not think what is the right and honourable thing to do. Once the enemy has been engaged in battle the soldiers must concentrate on killing the enemy. They have to kill or they will be killed."

Gwenllian was not happy with the answer but she said

nothing immediately. Philip, sensing that she was not satisfied with his answer and predicting another question, continued, "Yesterday, the war cry of the rebels as they started running at their enemy must have sent shivers through their own bodies as well as their enemies. Once they started running they knew they had to do their utmost to win and that meant trying to kill everyone in their path. The rebels did not have the luxury of having time to think about who to kill and who not to kill. I am sure they behaved honourably under the circumstances."

In her anxious state Gwenllian had many more questions on her mind and started by asking, "Why did the soldiers at the ford not wait until we were in the middle of the river before attacking?"

He replied, "They were young and inexperienced. Had they been a little more patient the result might have been very different. We were lucky to have only lost Hywel."

This shocked Gwenllian and she was silent for a while reflecting on his answer.

Disturbed by the experience at the ford and never having been present when Philip had killed anyone before, she wanted to know more about what soldiers did in war and so she asked, "Where do you stab a man with your sword when you intend to kill him?"

Philip, a little surprised by her question, replied, "In the heat of a battle you tend to swing your sword in all directions hoping you make any contact but in a one-against-one situation you push the sword into the body just below the ribs and then push it upwards."

She was concerned that the rebels had killed many of the young Flemish men unnecessarily and was worried that this would reflect badly on the rebels and their leader.

"After killing one man how do you stop?" she asked.

Philip understood her concern and felt that she deserved an answer. After a few moments of careful consideration he said, "Once they were engaged in the fight and the slaughter had started it would have been very difficult for the soldiers to return to normality immediately and much killing does take place after the battle is won – unfortunately it is normal."

He turned around on his horse to see how she was taking the answer. She glanced up at him and gave him a slight smile of approval.

This encouraged Philip to continue, "The soldier would not be sure that you had won and there is always confusion because you are not sure what is going on about you. Also, remember a soldier may have seen some of his comrades killed or injured and that will have made him very angry and he would inevitably be looking for revenge. The killing can continue for quite a while after the battle is won. The soldiers get so worked up they can't stop."

"I was concerned, having heard what Jenkin had to say, that their behaviour was barbaric," she said.

"Battles are battles," he said. "Don't worry about it – I am sure no one will be critical of the rebels or their leaders. Battles are not pleasant or honourable events."

He knew why she was showing so little concern about Hywel's murder by the ford: it was because she had greater concerns. She was anxious about the journey home and the safety of her eldest son. Members of her family would have been involved in the battle at Hyddgen and that would also be weighing heavily on her mind.

Philip, again turning around on his horse to look at her, reassured her further by saying, "Your father will have done all he could to control his men when it became clear that victory was theirs."

Again, she smiled gratefully at him.

"You must be hoping that your father and brothers have survived the battle without injury," he commented.

"Yes. I hope my father and brothers have survived the battle safely. I am pleased about their victory – I am delighted by it, really," she said as her thoughts drifted to think of her childhood, her father and the progress of the rebellion.

She realised that the rebellion would be boosted by the victory and in turn that could cause more difficulties for her and her family. Philip and Gwenllian had four sons: Rhys was seven years old, Dafydd was five, Ieuan was three and Meredydd was a year old. She was grateful that they were too young to become involved in the rebellion. She hoped and prayed that her boys would never become involved in any war and would not become victims of the present rebellion. She would do her utmost to keep them safe and out of harm's way.

Though she was not at the battle, Gwenllian was more involved than many in the battle at Hyddgen because her father, Owain Glyndŵr, was the leader of the rebellion.

Before he married, Glyndŵr had a relationship with Tudur ap Meredydd's daughter and out of this relationship Gwenllian had been born. She was brought up by her maternal grandfather and married at a young age to Philip ap Rhys of Cenarth, Gwerthrynion which was then part of the lordship of the Mortimer family and would, with the passage of time, become part of Radnorshire.

At the time of the battle of Hyddgen, Glyndŵr had been happily married to Margaret Hamer for many years and they had a number of children including Gruffydd, Meredydd, Alice, Janet and Margaret. It was a happy contended family and things were going well for them prior to the difficulties in north Wales when Owain had challenged Lord Grey of Ruthin over the possession of some land.

The news of the disagreement between Glyndŵr and Lord Grey had been brought to Cenarth by the poets and entertainers who visited frequently. Iolo, Gwenllian's favourite poet, was very keen on the story and thought it important but Gwenllian thought very little of it at the time and Philip gave it even less thought.

Then, on a date that she would remember for ever, the sixteenth day of September 1400, Gwenllian heard, from Iolo a few days after the event, that there had been a gathering of some Welsh nobles at Glyndyfrdwy and that Glyndŵr, her father, had been declared the new prince of Wales. Her father, a prince of Wales, it was difficult for her to absorb. She questioned Iolo numerous times during his visit, sure that he was pulling her leg and would tell her any second that it was a joke and that she could laugh. However, as he was leaving Cenarth, Iolo assured her that he was speaking the truth and she accepted his word.

She had no idea what it meant to be the daughter of a prince and far less what the consequences would be for her or her family. She was not always regarded as a member of the family anyway and so there were times when she would convince herself that it had nothing to do with her.

While attending the market at Llanidloes, she heard that three days after becoming the prince of Wales, Glyndŵr and a band of his supporters had attacked Ruthin, Denbigh, Rhyddlan, Flint, Hawarden and Holt. Her father was leading a full-scale rebellion. However, most people thought that it would be settled within weeks at the most with the king arriving at a compromise between all involved.

But a few days later, the rebels, under Glyndŵr's leadership, attacked Oswestry and Welshpool. This was bringing the fighting much closer to Cenarth and Gwenllian began to think it would not end as soon as she had expected. People were being killed and injured – surely there would be consequences. The king and his barons in the Marches of Wales could not continue to ignore this type of action for long.

However, shortly after the attack on Welshpool, the rebels were defeated in the Vyrnwy valley and they disappeared into the hills and mountains of north Wales. King Henry IV invaded north Wales in the October of the same year and went as far as Bangor without facing any significant resistance. On reaching Bangor, the king granted all of Glyndŵr's estates to the earl of Somerset. Again, this had no effect on Gwenllian and her family, and by the winter of 1401, even Glyndŵr's strongest supporters, with the exception of Iolo perhaps, thought that the rebellion was at an end. Many people felt pleased that someone had challenged the king's authority in Wales without causing too much death and destruction.

At times, it shocked Gwenllian to think that her father was at war with the king. There were other times when she was embarrassed by it but her overall feeling was of pride. She was proud that she was Glyndŵr's daughter and proud of his bravery.

Philip was calm about it all and decided that he would not get involved. He was only vaguely interested in political affairs and was happy with his life at Cenarth. He would have preferred better conditions from Sir Edmund Mortimer but he took the view that there was little point in complaining and he was content to carry on with things as they were.

Gwenllian, on the other hand, was much more closely involved in the rebellion since her father was leading it and her brothers were by his side. Since that September in 1400 she had questioned all visitors to Cenarth more carefully for any news of the rebels and was worried that her father and brothers might be killed in the fighting that was taking place. She was also worried that the rebellion might bring shame on them as a family or could even possibly bring retaliation on Cenarth and her boys. The king, it was generally known, was placing agents all over the country to find and capture Glyndŵr. There was no doubt that the king was furious that he had not been able to defeat the rebels in a pitched battle, capture Glyndŵr and make an example of him.

By the end of the winter of 1401 there was still no news of the rebellion and Gwenllian, like many others, thought that the rebels had either dispersed permanently or were hiding in the mountains waiting for an opportunity to strike again. There were numerous rumours about Glyndŵr: some saying he had been killed and some even claiming that he had been buried at Valle Crucis Abbey. Others were convinced that he was in hiding in the mountains. The stories brought by the poets and the entertainers were so outrageous at times that it was clear that they had been manufactured purely for entertainment. The stories around the market in Llanidloes from the prophets of doom and gloom were that he was about to attack Llanidloes and burn the town.

Gwenllian felt very uncomfortable with some of these stories and wondered if people knew who she was. She had never gone out of her way to tell anyone that she was Glyndŵr's daughter but some inevitably knew and no derogatory remark had ever been directed at her, at least not to her face anyway.

Occasionally, she received news, mainly through the poets who called at Cenarth, that her father and brothers were still alive and well and she was always glad and relieved to hear such news.

She had not seen any of her father's family since the rebellion had started over a year ago. Gwenllian hoped that one of them would call to see her soon or that if one of them were in difficulty they would ask her for help – after all, Hyddgen was not very far from Cenarth. Her half-brothers, Gruffydd and Meredydd, used to call by when they visited their father's family in west Wales, but Glyndŵr had only visited her after the birth of her first son, Rhys.

She felt that Glyndŵr was a little uncertain of her when he had visited Cenarth, particularly as he dismounted and walked towards her. Perhaps he felt unsure of how he would be received by her and her family or that he felt guilty about something. However, the tension, if there had been any, disappeared once he had taken her in his arms and hugged her.

She had met him a number of times when she lived as a child with her grandfather and knew that she at least looked like him. She was very glad that he had never tried to disown her but had always been open about the fact that he was her father. His last visit was a celebration and he had come to see her as a proud grandfather of her newly born son. It was at that meeting that Glyndŵr realised that, without question, Gwenllian was very much his daughter. She was tall like him and she was a very determined person.

It was the concerns about her own family that troubled Gwenllian as they moved eastwards up the narrow and difficult path out of Cwm Ystwyth and up to Blaen Cwm Elan. Gwenllian wanted to talk again but her train of thoughts were disturbed by the struggle she had with the oxen during the last hundred yards to Blaen Cwm.

Philip was also troubled by their experiences at the ford and was already pondering how he would replace Hywel. He appreciated the silence which allowed him to be alert and scan the rocky sides for any movement and signs of danger.

They reached Blaen Cwm Elan and the oxen were watered and given a break. The track ahead was now more level and the land around more open and consequently much less threatening. The lines of the hills were gentler and calmer for the eyes. Rhys woke up when they stopped and he was moved to sit next to his mother on the driver's seat. Gwenllian explained sensitively to Rhys what had happened while he slept, including how Hywel had been killed. Rhys was initially very tearful but under his mother's influence he soon concentrated on the journey ahead and on his parents' conversation.

"Are we safe coming this way?" asked Gwenllian. "Won't there be more of the Flemish soldiers hiding in these mountains?"

"No," replied Philip. "The Flemish soldiers will have gone south in as direct a route as possible and as quickly as possible. They have had a beating and will wish to go home in case your father goes after them to burn their farms and take their stock."

"What do you think he will do? Will he go south after them?" she asked a little uncomfortably.

"I really don't know," he said.

"But what would you do if you were him?" she persisted.

"I am not him and I don't know what he wants to achieve."

"I hope he stops and gives the injured time to be treated," she said. "Why was he in the Pumlumon area do you think? Did he know that there was an army coming up from the south and he waited for them in the mountains?"

"I don't know, Gwenllian. I can't answer any of your questions." He replied while viewing the track ahead and scanning the adjacent land. The attack at Rhyd-y-groes had unsettled him too and he was far more alert than usual.

After a few seconds delay, he continued, "I had heard that the rebels had been gathering in the Pumlumon area for some weeks and using it as a base to attack the south-west."

"You did not tell me," said Gwenllian in a hurt voice.

He calmed her by saying, "I thought it was just one of the hundreds of stories that are circulating about your father. You must hear many yourself."

Changing the subject, she asked, "What will happen now that my father has won a big battle?"

Philip was more interested in reaching Rhayader but he answered politely again, "I can't imagine but I would think that this will change people's views of your father and the rebellion. He will have to be taken more seriously."

"How do you think it will affect us?" she asked.

"I hope it won't affect us at all," he said. Then he drew her attention to basic and realistic facts: "Gwenllian, Hywel has been killed and we have to take his body to his family in Rhayader. Then tomorrow we will go back to Cenarth and in time we will have to replace Hywel and that will not be easy."

This turned Gwenllian's thoughts to Hywel and she asked, "Did Hywel feel any pain do you think?" Then, answering her own question as she would wish it answered, said, "I don't think he did because when I went to him there was no sign of life left. I think he died instantly and felt no pain."

"I am sure you are right and I am glad of it," said Philip, thinking that there would now be time to reflect on what had been said but, no, Gwenllian had another question.

"How much older than your father was Hywel?"

"I'm not sure. Perhaps he was ten years older. I can't really say," replied Philip.

Cwm Elan was endlessly long with numerous bends to be negotiated just like Gwenllian's questions and the oxen were very slow. Philip wished he had not taken the oxen cart and had instead relied on packhorses. However, the oxen, step by step moved steadily along the track. Gwenllian and Philip were happier after they reached the higher ground and were passing the stone erected to commemorate the murder of Einion Clud by the Mortimer family two centuries earlier. The journey from that point on was downhill to Rhayader, but it was a race against time because the sun was sinking fast behind them.

They reached their destination just before nightfall and took Hywel's body into the relative's small cottage. They stayed over night with the family in the cottage and helped to bury Hywel in the morning near the church. They started on the last leg of their journey in the afternoon and arrived at Cenarth in the evening.

The other three Cenarth boys were delighted that their parents and Rhys had arrived home safely. Beth, the housemaid, had just fed them all when the sound of the cart could be heard on the track leading up to the farmstead.

The boys rushed out to meet their parents and to have their hugs with their mother, but Beth could see immediately that there was something wrong and asked where was Hywel.

Gwenllian stayed outside with the boys while Philip took Beth into the house to tell her what had happened.

Beth was devastated. She had worked closely with Hywel for many years and thought of him as an older brother. Beth and Hywel were considered part of the Cenarth family and so Hywel's murder was a major blow to them all. After recovering a little from the initial shock Beth went out to talk to the boys and Gwenllian, and to explain to the boys that Hywel would not be returning to Cenarth and had gone to heaven. The boys accepted this reluctantly but wished that Hywel had come there to say goodbye to them – his best friends.

# Chapter 2

**30 June 1401**

THE MORNING OF the last day of June 1401 was sunny and calm. Gwenllian was driving the same oxen cart that she drove from Ceredigion a week earlier, but this time she was driving it home from the local mill.

She had collected six sacks of ground corn for bread making at her home in Cenarth, a little over a mile away. She loved driving the oxen cart along the track home. It was all in sharp contrast to her journey from Rhyd-y-groes. The pace of the oxen was such that she had time to enjoy the countryside around her and she did not have to concentrate on the oxen because they knew their own way home.

The cart rumbled across the river Dulas at the ford up river from the mill, squeaking and shaking as it moved up the track away from the river, the water dripping off the wheels and the oxen's hooves. She held her head high while standing on the driver board and enjoyed the moment as she started up from the river valley up the east side of Cenarth Hill with its rounded sides and its wide flat top. The slopes were covered in short old Welsh oak trees and a few weeks earlier the hillside had been covered with a carpet of blue bells.

She encouraged the oxen up the dusty track moving higher with every step at a gentle incline up the sun facing slope. As she got higher she could see more of the surrounding land and could now sit and enjoy the wider view opening on her left. Cenarth Hill obscured her view to the west, but to the east and south lay the open land, known as Waen Marteg, from which the river Marteg drew its waters. The Marteg flowed westwards to join the Wye just below Coed Nannerth about two miles away. Behind her were the hills, which separated her from the small town of Llanidloes about two miles away. She had a good view of them on the way to the mill earlier in the morning.

On this journey she could relax and enjoy the morning air and the solitude, even the smell of the beasts was sweet. She had recovered quickly from her experience at Rhyd-y-groes – she had to. Though it was not a hand-to-mouth existence at Cenarth there was no time to waste. The farmstead was a busy place and everyone had to participate in providing the necessities of life. She grieved for Hywel naturally and missed him greatly but her family was unharmed and that was the important thing for her.

Cefn Cenarth was a large, bulky rounded hill and as she proceeded higher up the side she could see the limewashed farmsteads to the east occupying positions on the top of rounded green lowlying hillocks, scattered as if by a giant and powerful sower in ancient times. She knew the farmsteads well and she knew the people who lived in them.

After a few minutes travelling, she noticed that there was a man on a horse a short distance ahead of her. He was travelling very slowly in the same direction as she was heading and she was surprised that she was catching up with the rider because her oxen were not known for their speed. However, she was gaining on him and could see that he was a rotund man sitting heavily on his horse.

Once she saw that he had a small harp hanging over his shoulder she knew exactly whom she was going to overtake on the track. The horseman ahead was Iolo, the poet and storyteller who frequently visited Cenarth to entertain the family. He was making very slow progress and it was obvious to Gwenllian as she caught up with him that he'd had a heavy night of drinking at Llanidloes the night before and was probably hoping for a similar, if not better time, at Cenarth.

She hailed him from behind, "Hello, Iolo."

He was startled and there was a possibility that he would topple off his horse but he somehow managed to hold on and performed a quick recovery. He stopped for Gwenllian to get level with him.

Clearly, he was waking up but he recognised her immediately and addressed her with, "Hello, Gwenllian. I see you've been to the mill."

He's sharp even with a hangover, she thought, and she replied, "Yes, I got up early and went to collect these sacks. Where have you been?"

"Well, I spent the night in Llanidloes though I had planned to reach Cenarth before night fall. I actually spent the night in the stables at the Castle Inn," Iolo said as he continued his waking-up process.

He was quite jolly as usual but his eyes were red and bleary; not just caused by an uncomfortable night's sleep in the stables. He had clearly spent some time inside the Inn drinking cheap ale supplied by those he entertained.

Iolo knew Gwenllian well. He knew her father, Owain Glyndŵr, and he knew her background. He also knew her mother's family. Nothing could be hidden from Iolo, he knew everybody and everything about everybody. He knew the Cenarth family well and had told her boys many a story; educating them in history, geography and social skills at the same time.

He liked Gwenllian and she liked him. She enjoyed his jolly company and he reminded her of her happy childhood in her grandfather's house where the poets were frequent and welcomed visitors.

Iolo admired this tall, slim, blonde attractive woman, who was in the same mould as the other Glyndŵr daughters. All the daughters were tall like their father but very feminine in form, which went some of the way to explain their extremely advantageous marriages, even overcoming risk to their husband's estates. English men were not allowed to marry Welsh women but Sir John Scudamore had married Alice Glyndŵr, Sir John Croft of Croft Castle had married Margaret Glyndŵr and Sir Roger Monnington of Monnington Court had married Janet Glyndŵr – all at a great risk to their own position.

When Gwenllian allowed herself to think of her half-sisters she did for fleeting moments feel envious and not quite equal to the others. Gwenllian was the other daughter – not mentioned frequently in the Glyndŵr household. But this did not impair her genuinely warm feeling towards her kith and kin, particularly her father and brothers.

Though Gwenllian, when she first moved to Cenarth, had appeared to many to be a somewhat snobbish person she was not. What people perceived to be a superior attitude came from her shyness and some people thought possibly from her own sensitivity about her birth. It was part of her defence system to cover what she perceived to be a weakness in her status. It was known that she was from a distinguished family on both her father's and mother's side and many knew that she was Glyndŵr's other daughter, though at the time she moved to Cenarth this was of no consequence and not as significant as it was to become.

The shyness of her younger days had left her and with the birth of each child her confidence had grown. Gwenllian was a pleasant person, a caring mother to her boys, an excellent hostess and a supporter of music and the work of the poets, all of which endeared her to Iolo.

She had received a privileged and cultured upbringing with her maternal grandfather and she endeavoured to provide the same background for her own family. Iolo enjoyed the welcome, the good food and drink he received at Cenarth.

Unlike her husband, Gwenllian was politically aware and was supportive of the revolt from the start and of her father in all he did. Iolo was fully aware of this and spent time during every visit talking to her about her father and the rebellion;he knew that he was pleasing his hostess by doing so.

They progressed upwards side by side where the track and open fields permitted and shared the views of the surrounding area as more came into sight.

Iolo asked her with a broad grin on his reddish circular face, "You've heard the excellent news about your father's victory?"

"Yes!" she replied. "Are my father and brothers well and healthy after the battle?"

"Yes! Not a scratch on one of them," he reassured her.

"We came very close to the action. We were attacked at Rhyd-y-groes by Flemish soldiers escaping from the battlefield. Hywel was killed by one of them."

Iolo could see that there were tears in her eyes and was for once at a loss as to what to say. Eventually he managed to say, "I am very sorry to hear that. Hywel was a great fellow and a great friend of mine. Oh! Dear me. I am very sorry."

Gwenllian nodded and smiled her thanks to him.He allowed a small gap of time to elapse, just enough for him to be able to return to the subject on his mind. "You must be very proud of your father – it's a victory for us all – it's a victory for Wales and the king has been given a bloody nose."

"Yes, Iolo, I am very proud of him."

Looking up at the farmstead he remarked, "Doesn't Cenarth look magnificent. You and Philip take great care of the place. Your father must be proud of you as well."

Cenarth farmstead, which was now in view, was a magnificent place: limewashed regularly under Gwenllian's instructions, it was the largest, the most conspicuous and most impressive farmstead in the area. The well looked after thatched roof, which came to view first, was shining in the morning sun.

The hall had been built about fifty years earlier on the south-facing slope of Cefn Cenarth in an ideal position to absorb as much sun as possible. It stood some distance above the valley floor and was perched end-on high on the hillside. It was built using local oak to produce the dark brown – almost black – beams, which supported the walls and roof and accounted for the shape and the strength of the structure. The main supporting beams were strengthened by lateral supports keeping the main uprights in a fixed and solid position. The spaces between the wooden supports were filled with interwoven hazel sticks and dried clay and the resulting uniform rectangular patches were limewashed. All visitors to Cenarth Hall and farm would realise instantly that the farmstead was looked after with great pride.

The hall was situated superbly on the brow of the hill facing the wide flat plain of the river Marteg and about a mile from the church of St Garmon. Cenarth was a well-established township in the northern part of Gwerthrynion, an area, as tradition had it, which was named after Gwrtheyrn the British leader reputed to have allowed the Saxons into

Britain 1,000 years earlier. The farmstead was at the heart of the Cenarth township.

Two tracks led to the hall and farm, both hugged the side of the hill as they rose gently, one from the east and the other from the west. Gwenllian and Iolo were now approaching the hall from the eastern direction of Tylwch and Llanidloes. The other track was from the direction of the church and Rhayader. Both tracks met in the yard behind the main house.

For the final 200 yards leading up to the hall Gwenllian took the cart ahead of Iolo's horse but when the track widened again near the top, he caught up with her. They stopped a short distance from the yard and looked at the countryside below them and admired the glorious view. The oxen could now smell the farm and were keen to get home.

The hall, with its accompanying buildings, looked down on a slightly marshy patch of land, which included a kidney shaped pool. This part of the estate had never been drained because of the benefits derived from having a pool so near. The pool was well stocked with fish which had made their way up from the Marteg river and the wild water foul came and went with a few resident moorhens and, of course, domestic ducks and geese. Apart from the human occupiers of Cenarth, their main enemies were the foxes, stoats and weasels, which roamed the area in abundance; their main protectors were the farm dogs, which never seemed to sleep with both eyes closed.

Beyond the pool was the track between Llanidloes in the north and Rhayader in the south. On the far side of the road the land opened out with the limewashed farmsteads dotted at random on this array of various shades of green. The view from Cenarth, because it was so high on the hillside, was stunning and provided an opportunity to see the countryside around through a very wide angle.

By raising their gaze a little from Waen Marteg to the horizon Gwenllian and Iolo could see the hill above Prysgduon to the north-east and moving their sight gradually southwards they could see Bwlch-y-sarnau with the gap in the hills allowing a track to lead down to Abbey Cwm Hir.

Bwlch-y-sarnau was in Maelienydd, another area that was also part of the Mortimer Lordship. The Cistercian abbey of Cwm Hir was situated about three miles from Bwlch-y-sarnau, out of sight of Cenarth but quite close and no more than six miles away, hiding in the deep Cwm Hir valley.

A short distance from Cenarth the early Welsh saints had established a small monastic settlement just above the river Marteg and there was now a small church on the site dedicated to St Garmon, whose military skills, learnt in France, had brought a great military victory to the Welsh centuries earlier as the poets kept reminding the Cenarth family.

Looking at the church Iolo asked her, "Do you think that Garmon is buried there near the church?"

"I don't know – all I know is that he was one of our greatest military leaders and he learnt his skills abroad," Gwenllian replied.

"Just like your father," Iolo said soberly and definitivly.

Gwenllian, glancing at him, smiled. Then, pointing beyond the church and slightly to the left where she could see the village, she said, "Baily Bedw can be seen clearly today."

"Yes. I think I can see the blacksmith's forge."

Gwenllian was impressed by Iolo's knowledge of the area, considering he had never lived there and visited only occasionally. He knew the names of all the surrounding hills and streams. He had something to say about all the land features that they could see from their vantage point at Cenarth. He knew who lived where and who had lived there in the past. He was an extremely knowledgeable person and had an impressive memory. It was no wonder that he had a massive store of poems and stories.

To the south and west in the direction of Rhayader they could see the low hills in the distance. They stood clear and distinct this morning and this raised Gwenllian's spirit even further because it was from this direction that the clouds came most frequently carrying the rain that was sometimes hated and sometimes loved as the saviour encouraging the grass to grow and therefore provide grazing for the stock. The cold wind would come over from the east and the north, over the hills above Prysgduon carrying snow with it in the winter months. Trees had been encouraged to grow on the east side of the farmstead to provide some shelter from this chilling and bitter wind. The high elevation of Cenarth exposed the farm and the houses to these cold wintry winds. However, the people and animals of Cenarth had hardened to those exposed conditions – as much as that was possible.

Gwenllian and Iolo arrived in the yard and were greeted by two of her boys, Rhys and Dafydd, with Rhys holding on tight to his younger brother's hand. Another two of her boys, Ieuan and Meredydd were inside the house in the care of Beth.

Iolo greeted the boys joyfully, "And how are my young eagles today?" Without waiting for an answer, he asked them, "Have you eaten yet?" This was a clear hint to Gwenllian that he himself was hungry.

Talking to the boys he said, "Let me tell you what the white crow told me this morning. It said it's going to be a beautiful day and there are going to be some boys swimming in the pond later."

Rhys said, "Hywel has left us and gone to live in the sky. We think he is happy up there but we miss him."

"Of course you do. He was a very good man. After we've eaten we'll go down to the pool and see if you can bounce a stone across it. Come on, first things first – food."

Gwenllian picked up the youngest and carried him into the house and the others followed her in.

The oxen, cart and sacks were left for one of the farm workers to deal with while Gwenllian went to prepare a welcome for Iolo and arrange the provisions for an entertaining evening. She was in good spirits having enjoyed her early morning excursion to the mill and having had Iolo's company on the way back. She now sat with Iolo to receive whatever news he had to tell her. Gwenllian used him and others like him to find out what was going on in the world. They gave her news about her family, her extended family, the politics of the day in all parts of Wales, Wigmore, where Sir Edmund Mortimer lived, and the latest royal gossip.

Compared with the outside it was very dark inside the hall, even with the fire burning, but the windows were of good dimensions and allowed a lot of light in and Gwenllian's eyes soon accustomed to the gloom when she went in with Dafydd and stood by the east window. In the mornings, Gwenllian would go to the east window to find out what the weather was like and what were the climatic prospects for the day. If the sun shone pink light through that window then it would rain before the day ended. She would check if clouds were moving from the west. If the wind was coming from the east then it would be felt at this window and she might decide to board it up until the wind died down or changed direction.

Beth was there in the corner feeding the two younger boys. Gwenllian loved these boys more than anything else in her life. She was proud of them but would have liked a girl and the thought flashed through her mind more than once – perhaps next time.

Beth who helped in the house was not married. She had been working at Cenarth for at least ten years. She was Gwenllian's greatest ally and helper and had learnt a lot helping her own mother with her siblings. Though Gwenllian treated and regarded Beth as an equal, Beth nevertheless knew her place. She was an excellent asset to the farmstead and did everything domestic at Cenarth and much more when needed.

The most noticeable feature in the hall was the central fire kept alight every day and night. There was usually a pot of some kind of broth gently boiling above the fire. This pot was Iolo's first port of call and Beth got him a cup of hot soup as soon as he entered.

Stoking the fire had been Hywel's job but since his death the work had been done mainly by Beth with all other workers lending a hand as best they could.

Having ensured all was well inside the house Gwenllian went out to see what needed doing on the farm, leaving the boys to be entertained by Iolo. She soon found that the horses were in need of being fed and set to do the task herself.

Philip would normally see to the horses at this time of the morning but today he had gone to Llanidloes to see if he could employ a replacement for Hywel. There was a desperate need for someone like Hywel who had seen to so many of the daily chores around the house and farm. Since Hywel's death, Philip, Gwenllian and Beth had been sharing Hywel's tasks and the strain was already beginning to tell on them after just one week. Philip knew that they were struggling to get the farm chores done each day with one man short. So, after discussing the situation with Gwenllian it was decided to employ a replacement for Hywel as soon as possible and Philip had left that day for Llanidloes at the same time that Gwenllian had left for the mill.

Later that afternoon, Philip arrived back at Cenarth with Cynwrig. He was delighted that he had been successful in his mission as he felt sure that it would be a very difficult task to get someone anything like as good as Hywel. Also, the rebellion had resulted in many workers going to England to work rather than face going to fight the rebels. Gwenllian was therefore surprised to see him back so soon with a strong-looking man who would obviously be an asset to the farm.

Philip introduced Cynwrig to Gwenllian, then to Beth who showed him his bed and took him around the farm introducing him to as many of the workers as possible and explaining to him what his tasks would be at the same time.

After talking to Iolo and giving him a warm welcome, Philip went for a walk with Gwenllian down the track to the pond. They took it as an opportunity to discuss the appointment of Cynwrig and also to judge how the new geese were settling into their new home.

Philip was of the same height as his tall wife with a pleasant open face and of a strong build. His broad muscular shoulders developed through lifting and pulling things on the farm, and he could also swing a sword powerfully and effectively. He was skilled as an archer and could throw a spear accurately. These skills he had acquired naturally and practised while hunting. Though he was a good and well-trained fighter he was not inclined in that way by nature and only got involved when it was necessary to defend himself or his family.

Philip had not joined the rebels, not because Gwenllian had prevented him from doing, but because on matters of disputes he kept his own counsel and out of trouble. Primarily, he did not wish to cross Sir Edmund Mortimer whose lordship included Cenarth. He was not one for taking sides and finding fault because he cared more for his family, more for his house and the farm, more for good food and good wine and he enjoyed music and socialising at the weekly market in Llanidloes and with the poets.

He was a very keen huntsman and would not miss a chance of going out with the dogs, sometimes he would be on foot and sometimes on horseback. Hunting, which was a weekly event at Cenarth, was regarded by Philip to be as important as his religion.

Philip and his family were well-respected people and, like his father, he was a kind man and there were numerous stories about him and his kindness. When the Cenarth carts were returning full from the fields having lifted turnips, he would stop the cart and throw a few into the gardens of the more needy as they passed.

He and Gwenllian were different in many ways but were well matched.

"How did you get someone so strong so quickly?" she asked. "I thought it was going to take us weeks to find anybody."

"I know," he said. "All I intended to do today was start the process by letting it be known that I was looking for a replacement for Hywel," said Philip. "But as I was dismounting by Maes-y-dre and before entering the town a man came over to me and said that he liked the look of my horse and that he was looking for a good animal. I told him that mine was not for sale and that I did not know of any but that when we wanted new stock introduced we always bought from the monks of Cwm Biga."

Gwenllian intervened with a question, "So, how did that conversation lead you to employ Cynwrig?"

"As part of the conversation with him I said that I had gone to town to look for a farm worker and he immediately said that he knew just the man, who had experience of working on a farm. So I went with him to a house in Short Bridge Street. He entered the house and came out with Cynwrig. He introduced us and I questioned Cynwrig carefully about his background. I thought he seemed reliable and a hard worker so I hired him. What do you think of him?"

"I like him," she said. "I'm sure he will be very useful and it's such a relief to have an extra pair of hands around. Beth was finding it difficult and I did not want to over burden her. She is so good."

They agreed that they had done well to employ Cynwrig with so little difficulties.

After checking the geese and seeing that they had settled well into their hut near the pond they decided to close them in for the night. They returned uphill to the house and looked forward to an evening with Iolo though the night would be subdued because of Hywel's death.

They had no doubt that they would receive a full report on the battle at Hyddgen. Gwenllian wanted to hear about the battle so that she could compare Iolo's account with that of the Flemish soldier.

Iolo was Cenarth's self-appointed bard. He called occasionally on his travels across Wales and would tell stories about what he had learnt on his journeys. In other words, he would relate the current gossip and pick up any new gossip in the Cenarth area to take to some other hall in some other part of the country. In return for sustenance he would sing in the evenings, write complimentary poems about the family and tell stories. Philip and Gwenllian always gave him good food and drink and he would stay for a few days before moving on.

Sitting, Iolo projected a spherical image but even standing he remained almost spherical. He was rotund, with a perfectly round face, a round body and bow-legged. He had a magnetic personality with an excellent sense of humour and given a few cups of ale, as he would be at Cenarth, he would entertain for hours on end.

Other bards visited the farmstead also but Iolo was the favourite because the family and their friends could understand his poems – well, most of them anyway. Llawdden's poems were so complicated and long winded that many lost track of what he was saying. The same was true when he told a story: he was too slow coming to the punch line. Lewis was another who called at Cenarth and his poems were good but he was a little unreliable, caused mainly by his fondness for women.

After Philip and Gwenllian returned to the hall from their walk they settled down to talk to Iolo. The battle of Hyddgen was, inevitably, the prime topic of conversation.

Gwenllian, like the others, was truly mystified by the victory at Hyddgen. There had been no omens, no white crows around, no more owls than usual at night, no dogs had been howling, nothing unusual had appeared in the heavens, there had been nothing seen or heard to signify that a major event was to happen. Some gossips at the local market, being wise after the event, had of course predicted it all.

All the people she had spoken to agreed that the battle was

a turning point in the rebellion and Gwenllian realised that her father was now more than an irritation: he was a threat to the king's rule in Wales and the name of Glyndŵr was now on everybody's lips.

Iolo was of the view that it was a cause for celebration but Gwenllian reminded him that Hywel had been killed by Flemish soldiers escaping from the battle and they were still upset by that loss. But Iolo insisted that they should have a small party because it was such an outstanding victory for her father and should be recognised as such and the only way to do that was to have a party. Gwenllian relented eventually and sent Cynwrig to kill one of the geese.

She was proud of her father's victory but she was also apprehensive as to how it would affect her family. The king and his agents were likely to retaliate and that made them as a family vulnerable. They would have to be vigilant for a while at Cenarth.

While the freshly plucked goose was roasting above the fire, the evening got underway. There was no formal start to the evening no more than a formal end. The farm workers, as they finished their tasks for the day, drifted into the hall, joining in the drinking while listening to Iolo's harp music and even dancing to some tunes.

As the smell of the roasting goose percolated to every corner of the room, Iolo put down his harp and delivered a very moving tribute to Hywel, comparing him to a faithful servant from the Mabinogion legends, and recited a poem in his memory, leaving many in the house in tears, including Gwenllian.

He then turned his attention to the recent battle at Hyddgen. He described how a very large army of heavily armed and well-trained and experienced Flemish soldiers from the south-west had been easily routed by a much smaller force led by Glyndŵr. He described it as the most important victory for Glyndŵr since the rebellion had begun.

He announced that he had memorised Glyndŵr's speeches at Hyddgen and climbed on a sturdy chair and repeated what he claimed Glyndŵr had said when rallying his troops before the battle. "Take heart all of you because the place we will fight at is of our own choosing and we will be attacking downhill. This mist is in our favour and is an omen of victory. God is on our side. The enemy will expect us to use this mist to retreat into the mountains but we will surprise them with an attack. We will use the mist as a veil to hide our advance. Silently and in battle order, with swords drawn and arrows at the ready, we will march towards our enemy through the mist. When you see our flag unfurling at the front with the dragon showing clearly start running at the enemy but stay silent until you hear the sound of our arrows going over head. At that moment scream and shout as loud as you can to frighten them and run at them hard. The archers will take out their soldiers on the left so charge into the centre and right."

"Our enemy thinks that, because we are outnumbered and he is better armed than us, it is ordained that he will win. Our forefathers, Garmon and Arthur were outnumbered and out armed in the battles they won. We stand here on the slopes of Pumlumon, our hearts full of hope for our future and the future of our people. Today we shall through our determination turn our hope into faith in our future, the future of our people and our country."

"As we charge into our enemy we will avenge the treacherous death of Llywelyn, our last true prince. We will fight our way to victory and we will beat our enemies. We will not give up. We will fight with all our might. We will win."

"Fight for the dragon. Fight for your future and your country."

The whole gathering erupted in uproar when he finished. He had delivered Glyndŵr's call to arms as if addressing an army and after a suitable pause he turned to Gwenllian and asked from his elevated position on the chair, "Well, Gwenllian, you must be very proud of your father?" Iolo was in his element and having the time of his life.

There were shouts of, "Yes!" and applause from the audience. Gwenllian had tears in her eyes as she nodded her head signalling that she was indeed very proud of her father.

Beth, helped by one of the farmhands, ensured that everyone had a jar full of ale. It was decided that the goose was cooked and it was removed to be carved. This gave Iolo time to down a jar of ale while still standing on the chair and the congregation discussed Glyndŵr's speech.

Full of pride, ale and fired by his audience, Iolo proceeded with his peroration informing his audience that after the victory Glyndŵr had stood on top of a large white stone and his army had gathered around him to listen to his words in total silence. He had first thanked them all for delivering a decisive victory. According to Iolo, Glyndŵr said, "The day is ours. We have won a famous victory. These mountains are ours now and we will never give them up. This battle has seen the triumph of our hope over what our enemy thought was ordained. Before this battle we had hope in the future of our people but now we have faith in that future. We have faith in the future of our country. Let this victory live forever in the hearts of our people and let them never be trampled by their enemies again."

There was enthusiastic applause, shouts and whistles at the end of which Iolo paused for a few seconds and then said, "Then there was an enormous cheer from Glyndŵr's men and they waved their swords and spears in the air."

His audience erupted again and cheered and shouted in support of Glyndŵr just as his soldiers had done. They marvelled at the speech and its delivery by Iolo who had his audience in the palm of his hand.

After gorging on a leg of the goose, he soon had them laughing and singing to his tunes on the harp. Later in the evening he resorted to telling them his stories, which he used to capture his audience's attention with tremendous skill. He seemed to be able to remember which stories he had said at Cenarth before and never repeated a story unless there was a special request, which there was often. Gwenllian drank a little more mead than was her practice that night but everybody else at Cenarth was also well inebriated.

Iolo, despite the fact that he spoke continuously for hours, ate more than his fair share of the goose and was able to consume a substantial amount of ale and mead. The party came to an end in the early hours of the morning when most of the people present, including Iolo, had fallen asleep.

# Chapter 3

A FEW DAYS after the party and about a fortnight after the battle of Hyddgen, Gruffydd and Meredydd, Gwenllian's brothers, rode into the yard at Cenarth.

They were well dressed, armed to the teeth and Meredydd was covered in dust. The first five days in July had been warm and sunny with hardly a cloud in the sky, so the tracks were very dusty. The horses were in very good condition but covered in sweat and ready for a rest. The two brothers had obviously been racing along the track from Llanidloes and Gwenllian was convinced that Gruffydd had won.

Gruffydd, the elder of the two, was more aggressive in appearance. He was tall and quite heavily built but not fat. He was all muscle on a strong and powerful frame. His eyes were dark and piercing with the lower part of his face covered in a thick, dark, short beard. He held himself straight. The immediate impression he left on anyone meeting him was that he was not a man to cross. He was however pleasant and far more amenable than his appearance indicated. He had a good sense of humour and could be made to laugh easily. One suspected that he could also be angered easily. It was noticeable that he was rarely separated from his sword even in bed.

Meredydd was of the same height as his brother but not with such a powerful frame and neither was he as heavy as his brother. Meredydd had a milder appearance. His eyes were calmer and pale greenish blue in colour. He had a higher forehead than his brother and his beard was slightly longer, which contributed to the milder image he projected.

Meredydd gave the impression of a more cautious man, more of a thinker. He was more willing to spend time playing with Gwenllian's boys, talk about poetry and spend time discussing the stock on the farm. It was easier to relax in his presence.

When she heard the clattering of hooves in the yard Gwenllian went to see who had arrived and her brothers greeted her with great warmth and dismounted. She was delighted to see them and hugged them both in turn and took them into the stables to meet Philip. After a while, Gwenllian left the men in the stables to admire the horses and went into the hall to help Beth prepare food.

Later Philip brought the brothers into the hall to eat. All who saw them congratulated them enthusiastically on the victory at Hyddgen and Beth was no exception. They were proud and happy to be congratulated and their reply to everyone was that they hoped there were greater things to come. Neither did they say much about the tactics used. They had no intention of giving away any secrets.

As soon as they were alone with Philip and Gwenllian, Gruffydd said in a slightly quieter voice than usual, "We came here to see you and Philip mainly but we are also recruiting in the area. We are drumming up support for the rebellion and hoping to get some men to come with us as soldiers or to be one of our reserve soldiers, so that when the call comes they can join us wherever we need them. It would be ideal for us to have soldiers based in this area because you are so centrally placed here that any reserves based here could be moved quickly to any part of Wales."

Gwenllian and Philip were nodding their heads at this and Gwenllian said, "Yes," in a very positive manner. Philip's welcome for Gruffydd and Meredydd had been genuine and warm but he was a little unsure of their desire to involve Cenarth in the revolt.

Gruffydd made the case for them to declare their support for Glyndŵr by saying how badly the Mortimers had always treated their tenants and how they could not be trusted. While Philip and Gwenllian agreed with him, it was not with great enthusiasm.

Sensing this lack of keenness, Gruffydd asked, "What do the people of this area feel about the rebellion? Are they very supportive?"

"They are very supportive," replied Gwenllian immediately, but Philip was more cautious with his reply of, "Some are and some are not."

"What families could we rely on?" asked Gruffydd.

Gwenllian and Philip looked at each other briefly, both sensing that they would have to name people and even Gwenllian was reluctant to do this.

Meredydd sensed the unease and said, "I suppose in a community like this people are reluctant to disclose their allegiance too openly."

Philip was quick to take advantage of the opportunity offered by Meredydd's lifeline and replied, "Yes. People in this area have a hard life making a living from their farms and are not too willing to see their hard work lost by taking any hasty action."

Meredydd could empathise with that view and nodded his head in agreement.

"Don't they realise that they would get a better life if the rebellion is successful?" asked Gruffydd.

There was a silence that lasted a little too long for comfort followed again by Gruffydd saying, "You would not have to submit to Sir Edmund Mortimer's whims or pay his high rent demands."

Philip ventured, "Sometimes, it's better the devil you know than the one you don't."

"Many of the locals feel like that though many of them despise Mortimer," added Gwenllian quickly.

Meredydd, always the peacekeeper, said, "I suppose people know who you are Gwenllian and will not speak the truth in front of you. They may say that they support us in your face but say something very different behind your back."

"That is almost certainly true," said Gwenllian. "I have no means of finding out what people really feel about the rebellion and where their loyalties are in reality."

After a pause, she continued to direct her words at Gruffydd, "We wish to support you and father but we are very exposed to retaliation here by locals who are against you never mind Mortimer and the king. If we gave you open support we would lose Cenarth. Mortimer would send us out of the farm and where would we be then? Father's support in this area, so close to the border and so firmly a part of the Mortimer estates, is weak and he could not defend us here if we were attacked. Also, we have very young children to think about."

Philip agreed with her strongly and was delighted to hear her speak so clearly and definitively on the matter. It was easier for her to say it than for him.

While Gruffydd was gathering his thoughts and reflecting on how like his father Gwenllian was, Philip said, "Be that as it may, you and your father and all the rebels are welcome to use this farm as a safe house. I want you to convey that to your father. We will do all we can for you and we can be of more support to you working with you covertly than if we were to support you openly."

"Yes," confirmed Gwenllian. She had been a little uncertain about speaking her mind in the presence of her brothers and she was happy that Philip had made such a clear statement of support. She was also genuinely uncertain about becoming too involved in the rebellion – her feelings veered between pride in her father's achievement and fear of what it might bring.

Gwenllian sincerely wanted to impress and please her brothers. She had met them numerous times before at Cenarth and at her maternal grandfather's home before that. They had always treated her as an equal. They had never spoken down to her; if anything, they had showed great deference to her and had always listened to what she had to say. She sometimes thought that they were slightly in awe of her as their older sister. Her obvious facial similarity to their father no doubt unsettled them. Had she been brought up with them at their home in Sycharth she would have had considerable influence on them both. They treated her as they would their other sisters.

She did not know her sisters as well as these two brothers and often wondered what they were like physically. She wondered if they were as pleasant and as easy to talk to as these two.

Gwenllian always knew that these two brothers were close and often together. She never felt in competition with the brothers for Glyndŵr's affection but there was some rivalry in her own mind between her and the sisters. Glyndŵr had control over his daughters by Margaret Hamer but not over Gwenllian. He decided who they married not knowing whether or not that marriage would be a happy marriage.

Gwenllian was able to negotiate with her grandfather and she believed she was much happier in her marriage for having been given that freedom. Her sisters were in more exalted positions than she was but there were more important things in life for Gwenllian than pomp and power as she kept on reminding herself.

There were many times when she had wished that she had been brought up at Sycharth with her brothers and sisters, but there were other times when she was glad that she had not, particularly when she recalled how happy she had been at her own home. She would not have wished to miss that for anything in the world.

While she was very supportive of the actions of her father she did not wish Philip to feel obliged to take part in the revolt just because she was Glyndŵr's daughter. But she need not have worried because Philip was very cautious about making any commitment to the cause. He had to make sure that he did not commit himself to a revolt that would last a year and then peter out. He did not wish to challenge the Mortimers. He, like Gwenllian, had their children to think about. Gwenllian did not wish to see her husband go off to fight, leaving her to bring up very young sons and look after a farmstead like Cenarth.

Gruffydd and Meredydd were a little disappointed with the result of their visit to Gwenllian and Cenarth. Other visits to other families in Gwerthrynion had been equally noncommittal. These were practical people not used to making rash decisions and more likely to weigh matters carefully before committing to anything. One or two homesteads had been more enthusiastic than others but the two brothers were a little downcast riding carefully at dusk from Cenarth north to report to their father. He would not be pleased but they would have to tell him that it was difficult to sell the cause because no one was sure about their aims and what would be achieved because Henry IV had already made it clear by invading north Wales that he would not give in to any demands.

# Chapter 4

L IFE AT CENARTH was busy in July with many seasonal
tasks to be completed and the good weather they had
been experiencing was not helping matters. The streams
were low and there was concern about there being enough
water for the animals. Water had to be carried to fill up some
troughs.

The boys were still too young to do much work but they
helped in their own way with Cynwrig just as they used to
do with Hywel. Drinking water for the family had to be
collected in pails from the well just above the hall and the full
pails carried downhill.

Washing water and water for the animals was taken from
the stream running by the house; though it had little water in
it, it was not dry. The stock had to be checked and fed. All
this meant that there was a lot of work to be done every day
and Saturdays were mainly occupied in taking produce to be
sold at the market in Llanidloes.

Occasionally, someone from the farmstead would visit the
abbey at Cwm Hir to purchase honey, mead or grain sold by
the abbey. In the past, Hywel had taken the two older boys
with him in the cart. They would have a slice of cured ham
and a piece of bread and they always enjoyed their day out at
the abbey.

In mid-July the two elder boys, Rhys and Dafydd, were
allowed to go on a visit to Cwm Hir with Cynwrig. He
was reliable, there were no military problems in their area
and they had been with Hywel many times before. It was a
beautiful morning and after all the chores were completed,

Cynwrig, Beth and the two boys set off for Abbey Cwm Hir for some of the monks' special honey and mead, the stock of which had been depleted at Cenarth after the celebrations of the victory at Hyddgen.

The cart was pulled by trusted oxen which were past their prime but most unlikely to panic if frightened or surprised by a farm dog or anything else. The animals struggled on the climb up to Bwlch-y-sarnau but picked up speed on the journey downhill from then on. The boys played on the straw in the cart: one minute they were play fighting and wrestling and the next laughing happily about something or other. They were enjoying the trip and looking forward to seeing the abbey and the monks.

The cart trundled its way down the valley towards the abbey with Cynwrig and Beth taking their time to take in the countryside. They stopped once for a cart coming towards them driven by a monk. Cynwrig pulled the cart slightly off the track to allow the monk to drive past. The monk nodded to Cynwrig as they passed but did not exchange any greetings. The monk's cart was empty; probably on its way to the abbey's farm at Llaeth Dŷ. The boys went quiet as the monk passed because they had been taught to respect monks and all Christian people. However, once he was behind them they exchanged a naughty smile and then started laughing.

A little further on, they came across a man dressed as a stockman walking towards them. As they approached the man, Cynwrig exchanged greetings with him. Cynwrig, who was obviously in no hurry to complete the journey and clearly knew the man, at least by sight, stopped the cart to talk to him. He told the boys to stay in the cart while he went down to stretch his legs and exchanged a few friendly words with the man. It wasn't long before he was back in the driver's seat next to Beth and they continued their journey.

In a very short time they arrived at the abbey. It was a magnificent building on the floor of the valley, snuggling closely to the side of the hill and the river Clywedog. In addition to the church building it had cloisters, a garden and a fish pond. The boys were as impressed as ever with this place – it was so different from Cenarth.

"I have been here many times," said Beth. "But I am still surprised at the beauty of the place. It's so big and the tower so high. It's in a wonderful location and it's so peaceful here."

"I haven't been here before but I have heard a lot about the place and I can see it's all true," Cynwrig informed her.

"I've met many of the monks here and they produce excellent mead and wonderful herbs."

"I've met some monks but none from this place," Cynwrig replied. "We had better go in and get the mead and honey."

The church had a very long nave, a north and south aisle with beautifully constructed arches. The top floors of the tower contained the belfry and were constructed of wood but based on a solid stone structure. The tower had two bells, one large, one small, which could be heard some miles away on a very quiet day or when the wind carried the sound up the long, narrow valley.

As an institution, it had been supportive of the local Welsh until recently when under the influence of the Mortimer family it had lost that close link with the surrounding area. The Mortimers had been influential in appointing the recent abbots and many of the locals felt that the sympathetic attitude of the abbots had declined with each succeeding abbot.

Cwm Hir Abbey was a large, complex organisation. Its numerous granges, such as Bryn Biga, Galon Manor and

Dolhelfa were well run and reared cattle, sheep and horses. They produced dairy products and had fulling and corn mills. They were famous for their bees and were major producers of honey in Mid-Wales. This was a wealthy establishment and played a crucial role in the local economy.

It was quite common to see individual monks and small groups of monks walking to the local markets to sell their products or going to other abbeys or visiting their various granges. The Cistercian monks were easily recognised in their white habits. The monks were generally welcomed but the attitude of reverence towards them had declined somewhat for a variety of reasons. Some did not like the abbot and, therefore, did not like the monks. Others disliked them because they felt they were too wealthy and that it distracted from their Christian role. People who knew the individual monks personally spoke highly of them, as indeed did Philip and Gwenllian.

Cynwrig and the two boys were allowed in through the side gate into the gardens by a monk dressed in his white habit. The boys were very excited by the place. The garden was peaceful and the sunshine added to the wonderful feeling of well-being and satisfaction. The small pond could be seen just beyond the garden. The monks had diverted some of the water from the river Clywedog flowing at the base of the hill to form a small pond.

Being fairly familiar with the layout of the abbey and possessing the natural confidence of young boys, Rhys and Dafydd soon went exploring on their own. Beth went with Cynwrig to supervise the loading of the cart with barrels of mead and pots of honey.

Once the loading was finished they went to look for the boys. After some searching and shouting they found the youngest accompanied by a monk walking from the direction of the pond but could not see Rhys. Dafydd said that he had been with Rhys in the abbey and when they were under the tower where the bells were, Rhys had climbed up some stairs with a monk and hadn't come down again. Dafydd hadn't seen him since he went upstairs.

While Cynwrig stayed with the cart, Beth took Dafydd into the room at the bottom of the tower, where he had last seen Rhys. She could see the steps that led to a higher room. She questioned the young boy again as to where Rhys had gone. Dafydd pointed to the stairs and repeated that Rhys had gone up the stairs with a monk while he had gone to another part of the church. He had returned to the bottom of the stairs and because Rhys was not there he had shouted for him up the stairs. Then a monk had come and told him that his brother was out in the garden. The monk had then taken him out into the garden and that is when he heard Beth calling his name and he had left the monk and gone to her. He was adamant that he had not seen Rhys since he went up the stairs.

Holding Dafydd's hand, Beth went up the stairs. The steps were steep and Dafydd struggled to go up them but Beth was not going to leave him behind. The higher up they went the more the steps squeaked. At the top, the stairs opened into a room, which had tables and chairs and the bell ropes hung on one side. There was another staircase leading up to a higher room. Beth went to the bottom and called Rhys's name. Dafydd was uneasy, silent and stood still.

"Who's there?" a man's voice called down to them.

"Beth, from Cenarth Hall and I am looking for Rhys, a seven-year-old boy who, I am told, came up here," said Beth. Upon hearing this there was a series of whispers and three monks dressed in their white habits descended the stairs in an arrogant and purposeful manner.

The leading monk said in a very authoritarian voice, "There hasn't been a boy here and no one should enter the abbey, never mind these rooms, without permission."

It was made clear to Beth through gestures but in no uncertain terms that she and Dafydd were to go downstairs to the ground floor. They were escorted downstairs by the three monks and taken out of the church and back into the garden where the three monks abruptly left them. Beth took Dafydd to look around the lake and she peered into the shallow pond with Dafydd.

As Beth and Dafydd were leaving the pond a monk came running towards them to say that the boy had been given a lift home by a monk, who was going in the Cenarth direction.

Beth was initially greatly relieved when she heard this and went with Dafydd to the cart to tell Cynwrig. Cynwrig was of the opinion that they should start on the journey back to Cenarth. Perhaps it did not occur to him immediately that Rhys would not have gone anywhere without his brother and that he would not have gone without telling Dafydd or Beth that he was leaving. Beth was less certain as to what was best to do but reluctantly climbed on to the driver's seat and she told Dafydd to sit next to her.

Cynwrig checked the packing of the barrels then climbed into the driver's seat next to Beth and Dafydd and ushered the oxen on their way. Beth was hoping that they would catch up with the monk and Rhys. The journey back was uphill all the way to Bwlch-y-sarnau and the oxen were making heavy weather of the journey on what was turning out to be a very hot day. The flies were bothering the oxen as they plodded upwards and Dafydd was feeling lonely and upset. He was never separate from his big brother. Beth and Cynwrig were pensive and too absorbed in their own thoughts to be able to talk much to Dafydd, but Beth did try to reassure him occasionally.

Once they passed Bwlch-y-sarnau the journey was downhill with Cenarth in their sight and within a short while they were climbing the track towards the hall. The house looked magnificent in the bright sunlight.

Rhys did not come running nor walking towards them. Cynwrig stopped the cart in the yard when Gwenllian came out of the shed and, before Beth had time to say anything, she asked instantly, "Where's Rhys?"

Cynwrig replied, "Isn't he here?"

"No," said Gwenllian. "He left with you to go to Cwm Hir. Are you losing your mind or are you and those two playing a joke?"

Beth, between sobs, told her what had happened.

Gwenllian was distraught and said that she had heard of a monk in Cwm Hir that was overly fond of little boys. Beth confirmed that she had also heard that there was a bad monk in the abbey.

Dafydd was crying, Beth was crying and Gwenllian was in a frenzy. Philip was out with the animals.

Gwenllian was in a state of shock but knew that Philip must be fetched immediately and she sent Cynwrig to get him.

Within a few minutes Philip was in the hall having already heard the news from Cynwrig. They got horses out and soon Philip and Cynwrig set off for Cwm Hir. Cynwrig did not wish to go but realised that he was needed. Beth and Gwenllian stayed at Cenarth consoling each other and the children and hoping that Rhys would turn up with the monk having possibly made a detour to Llaeth Dŷ or some other property owned by the abbey.

Though it was late afternoon the abbey gates were open and Philip and Cynwrig dismounted and, leaving the horses outside, entered the abbey grounds. Philip demanded to see the abbot who eventually came reluctantly from his sanctuary. They told him what had happened but he reiterated the story that Rhys had left with a monk who was taking some provisions to their grange at Cwm Biga and since he was passing Cenarth had given Rhys a lift home. The abbot did not think there was any need to be concerned.

On the journey to the abbey, Philip had thought of all the questions he needed to ask of the abbot and he questioned him carefully, adding that he did not believe that his son, at the age of seven, would have left without letting Beth, Cynwrig or his brother know he was going. Philip told him that it did not make sense to him.

"Also," Philip said. "His brother last saw him climbing the stairs to the belfry."

"Oh! He must be mistaken," said the abbot.

"How do you know?" asked Philip.

"Nobody goes up there without permission," said the abbot.

Philip replied "I'm told that there were three monks in the top room when Beth was there looking for Rhys."

The abbot replied, "You are most definitely mistaken."

"I have known Beth for many years and she does not make mistakes like that and neither does she lie," Philip said, forcefully.

"If as you say he was taken home by a monk in one of the abbey's carts what is the name of that monk?" asked Philip.

"I don't know his name but I can find out."

The abbot went away for a while and came back to say, "The monk was called Benedict and he will not be back from Cwm Biga for a few days and might well visit some of the other granges before returning."

Philip was getting more and more irate and desperate. On the one hand, he had Dafydd saying that Rhys had climbed the stairs. But Dafydd was only five years old and he could easily be mistaken or telling a fib as he sometimes did. Beth was reliable but she was also relying on the words of a five year-old. He wished he had brought Dafydd with him, to ask him exactly when and where he last saw his brother.

The abbot said he would have the abbey and the grounds searched and would take Philip to see the belfry. True to his word he got the bell rung and all the monks gathered. They were organised into pairs and sent to search for Rhys. In the meantime, the abbot took Philip to the belfry and to the top room.

Having shown that there was nowhere to hide in the belfry the abbot took Philip and Cynwrig around the church checking every nook and cranny. But they did not find Rhys.

The monks returned gradually from their various searches but they had not found any trace of Rhys. Further, one monk claimed that he had only seen one boy going into the bell tower and that was the boy he had later seen leaving with Beth and Cynwrig. This threw doubt as to whether Rhys had entered the tower or not and also increased the possibility that perhaps Dafydd was confused.

Philip was mystified and desperate. He wanted to pin the abbot against the abbey door with his sword and demand that he did something to find his boy but he did not think that it would do any good. The abbot said that he had done all he could to find the child and that it was more likely that the boy would be found at home and he advised that they go home and look for the boy at Cenarth.

They had no choice but to leave, with Philip hopeful that Rhys would be home when they arrived back at Cenarth.

When they arrived home they found Gwenllian and Beth anxiously waiting for them. Rhys had not turned up. Philip related their story. The evening was approaching and it would be dark soon but they did not go to bed. They waited for Rhys's cry at the door but it never came. It was a long and anxious night though the dawn came early.

At dawn Philip gave Gwenllian, Cynwrig and Beth the task of searching the Cenarth buildings and fields for the little boy and if they failed to find him by mid-morning to alert their neighbours to the fact that he was missing and to ask for their help in searching for him.

Philip took a fresh horse and said that he would go to Cwm Biga to see if Rhys had been taken there by mistake. It was mid-morning by the time he arrived at the grange on the side of Pumlumon and the monks were, as he had guessed, at work. Some he thought would have gone into the hills to tend the sheep, some would be seeing to the horses and others would be with the bees on the hillside. One thing was clear: there was no one at the farmhouse whom he could question and so he went up the hill on foot to where he thought the beehives were kept. He had been here before but only a few times.

Eventually, he came across the bee keepers. There were two monks there and he immediately went to ask them if a little boy had arrived there the day before with a monk from Cwm Hir. They knew nothing about the arrival of a monk driving a cart from Cwm Hir. They said they had not seen a cart arriving there the previous afternoon but some honey had been picked up early in the morning by a local person on a horse. They said that they had been very busy the day before with their bees and had not been down at the farm all afternoon but that perhaps some of their fellow monks would have seen something.

Philip waited until late evening for all the monks to return to the grange farmhouse and asked each one as they returned had they seen the cart or the little boy. They were more helpful than the monks at the abbey but no one had seen the cart or the little boy.

Philip left as night was falling and had a very difficult journey home in the dark walking his horse for most of the journey. He did not arrive at Cenarth until after midnight but the whole family was waiting for him desperate for news about Rhys. Gwenllian was inconsolable at the news that Philip brought back. She and Beth had cried for most of the day and were now exhausted.

During the day Philip had spent at Bryn Biga, the Cenarth estate had been searched thoroughly including the pool. The road between Cwm Hir and Cenarth was searched. The hillsides near and far were searched over the next few days by neighbours but to no avail. Rhys had disappeared, whatever that meant.

Gwenllian was in a desperate state made worse by the fact that there was nowhere else to search. Beth, on the third day of the disappearance, came to her and reminded her of the rumour she had heard about one of the monks being fond of young boys. Gwenllian spoke to Philip about the suggestion and he said that he would go immediately to the abbey and challenge the abbot. He would like to have taken Cynwrig with him but the farm had to be looked after and so he rode off as soon as he could to Cwm Hir.

He arrived at the abbey within the hour having ridden the horse hard. He was requested this time to remove all his weapons, which he did rather grudgingly. He had to wait before he could meet the abbot, a man he did not take to on a personal level. After the abbot had completed his devotional duties he met Philip in the presence of another monk.

Philip came straight to the point and asked, "Has Benedict returned yet?"

The abbot replied calmly, "No, he hasn't. We've heard that he has gone to Ystrad Fflur."

Philip stared at him in disbelief.

"Alas," the abbot continued. "Benedict is a lay brother and, as such, he is very reliable."

In fury with the abbot, Philip's attitude became more threatening and with his fists clenched, he took a step towards the abbot.

The abbot immediately reacted and demanded that he behave himself in the abbey and that he would have to report his threatening attitude to the abbey's provider and supporter, Sir Edmund Mortimer. He assured Philip that the abbey had nothing to do with the boy's disappearance and that he did not want to see him at the abbey ever again. The abbot said that Philip should look elsewhere for his lost son: the abbey had done everything it could to help him and his family.

Having calmed a little, Philip raised the other issue, which was playing on his mind. He asked if the rumour was true that there was a monk in the abbey who was known to befriend small boys. The abbot looked shocked initially but replied by saying that there indeed had been that rumour but that monk had been moved to an abbey in Gwent some months previously. He also stressed that the whole story regarding that particular monk was reliant entirely on rumour and that there had been no complaints.

The abbot made it clear that their meeting was over and reiterated his view that the abbey had nothing to do with his son's disappearance. He wished Philip well in his search and departed with the other monk.

Philip had no option other than to go home, which he did slowly and with a very heavy heart. He reported on the meeting to Gwenllian and Beth. Gwenllian was in despair.

The message given to the children gradually changed from "we are waiting for Rhys to come home" to "we hope he will come home". After a few weeks of despair, tears and heartache it became "we are praying for Rhys".

Philip was grieving quietly. He did not talk about Rhys and he did not mention his name. Gwenllian was desperately unhappy and as hope faded she sank further into the gloom of depression. Time is meant to heal, but this wound was too deep to ever heal. Every night she went to the empty bed and laid a single wild flower on it and then removed it in the morning.

She visited St Garmon's church most days. The church had a low wall surrounding it and the Cenarth family members were always buried there. It was a small limewashed wooden building and was centuries old. The inside was of simple construction with the wooden cladding giving it a warm feel that was often missing in stone structures. Philip played his part in ensuring that the church building was well maintained and limewashed as frequently as it was required. He and Gwenllian were regular users of this wonderfully peaceful building. As Gwenllian knew quite well, the church contained St Curig's staff, which was believed to have some magical powers. She prayed for Rhys and all her sons. She prayed that she would have Rhys back and that her other sons would be kept safe. She prayed at the altar and made wishes at St Curig's staff.

She prayed initially for the safe return of Rhys but as the weeks went by her prayer changed to requesting some hint of information about Rhys. Gwenllian went to the edge of despair and it was only the thought of her other children that kept her sane. Having prayed daily for some news of Rhys she began to question why had not one of these prayers produced something. The loss of a child is the worst loss of all and not to know what has happened to that child is even worse. Her grief had no means of being released at a grave side. There was no end to it.

Why had her prayers not been answered? Surely she had led a good life and deserved some help. She began to question the existence of God as a kind individual.

She had very low moments and then the next day, for no apparent reason, she would feel a little better. However, a better day was always followed by a sense of guilt. Guilt that she was there and Rhys was not, guilt that she had allowed him to go to Cwm Hir, guilt that she was not grieving all the time.

Her daily prayers would also contain statements directed at Rhys, telling him "I am still looking for you". Daily she would whisper this to herself first thing in the morning and last thing at night. Philip was not aware that she was saying this to herself but he noticed that she no longer kept the nightly vigil at Rhys's empty bed.

Iolo somehow got wind of Rhys's disappearance and came to Cenarth to see if the rumours were true. He only stayed for a few hours and moved on having experienced the sadness and anxiety in the family. Before leaving he intimated that he might see her father and would tell him about Rhys.

Then on the tenth day of August Owain Glyndŵr moved his army to the east of Wales passing southwards to Maelienydd and attacked the abbey at Cwm Hir. His men were instructed to search the abbey for a body of a young child. The abbey was regarded as being in Mortimer's camp and supportive of the king with some of the monks being Mortimer's spies. Little respect was shown for the abbot. The abbey was badly damaged in the search and also some parts were put to the torch.

Having exacted his wrath on Cwm Hir, Glyndŵr dispatched his army back north under the leadership of Rhys Gethin. Owain and his two sons, Gruffydd and Meredydd, called at Cenarth. He wanted to see Gwenllian to talk to her about her loss, sympathise with her and hold her.

As soon as he was off his horse she ran to him and collapsed into his arms. Owain was also suffering: he had lost a grandson and was angry and puzzled by the whole event.

He told her that despite a thorough search of the abbey building, outbuildings and gardens they had failed to find any trace of Rhys. They had also questioned the abbot, a supporter of Sir Edmund Mortimer. They had removed the abbot from his position together with his followers and given him a place to live at Mynachdy near Kington.

Glyndŵr deeply regretted that he had no additional information about Rhys and that he could not tell Gwenllian anything that would help solve the mystery.

Still in her father's arms Gwenllian continued to cry

openly saying through the tears, "I think of him every day".

Overhearing this, Gruffydd said a little awkwardly, "We were all very shocked when we received the news about Rhys. We are very sorry, Gwenllian."

Meredydd added looking at Gwenllian and then Philip, "We wish to commiserate with you Gwenllian and you Philip and we are very sorry that we have not been able to help you find Rhys. He was such lively and strong little boy when we met him during our last visit."

Gradually they moved into the hall and the conversation turned to the revolt. Glyndŵr spoke at length about the battle of Hyddgen and was very optimistic about the success of the revolt.

He appreciated that the Cenarth family were vulnerable and Gwenllian particularly so, but he suggested to Philip and Gwenllian that they could be of assistance to the revolt by spying on Mortimer and finding out what were his plans. Philip said that all the information they had was from rumours circulating in the market at Llanidloes or from the poets when they called, particularly Iolo.

Glyndŵr understood that this was the case but any information was always useful and he would like them to pass it on when possible. Information was vital for the success of the rebellion.

Gruffydd and Meredydd supported their father but only by saying the occasional "Yes!" at appropriate times in the conversation. They had been over this ground before at Cenarth.

Gwenllian agreed to act on the revolt's behalf and to find out more information about the opposition. In fact Gwenllian was keen to be involved. She wanted to support her father but she also wanted something to take her mind off Rhys. Philip was more cautious.

Her father told her that she could trust Iolo. He said to her that while Iolo likes his ale he never gets to a stage where he does not know what he is saying unlike some of the other poets. So he advised her to tell Iolo if there were any important bits of information she wanted to pass on to Glyndŵr. Iolo had direct access to the rebels through the safe houses system they had arranged.

He said they avoided using written messages because of the risk of these falling into the hands of Mortimer's agents or even the king's agents who were growing in numbers.

She wanted to know what she should do if there was some urgent information and Iolo was not at Cenarth.

"If things heat up in this area – which might happen after our attack on Cwm Hir I will get one of our agents in Llanidloes to contact you."

He would contact her, probably through one of her brothers. She agreed that this would be sensible and would avoid her getting into contact with people that might not be trustworthy.

Glyndŵr was glad of the opportunity to have met Gwenllian again and promised that he would call and see her again soon.

Their horses had been stabled, fed and rested and were brought out to the yard in front of the hall.

Horses of this quality were not seen in Cenarth or the surrounding area very often. They were strong, well groomed horses with fine leather harnesses and saddles. Philip commented on the stature of the horses, particularly Glyndŵr's, and asked if this was his famous charger, Llwyd y Bacsi. Glyndŵr said that this was not that horse but it was a good horse and almost as reliable as his favourite. His two boys, however, were quick to claim that their horses were better and that they could race him at any time.

The three mounted their horses with Gwenllian a little tearful because she did not wish to see them leaving. The three warriors left late in the afternoon in the direction of Llanidloes, going north to join their army.

Soon after they left Cenarth, Gwenllian also left to walk to St Garmon's church to pray. She needed the peace of the church. Their visit had raised hope and memories. Philip saw her go and allowed her time to reach the church before he followed her there slowly on horseback.

In the empty building she cried and prayed for Rhys, though the continued failure of her prayer to produce any result was at times weakening her faith. She was about to leave the church when Philip walked in quietly. She was standing near the ancient font. He came to her and without saying a word held her tight in his arms and there was a precious magical moment between them in the church, perhaps stemming from shared experiences or possibly there was a deep integration of their souls. Her spirit rose, giving her strength and restoring her faith in another world where she would meet Rhys again.

They went out of the dark church into the gloom. The sun had already set behind Cenarth Hill. They spent some time among the yew trees and graves and returned to Cenarth with Philip's horse carrying them both. She felt renewed.

In the autumn months that followed Rhys's disappearance, Philip put all his efforts into the farm and ensured that all the crops were safely gathered and stored while Gwenllian concentrated on her boys and the daily chores with Beth.

Philip heard from many sources how in many parts of

the country, particularly after the battle of Hyddgen, many of the homesteads had lost their bondmen and their labour during the rebellion because they had escaped to safer parts of the country. This was particularly true across the north of the country, but the problem was now spreading to many other parts and he was very pleased that they had managed to employ Cynwrig. They were not involved in the rebellion so he was hoping that there would be no attacks from the king's forces and agents. Clearly, from the visit by Glyndŵr and his sons, no forceful pressure was coming from the rebellion side on the Cenarth family to join the rebels. This is what Philip wanted, but Gwenllian was torn by her loyalties to Cenarth and her husband on one side and her father on the other. She had a deep desire to show to her father that she was as loyal and as supportive of him as his other daughters.

So, Cenarth remained unaffected by troops from either side to any significant extent. Philip's reputation as a person who was not politically active and his desire not to be involved kept the troubles at bay. There had been the occasional group of armed men from both sides who had called at Cenarth and Philip had always supplied them with good ale and plenty to eat and they had all left thinking what a fine welcome they had from Philip and Gwenllian.

# Chapter 5

A s THE WINTER months of 1401 approached, Gwenllian
fought her own battle between despair born out of grief
and the gradual decline of hope against her desire to remain
strong of mind for the sake of her other sons. The latter force
gained ground as the new life began to grow inside her, slowly
giving her new hope.

She still felt guilty when, during her chores, she realised
she had not thought of Rhys for a while. She prayed for him
every day believing that the prayer would be answered soon
but also believing that it would somehow bring her and
Rhys closer together. She prayed for Rhys to forgive her
for having lost him. She prayed that one day soon he would
arrive back at Cenarth and call her name as he entered his
home. This cruel hope was everything to her, though it was
dashed every day.

The autumn months were tiring her with the winds from
the south-west howling like dogs in the trees and the rain
smashing horizontally into the walls of the old hall. The
hours of darkness increased day by day and with the life and
soul of Cenarth dented and damaged the forces of despair
gained strength.

Her resilience to these attacks was boosted as she learnt
to lean on her religious beliefs to carry her through these
months. She used these beliefs to rest her soul on when she
felt her mind was tired from the strain just as she used to
lean on tables and walls in the latter part of her pregnancy
with Rhys and the others. The little church of St Garmon
had been of assistance to Gwenllian during this time and its

association with the conception of her new baby had given the place greater meaning to her.

It was the not knowing where Rhys was or what had happened to him that made it so unbearable. She often thought of the parents of those Flemish soldiers killed at Hyddgen. Their loved ones killed in a battle far away from home and left on the battle fields or in shallow graves for the crows and foxes to devour. Gwenllian had to come to some kind of acceptance of the cross she had to carry – it would take time.

Unlike Gwenllian, Philip remained angry: angry at the abbey, angry at God and angry at the world. He could not get it out of his mind that he did not trust the abbot whom Glyndŵr had displaced. He visited St Garmon's church occasionally but did not derive the same level of comfort as Gwenllian. He went mainly because Gwenllian wanted him to accompany her. Philip's main source of relief was in his work and he put all his energy into the farm and the stock. He had thought of joining the rebels in their northern hideouts but felt he had an obligation to his other boys and the new baby.

Beth was also devastated by Rhys's disappearance – after all she had brought him up. She had fed him as a baby, seen him crawling about the house and taking his first steps. She was there when he said his first words. Gwenllian thought that his ma–, ma–, ma– was an attempt to say mam while Beth was quietly sure that his be–, be–, be– was his effort at saying Beth. She poured her attention and love on to the other boys and gradually for her Rhys was becoming a memory.

Cynwrig, though strong and healthy, gradually lost interest in his work on the farm and the quality of his work declined. Gwenllian noticed this and asked Philip, "Have you noticed that Cynwrig is not as committed to the farm as he was at the beginning?"

"Yes, he is often distracted and absent-minded," replied Philip.

"Do you think he feels guilty about Rhys being with him when he went missing?"

"I don't think so. Beth does not feel guilty, does she?" said Philip.

"No. Beth seems to have coped well." Gwenllian said thoughtfully.

"I accidentally overheard some of the farm hands talking a few days ago about Cynwrig. They were of the opinion that he wishes to leave and join your father's army in the north. I would be very disappointed if he were to leave us because when he is at his best he is very good and he has learnt our ways well. He never gives me any trouble," said Philip.

Gwenllian, shocked, said, "I had no idea that he supported my father."

"Neither did I, but apparently he has held these feelings for a while but did not tell us so as not to appear to curry favour with us," Philip told her.

"When is he leaving?"

"The farm hands seem to think he wants to leave at the end of the month," Philip replied.

"He has never said a word to me or Beth," she said. "If he had told Beth she would have told me."

"I will go and see him now and talk to him about it. He is as much use to you as he is to me. Do you want me to dissuade him from leaving?" he had to ask knowing that it would cause a dilemma for Gwenllian.

She hesitated for a few moments, "No, encourage him to

join my father's men. He has probably made his mind up and my father needs good men like him."

"I'll let you know what he says," he said as he walked across the yard to where Cynwrig was cutting logs.

Gwenllian went immediately to find Beth in the hall. Discovering her stoking the fire she asked her, "Did you know that Cynwrig wants to leave and join my father?"

Beth looked at her in shock, then, reflecting a little, she said, "Well now that you say it, I did hear two of the farm hands mentioning it a day or two ago. I didn't think anything of it because I thought it was just empty gossip."

"So there may be something in it. Well, Philip has gone to ask him. He'll be back soon."

Philip came into the hall to confirm that Cynwrig would leave soon and join the rebels in the north.

By October all the crops were safely gathered and stored. The family and all the farm workers gathered in the yard to wave farewell to Cynwrig. The parting with Beth was emotional with Beth crying into her apron and Cynwrig giving her extra hugs. He left walking down the track towards Llanidloes. The boys stood at the top of the track waving him goodbye until he was out of sight.

The boys were very sad to see him go but were told he would be back once their grandfather's war was over, but the adults knew it was unlikely that they would ever see him again at Cenarth.

Philip, through choice, was more involved in the farm than ever before and he did not make much of an effort to find a replacement for Cynwrig immediately. Apart from the difficulty in finding men to work on the farm, Philip knew that it was not wise to bring a stranger into the household for fear that he would be an agent of Sir Edmund Mortimer, who was constantly seeking information on behalf of the king as to Glyndŵr's intentions and whereabouts. Where better to place an agent than at Cenarth?

Unfortunately, Cenarth could not be managed for long without getting a replacement for Cynwrig and so Philip had to go to Llanidloes again to find a suitable farmworker. This time there was no helpful man waiting to find him a suitable person. He visited the inns in town and let it be known that he wanted to hire a farmhand. He soon realised that it was not going to be easy to replace Cynwrig and he returned home without any success. However, at the Llanidloes market the following Saturday a local farmer told him that he had a spare man and would release him to Philip. In a week's time the new man, Simon, started work at Cenarth. There had been too many changes in recent months and the boys did not take to Simon immediately, but with the passage of time and a month on Simon was on the best of terms with all the Cenarth people.

The rebellion continued with Glyndŵr's men attacking Welshpool at the end of October. At Cenarth they wondered if Cynwrig had been there at the attack. Gwenllian wondered if he was still alive because she knew there are always casualties in wars.

The king retaliated by killing, in a horrific manner, the brave and much-respected Llewelyn ap Gruffydd Fychan in Llandovery, which did not do the king's cause any favours in west Wales. It gave the poets a subject to write about and to win more men over to Glyndŵr's banner.

Then, in November, the king established his headquarters in the abbey at Ystrad Fflur, sending the abbot and monks to find other accommodation. Some went to Cymer Abbey and some came to Cwm Hir.

The Christmas celebrations at Cenarth in 1401 were more subdued than normal because of Rhys's absence. It was their first Christmas without him. Iolo and the other poets visited but the usual high spirits were not present at the farmstead.

Christmas and the beginning of the year was a bad time for Gwenllian. Though she was carrying the new baby inside her giving a new hope for the future she still had vivid nightmares about Rhys. She still wondered where he was. She often thought in the middle of the dark nights if he was dead, where was his body? She could see and hear him in her dreams calling for her to help him just like she had heard the wounded soldier at Rhyd-y-groes.

The nightmares were disturbing her and causing her to lose sleep. She had long learnt that when they came they would not go away and she would get up from bed quietly without disturbing Philip and pick up her youngest boy, Meredydd, and without waking him go and sit with him on her lap by the embers of the fire in the otherwise dark room. During the dark autumn and winter months she did this almost every night and the lack of sleep would affect her feelings, lowering her spirits and making her too tired to think. Before dawn, she would return Meredydd to his bed, again without waking him. She could not imagine what she would do if she did not have Meredydd to nurse at night and a new baby to think about.

She would sit there, turning things over in her mind waiting for the dawn to come and would feel relieved when the first suggestion of the dawn came at the east-facing window. Then she would have the day to endure worrying about the next night that was coming. This sometimes repeated itself for days and sometimes for weeks. It was draining her energy and happiness seemed another life away. There were moments of deep despair that winter.

As the days went by, hope, sometimes her friend and at other times her greatest enemy, died slowly, imperceptibly slowly until it came that there was no hope and with that a sense of some relief. This did not make Gwenllian feel better but the anxiety coming from hope reduced a little and this afforded her a better chance of sleeping, which in turn made her feel less tired and so she could get on and do some of the chores around the house and farm. Most around her thought they saw an improvement at the turn of the year and the lengthening of the day helped. Christmas is always difficult when there is a bereavement and there is a relief in getting it over and done with. Gwenllian felt this relief, which added to the improvement in her spirits.

It was during this period that the concept of searching for Rhys had gradually changed from finding Rhys alive to finding out what happened to him.

Then in February a bright new star appeared in the sky just as the gospels said had appeared in the sky at the time of the birth of Christ. The large new star was vying with the moon for the night sky and there was a natural candidate for the role of honour. The general view in the towns, villages and farms was that it was a signal favouring Glyndŵr. It was a signal from God that the promised deliverer of the Welsh had arrived. This was the man whom the prophets of the nation had spoken about for centuries. This was the signal waited for so patiently. It is true to say that Glyndŵr and his co-conspirators encouraged this idea at every opportunity, perhaps because they did genuinely believe that it was an omen of success to come.

Of course everyone had his and her own interpretation

and hope linked to the star. Gwenllian saw the star as a personal signal to her from Rhys and she puzzled for days as to what the star was trying to say to her. After a few weeks, however, of puzzling, praying and making wishes at the staff of St Curig and in old magic wells with no effect, her belief waned again and she rationalised that this star was not there as a signal to her but more likely to the glory of her father and the uprising.

In April, Gwenllian gave birth to her fifth son Owain. The baby was a little early but it was an uneventful birth and it brought joy to Cenarth at last. The pace of life quickened. Gwenllian felt the relief that every mother experiences of having the event over and the baby healthy with all fingers and toes in place. She would have liked a daughter perhaps but a son did go some way to amend for the loss of Rhys. She flatly refused to name the new baby Rhys. Beth also discovered a reason to be happy again and she enjoyed looking after the new baby.

Life at Cenarth picked up, with neighbours calling, exchanging views and discussing life in general. The rebellion was again discussed though it was felt that what action was taking place was far away. As in the previous year, the rebels were quiet over the winter months but started their activities again in the spring.

To everyone's surprise in April the bright star that had lit the night sky disappeared as quickly as it had appeared. People were used to the star so that when it went mysteriously people were now concerned that it had disappeared as much as they were concerned when it appeared.

Iolo called at Cenarth to first congratulate Gwenllian and Philip on the birth of baby Owain, and secondly to deliver news about the rebellion, and thirdly because he was thirsty and hungry. Perhaps his priorities were in the reverse order but he told everyone otherwise.

"I am so pleased that the new boy has been named after his grandfather, the prince of Wales," he said, full of joy with a smile the shape of a crescent moon appearing on his round face. He drank to the health of the new baby and recited a poem for the baby and his parents.

There was a general raising of mugs and shouts of congratulations.

He had a mixed bag of news about Glyndŵr. "Glyndŵr attacked Caernarfon but after causing much damage in the town he failed to take the castle. They were very disappointed."

"Was Cynwrig involved?" asked Beth.

"I don't know. But if he has joined Glyndŵr's men then he surely was because Glyndŵr threw everything at that castle. Thankfully, the casualties on our side were low."

"Good," said Gwenllian loudly as did many others.

Iolo continued with his report, "That traitor Hywel Sele, Glyndŵr's cousin, tried to kill Owain but Owain had got the better of him and dispatched him, thank God. Glyndŵr was unharmed."

Gwenllian was shocked. She knew Hywel Sele of Nannau, near Dolgellau, from the time she was a child in Meirionydd. "Are you sure my father is unharmed?"

"Yes. Yes, Gwenllian. He was not even scratched by the traitor. But it does show how careful we need to be – there are enemies everywhere. Sele was trying to curry favour with the king," Iolo announced loudly and with derision.

"Let me give you some more good news," Iolo said. "Glyndŵr has captured Lord Grey and has imprisoned him in Dolbadarn Castle. This is a great success for our side. The king will have to pay a ransom for the lord."

Iolo, sensing that a little of the dark cloud that had descended on this farmstead was clearing a little, ventured some storytelling and encouraged them to sing.

He was able, during a chat he had with Philip and Gwenllian, to put some things in perspective for them by telling stories of families devastated by the Black Death and young sons killed in the rebellion. Iolo stayed for a few days and left the family in a better frame of mind than when he had arrived.

On the morning that he left, Iolo had a word with Gwenllian on her own. He could see that she had made a rapid recovery from the birth of Owain and had been boosted by the birth of a healthy son. She was beginning to emerge from her grief after the loss of Rhys.

"I can see that you are recovering," he said to her gently.

"Yes," she confessed to him. "And now that I am a little better, I would like to support my father with the revolt in the same way as my brothers and sisters are supporting him. I realise I can't go into the mountains and fight with his men but I would like to find out things about what his enemies are doing and planning and pass the information back to him through you. I would like to become his eyes and ears in this area."

"Well, your father has told me that there is nothing that he would like more than for you and Philip to keep him informed about what is happening in this area. As tenants of the Mortimers you are ideally placed to get information about the family. Find out if he is gathering an army, find out if he is totally supportive of the king. Find out everything you can about him and about anyone of interest to Glyndŵr."

Hoping that Iolo could enlighten her she said, "I don't

know much about the Mortimer family other than the name and that Cenarth is on their land."

As she had expected, Iolo could not be stopped. "Well, where shall I start? The Mortimer family is a very important family in Wales and in England and it is also a very complex family with aspirations to rule Wales and England. Roger Mortimer died at a young age in Ireland in 1398 when his two sons, Edmund and another Roger were very young. The Roger Mortimer, who had died in Ireland, had a younger brother Edmund and he is now in charge of the Mortimer estate until his nephews come of age."

"When will the nephews take over the estate?" interrupted Gwenllian.

"Well, this is the interesting point, you see," said Iolo moving his chair closer to her as though he was about to divulge a state secret. "Since the nephews have a good claim to the throne of England they have been imprisoned in Windsor Castle by their rival, Henry IV. The elder of the two boys was the fifth earl of March and is a descendant of Edward III and thus the heir to the throne of England."

"The Mortimers are of royal blood then?"

"Yes. Some say that the young Mortimer is the rightful heir and that, the present king had murdered the rightful king – King Richard. So, the position of the Mortimers is an interesting one and they will have to support the king while the two boys are imprisoned."

Iolo had managed to grip Gwenllian's interest and she could see that Cenarth was in a good position to spy on the Mortimer family.

She decided that she would indeed gather as much information as she could about this influential family and pass it on to her father.

Unknown to Iolo there was another driving force behind Gwenllian's decision to subvert work for her father and that was that the more she knew about what was happening around her, the more likely she was of finding something out about what happened to Rhys. This last motive was to prove to be the most influential and enduring of all, encouraging her to persevere.

"If I do find things out about Sir Edmund Mortimer then how do I get the information to you?" she asked.

"Pass what you can to me directly when you can. Glyndŵr has an agent operating in Llanidloes and he collects information and has his own system of contacting Glyndŵr."

"What's his name?" asked Gwenllian immediately.

"I don't know," said Iolo. "His name has to be kept a secret. Your father may be the only person who knows his real name. For the time being give me the information."

Gwenllian was content with this arrangement and they were soon parting with Iolo disappearing down the track south towards Rhayader.

Gwenllian was pleased with the day's achievement and started to plan what she would do to aquire the desired information. She needed to be well informed herself, she argued, if she was to help her father. She needed to know what the king was up to, and what Sir Edmund Mortimer was doing.

She took more notice of what was said at the market in Llanidloes on Saturdays, indeed she made sure that she attended the markets and listened in on others' conversations. She paid far more attention to what the poets who visited Cenarth had to say and in this way she gathered a good understanding of the state of affairs in Wales. It also improved her knowledge of her own family, particularly of her own half-sisters in Hereford and Gwent.

What she was gathering in this way was no more than tittle-tattle and she did not get any information of significant value to her father. There was nothing of sufficient importance that she felt that she should inform Iolo about and certainly there was no reason to contact her father.

Philip showed no interest in the information she gathered and thought it no more than gossip. There were times when Gwenllian found this irritating but then she would remember that he was a good man and was only mildly interested in things that happened outside the boundaries of Cenarth.

Philip recognised her keenness for information for her father was a part of her need to be accepted by the Glyndŵr family and it was a substitute for the loss of Rhys. He had taken to doing more work on the farm as a means of keeping his mind busy and so it was only right that Gwenllian did something that interested her and shifted her mind from Rhys. He was content to condone what she was doing provided it did not bring any trouble to their family.

# Chapter 6

M ANY LOCAL FARMERS and their wives attended the weekly Saturday market in Llanidloes not only to sell their produce and buy goods but also to find out the latest gossip – who was ill, who had died and what had they died of other than lack of breath. Philip was a regular attender at the market and would have a cup of ale in one or other of the many inns. Gwenllian was an irregular attender until she decided that it was a good place to gather information.

On the Friday evening, Philip and Gwenllian would decide on all they wanted to take to sell and either a cart or a horse would be loaded ready for an early start. If there was stock of any kind to be sold then the stockman or the shepherd would accompany the stock to the market starting at dawn, usually leaving slightly ahead of Philip and Gwenllian. If they were taking the ox cart then Dafydd the now eldest son would sometimes accompany them. Dafydd would stay with his father all the time at the market. This was normal practice for boys to be with their fathers and thus learn the ways of the market early on in their lives. Gwenllian insisted that Dafydd stick close to Philip but she need not have worried because his father kept a close eye on him anyway.

Dafydd would happily sit in the cart with Gwenllian while Philip drove the oxen. It was a rocky ride along the stone track leading down the side of Cenarth Hill and then down to the river Dulas, which they would cross at the ford just above the mill. Rarely was the water in the river higher than a foot deep but following a heavy bout of rain this ford could not always be crossed safely and Philip would not take the cart but instead he and Gwenllian, if she was so minded to go to the market, would go on horseback.

After crossing the Dulas they followed the track around the side of the Wenallt to Tylwch and then continued on the west bank of the Dulas until they could ford it again less than a mile from the town. The section of the track at Tylwch was dark and somewhat foreboding in the wooded narrow valley. With Philip, Gwenllian had no concerns but like many others if she were on her own on a horse or without an armed man she would take a different route. On her own she would not go all the way down to Tylwch but ford the Dulas to the east bank higher up the river and go around Llwydiarth, pass above the old Banhadlog Chapel and then descend past Bryn Du down to the southern outskirts of Llanidloes.

Whichever route they took they would usually leave the cart or horses near Maes-y-dre and walk into town. On a normal Saturday market day there would be many such carts there and several horses with a few local town lads paid in kind to look after them.

Llanidloes was a thriving market town with close on seventy burgesses, making, buying and selling a wide range of goods from leather mugs to garden produce. The town had also expanded on to the far side of the river with almost as many inhabitants in that part of the town as were living within the town's boundaries. These people living in Frankwell, as that part of town was called, were disliked by the burgess and regarded as no better than country people.

The houses were mainly timber framed with limewashed wattle and gaud filling the gaps. The town looked bright and clean. On Saturdays the town's population would at least treble with people coming from the countryside farmsteads to sell their produce and to buy what was for sale at the numerous stalls.

The Cwm Hir Abbey was always well represented with monks coming from the abbey itself as well as the outlying granges that they owned in the surrounding district. The Cwm Biga grange always had stock and produce to sell, ranging from horses and sheep to honey gathered from bees feeding on the Pumlumon heather. Their honey and the mead made from it were always sought after and of a high quality. The mead produced from this honey was probably the best mead produced in the area and bought only by the more affluent farmers.

The market hall was situated at the cross roads in the middle of the town and was built on large squared tree trunks with a thatch roof and was open on all sides. This was used on market days to sell eggs and dairy products though as the town had expanded these products were now also sold on Long Bridge Street. The market hall was the centre of activity on all days but particularly so on Saturday mornings. Good use was made of the old hall by locals and visitors alike and on a rainy day people usually crammed under it for shelter.

Cups and plates and other eating and drinking utensils were sold and bought on the street linking the market hall to the disused castle. This was always a busy part of town with people eyeing the products displayed and deciding which mug or plate to purchase.

The castle, at the end of this street had been left to go to ruins over the last hundred years and many of the stones had been used to produce solid bases for the burgess' houses. Other stones had even been taken secretly to secure bases for the houses at Frankwell but not with the approval of the burgess. The wall of the castle facing the market hall had been added to and converted into an inn, called very appropriately the Castle Inn and was the largest inn in the town with a long frontage. Its floor was cobbled from its castle days.

The street leading east, named Long Bridge Street led to the river Severn and the long bridge crossing it. This was the street by which the people living in Frankwell entered the town looking for bargains at the numerous stalls on the street. As they traversed the long bridge they would pass the church of St Idles on their right standing there above the confluence of the Clywedog and the Severn rivers in an idyllic and quiet spot even on market day.

The wide street leading south from the centrally situated market hall had an oak tree at the top end, hence its name Oak Street. The old oak tree had been there for a long time and was now well past its prime. The farm animals were bought and sold in this street. On a typical market day there would be cattle, sheep, pigs, geese, ducks and hens for sale. This was where Philip would come: this was where his interest lay. Gwenllian, however, preferred to spend time in the street leading from the old Castle to the long bridge. She would also visit the church and say a brief prayer.

The first Saturday in April 1402 was a fine dry day and the weather during the previous week had been fairly dry apart from one or two heavy showers as was usual at this time of year and the rivers were relatively low. It had been cold with the first light of the day but the sun was warming up the land and it promised to be a nice early April day.

Gwenllian knew many of the people at the market by sight and knew the people from the Cenarth and St Garmon area very well. She would stop to talk to some but exchanged only nods and greetings with others. She stopped with women of her own standing and they talked about their respective families, their weekly ups and downs, the weather and occasionally the taxes and tolls. As always the latter were objected to and were always too high. If a local collection had taken place recently there were always moans and groans all round and the collectors' physical appearance found to be wanting and denigrated generously.

Gwenllian had alluring qualities, she was her father's daughter, but there had been no knightly marriage for her. But she had done well for herself: Philip was pleasant, kind and her marriage had considerable status in the community. She was generally liked. She did have self doubts and there were times while walking around the market she thought that people might be talking about her and making snide remarks. She often wondered if some people were asking why was her husband not in the mountains with the rebels and her father.

Gwenllian had been listening carefully to what people were talking about as she walked around the market but she was also constantly looking at the young boys running around dodging between people. She could not help herself from searching for Rhys, knowing that she would not find him. He was always on her mind. She had not accepted the disappearance as well as Philip seemed to have done. She kept returning to the determined thought that she would not give up looking for him and she had certainly not given up hope of finding out what had become of Rhys and never would.

During her meandering around the market she exchanged glances with a man of about her own age and about her own height with, from what she could see of his face not covered by the slightly ginger coloured beard, an open and friendly face. He was well dressed and was only mildly interested in the market. She thought no more about it and went on to see what was on display under the market hall.

She had been there for a few minutes looking at the young chicks for sale when for no real reason she picked her head up to again meet the glance of the same man. He held her glance for longer than was natural and did not move away but lowered his eyesight only to raise it again almost immediately to again meet her eyes after she had done exactly the same thing.

Gwenllian was unnerved slightly by the eye contact and moved away from the roofed building "No, this is my imagination playing tricks on me" she said to herself. "He only did exactly what I did myself. There is no significance to it," and she moved on in the direction of the Castle Inn to view the mugs and plates.

She leant forward to view a plate on a stall to see if it was free of faults and rested well on a flat surface. She decided that the plate met her standards and she would buy it. She straightened up, moved back half a step and found herself next to the man she had exchanged glances with earlier. He was looking at her and before she had time to move away he said, "Very nice stable plate."

"Yes."

"My name is Robert Fox. I would like to talk to you. If we step back here it will only take a minute."

Seeing no reason not to talk to him she obliged.

"I have some mulberry wine in this flagon. If you take some in this small mug it will look as though I am selling you some," he said pouring her some wine.

She accepted the small mug and drank from it.

"Your father has asked me to meet you and talk to you," said Robert Fox.

Gwenllian was shocked and replied sceptically, "Oh, yes?"

Then she started questioning him, "How do you know my father? When did you speak to him?"

Fox was not perturbed by the questions. "You are Glyndŵr's daughter and I spoke to your father a few days ago. He wants you to get some information for him."

This bold statement surprised her and she asked again, "Where did you meet him?"

"I can't tell you that for obvious reasons," he replied.

"Are you the one he told me was his agent in Llanidloes?" she asked remembering what her father had told her the previous summer.

He hesitated a second before replying, "Yes."

"What does he want to know?" she asked.

He looked at her for a few seconds and with a lowered voice he said, "He wants all the information you have gathered."

"I have nothing to pass on today," she said, admitting with that statement that she was indeed gathering information for her father.

"No. I didn't think you did but it's important that we meet every week when you attend the market. This is not a good place to meet: too many people can see us and hear us in this place. I'm always here on market days and I hire a room at the back of Castle Inn," Fox explained.

He noticed that she had finished the wine and asked, "Did you enjoy the mulberry wine?"

"Yes, I did, thank you," she said smiling at him.

He nodded with a smile at her and just as he was moving away from her, he said quietly, "See you next week by the old market hall."

She left the inn soon after, being unable to contain her

interest and went again towards the market hall. The bustle there had reduced, the chicks had been sold and the women there were clearing up ready to go for a drink before making their way home. She walked around hoping to see Robert Fox again to get a better look at him but she did not see him again.

The morning at the market always passed quickly for Gwenllian but it had been a particularly exciting morning that day and when it was time to return to Cenarth she went to seek out Philip in Oak Street, his stamping ground on market day. He was usually to be found with a cup of ale outside one of the inns in that street and that Saturday was no different.

On the way home for reasons best known to herself she decide not to tell Philip about the meeting with Robert Fox, perhaps it was because she did not think that he would approve.

Gwenllian was quite excited about her contact with Robert Fox and gave it much thought during the week. She wondered how she could find out anything that would be of use to her father and also it raised her hope of finding some information about Rhys. It never crossed her mind not to meet him the following Saturday.

The following week, Gwenllian and Philip went to the market but despite walking around the market and staying an inordinate amount of time in the street leading from the market to the Castle Inn she did not see Robert Fox. The same thing happened the following week and the week after that. She spent a long time by the market hall and was very disappointed and was beginning to think that she had imagined it all. She wondered if he had gone to see her father or had been involved in a skirmish with the king's supporters or had even been apprehended or murdered by those supporters.

Then, on the first market day in May, she was thrilled again when she caught a glimpse of him near the market hall. It was raining and it was very crowded under the shelter of the old hall. She wanted to meet him again but people were moving about quickly with their heads down and it was difficult to see where he had gone. So, she thought the best thing was to again go to the stall where they had met four weeks earlier.

No sooner than she had reached the stall than she was face to face with Robert Fox. She was delighted and relieved knowing now that she had not imagined the first meeting. But her delight soon changed to anxiety when Robert Fox said to her nodding in the direction of the Castle Inn, "It's far too crowded and wet here to talk. I have hired a room in the Castle Inn and will be staying there tonight. Come with me to my room and we can talk there. It's important."

Gwenllian was initially shocked and unsettled by the suggestion, but she calmed herself a little and said to herself that if she was to work for the rebels she would have to take risks and not be surprised about what she would be asked to do.

While Gwenllian hesitated, Fox himself had already turned his back on her, clearly expecting her to follow him and in the bustle of the busy street and rain she would have had to shout after him that she was not going otherwise he would not have heard. She followed him, pushing through the crowds towards the inn. He entered the inn through the low dark door and disappeared into the darkness leaving the door slightly ajar for her to follow.

As she took the first step over the threshold she again had second thoughts. She feared that someone would see her enter and recognise her. She looked back over her shoulder and overcame her fear when she saw a boy with his mother running towards the door. The boy reminded her of Rhys and they were going to enter the inn for shelter from the rain and a drink. She had been in the inn before anyway and she entered just before she was pushed in by the boy and his mother.

It was hot and sweaty inside and she initially could not see what was ahead of her. As her eyes became accustomed to the gloom she saw Robert Fox about two yards away talking to the inn's landlord. There were a few people separating her from Fox and they were asking her, "Come in from the rain have you?"

She nodded her agreement to them and moved slowly towards Fox. The landlord had lent over the serving bar and given Fox something in his hand, which she assumed was a key to the room. Fox turned towards her and indicated to her to follow him. Another pang of anxiety came over her fearing now that she would be seen going up the stairs with Fox.

But Fox passed the stairs and went out through the back door and she allowed a minute or two to pass before she followed him. Once she was outside in the square yard separating the back of the inn from the inner part of the old castle she saw that he was there waiting for her. He pointed to a stone staircase on the right hand side of the yard. This yard was new to Gwenllian and she could see that the inn's stables were on the left, the remains of a castle wall on the far side and a small two-storeyed building with the external stone staircase on the right.

The staircase went up to a timber-framed room with faded wattle and gaud filling. The upper room rested on top of a stone-built storage room. Gwenllian followed him up the staircase without thinking. The steps were steep but she was up in no time. He unlocked and opened the door for her and in they went. Gwenllian was very unsure of what she was doing but knew she could not afford to hesitate outside the door.

As she stepped in, she noticed that the stable door on the opposite side of the yard was open and told Robert Fox. He told her not to worry about being seen because he had checked that there was no one in the stables. He knew that the stable lad was not about because he had been sent on an errand for the landlord. Gwenllian was not so confident for she had probably much more to lose than this stranger.

The room was small with a narrow wooden three slit window, which because of its height above the ground no one from the outside could see into the room nor listen to the conversation in the room. There was a small table, a chair and a bed lifted a good foot off the floor and against the wall opposite the window. There was no fireplace. It took her a while to get used to the darkness. He indicated that she should sit on the chair and he lent on the wall adjacent to the door. He had a friendly and likeable manner.

He said in a very business-like manner that he had been away meeting the rebels. He told her a little of what had happened across Wales in the last few months and how Glyndŵr had attacked many places in the Ruthin area including properties belonging to Lord Grey.

"I have not got any wine or mead to offer you but I don't suppose you want to be here long anyway."

"No," she replied firmly.

"Let me come straight to the point. How are you going to set about gathering information for your father?"

"I just gather information I pick up around the market here at Llanidloes mainly," she replied.

"How often does your father call to see you?" he asked.

While still looking around the room she replied, "Not very often. If he is passing near us he will call at Cenarth."

"And how often is that?" he asked.

"Not very often," she repeated.

"Every month?" he asked, determined to get the facts correct.

"About once a year," she replied.

He was hanging on to every word she said. He was giving her his undivided attention and it pleased her to be able to answer his questions and to be made to feel important.

"I would like to meet you again next Saturday," he said. "We can meet in this room. It's quite safe for you here. There is no need for you to walk through the inn: you can go round the side and across the yard. Just check that the stable lad is occupied in the stable or not there at all."

"I am uncomfortable crossing the yard and climbing the stairs," she said with concern in her voice.

"Next Saturday," he said, "I will see you by the market hall and I will signal you that I will wait for you in this room. If there is anything different I will tell you. I will check the stables first and if you are seen behind the inn or on the stairs, tell whoever sees you that you have lost your way."

"How can I be sure that you will be at the market next week?" she asked reminding him that he had failed to meet her in previous weeks.

"We are having information that there is something afoot in this area and we want to know exactly what is going to happen," he said.

She nodded her head in acceptance.

"Thank you for seeing me," he said. "Your father will be very pleased with you."

As she was leaving she quietly bid farewell to him then

moved quickly out of the door, down the stone steps, across the yard and was around the side of the inn and out into the street without anyone taking any notice of her.

She realised that as long as there was no one coming out of the stables as she was going down the stairs and crossing the yard then no one would see her. Thinking of her next visit, Gwenllian was not confident, first that Fox would check the stables thoroughly and secondly that saying to someone you were lost would be believable. So, she decided that she would check the stables herself before going up to the room and would think of something better to say if she were caught in the yard or on the stairs. However, she was determined that she would visit him again, as agreed on the following Saturday.

On the way back to Cenarth, Gwenllian felt more alive than ever and the excitement was helping to nullify a little the loss of Rhys. She again decided not to tell Philip but he did notice that she was in a happier state of mind and was pleased to see this improvement.

# Chapter 7

G WENLLIAN WENT TO the market again on the following Saturday, the eighth day of May 1402. She saw Fox by the old market hall as agreed and after a while went around the back of the inn, checked the stables and finding no one there she went quickly up the stairs to the door of Fox's room. She knocked gently; the door opened and she went in.

The room had not changed. The bed was there and she was not sure whether she found it threatening or part of the excitement that helped to propel her on her mission.

Gwenllian was a little nervous and explained, "I feel very exposed coming up the stairs and the seconds I stand to knock on the door feel like hours. I know that it is unlikely that anyone would come round the back, but it is possible and I would find it difficult to explain what I was doing round the back, never mind up the stairs. If I saw someone who knew me and many do, it would be difficult to explain. Certainly it would be impossible to explain to Philip if he saw me."

She continued, "Country people see everybody while the town people see nobody. What's more, they like talking about everything they see. I'm afraid of being seen on the steps. It makes me nervous."

Fox reassured her, "You don't have to knock just walk in. I can leave the door ajar. Also, if people are going to think the worst perhaps we should behave in that way."

Gwenllian was shocked and Fox realised he had gone too far too quickly and said, "I'm only pulling your leg. I do agree we need to find other places to meet. We could meet casually around the market and exchange information."

A casual meeting in the street would be less conspicuous but was that what she wanted? Didn't she also like the thrill that came from climbing those ten steps with her pulse increasing with every step? It definitely gave her a buzz.

"Yes," she said, "a casual meeting in the street would be less risky." Her reply was not totally convincing and she added "I mustn't stay long," wishing now to cover up for the lack of conviction he must have noticed in her previous statement.

He made no comment but motioned her to sit on the bed. He stayed in his chair.

"Have you heard anything from your father?" he asked.

"No," she replied. "But generally people are saying that he and his friends are very active in the north and are unlikely to come to this area for a while."

"I'm not so sure. People I've spoken to think that your father is planning an attack into mid Wales."

Gwenllian was quick to respond, "They are always speculating in that way. I've not heard any more talk of it than usual."

Fox then said "Your father would like to know what Mortimer is planning, that is if he is planning anything. We would like to know what his response would be if Glyndŵr attacked this area."

"How can I find out without meeting Mortimer or his friends?" asked Gwenllian, knowing that she had no contacts with such an important family.

"There is talk that Mortimer is discussing what to do and may meet some of his tenants to demand their loyalty and support," said Fox. "If he calls a meeting it would be useful if you got involved. I think you could learn a lot and we could pass the information to your father."

"I will do my best," replied Gwenllian. "If such a meeting is called I will go with Philip but I have not heard that Sir Edmund has any intention of calling a meeting."

"We will need to meet next week for me to know if Mortimer is making any move," said Fox.

"What if we meet casually near the honey sellers in Long Bridge Street, on the left as you look from here about halfway along the street, about midday?" she enquired. "I always need honey, because our own yield was low this year and everyone at Cenarth has a sweet tooth and it's good for the boys anyway."

Fox agreed to this arrangement and Gwenllian got up and moved to go. Fox suggested that she could stay a little longer. Though she was at ease in the room and was pleased that she now had a clear task, she was too concerned about meeting someone as she went down the stairs to stay any longer. Also, she could never be sure that someone had not seen her enter the room and might be watching to see how long she would stay. It would be easier to explain five minutes than thirty minutes.

That anxiety did not leave her until she was back with the people milling around the market hall.

She felt quite exhilarated as she moved with a spring in her step to the honey stall. She quite liked Fox. She bought a pot of honey and went to meet Philip.

On the Tuesday, the eleventh day of May following Gwenllian's last meeting with Fox, Philip received notice from Sir Edmund Mortimer demanding a meeting in a week's time with his main Radnor tenants at Rhyd Ithon, a ford on the river Ithon, west of the Radnor Forest and south-west of Knighton.

The demand was delivered by two men, estate administers of the Mortimer lands, and they were careful to remind Philip that the Mortimer estate had been very lenient in taking up the rents and services for a few years. They explained that the meeting had been arranged to organise a resistance to the increasing threat of Glyndŵr's rebels and the possibility that they might attack the Mortimer lands again and this time with more devastating effect. Philip had met one of them before and while the farmers did not like these people he considered this man to be a reasonable person. Philip wondered if the visitors knew the link between Cenarth and Glyndŵr but did not say anything and Philip accepted the demand without any resistance.

Philip and Gwenllian discussed the missive from Sir Edmund and it was agreed that Philip would meet with other tenants in the area to see what they were going to do. A meeting was held outside St Garmon's church on Sunday evening. There was a considerable amount of hot air with arguments put on both sides but the general consensus was that in recent years the Mortimers had been reasonable landlords, though this could be because Sir Edmund was afraid of annoying his tenants in case they sided with Glyndŵr. The other tenants were of course aware that Gwenllian was Glyndŵr's daughter and therefore were very interested to hear what Philip was saying about the gathering. They knew that he was a cautious family man who would weigh matters carefully before making his mind up and after he came to a decision, they knew he would keep to it.

Philip was of the opinion that they should obey Mortimer and attend the meeting. His was an influential voice and it was agreed that they would meet Mortimer at Rhyd Ithon. Some questioned whether they should take all their armour and weapons with them. Others wanted to know how long they would be away from their farms. There was the inevitable question concerning the whereabouts of the rebel army – were they likely to attack the gathering? Philip expressed the opinion that Mortimer would not have called the meeting unless he was sure that Glyndŵr's men were occupied in some other part of the country.

Some farmers said that since there was no possibility of any fighting they would take their wives with them and only the minimum of weapons. They were going to deal with the call as if they were going on a long hunting trip.

Later that evening Philip and Gwenllian discussed the results of the meeting and they decided that they would both go to Rhyd Ithon. Gwenllian was keen to be involved and Rhyd Ithon was not very far away.

Philip was going to take most of his armour and weapons with him and as many of the farm workers as could be spared at Cenarth.

The following Saturday, the fifteenth day of May, Gwenllian met with Fox by the market hall and told him about the meeting to be held at Rhyd Ithon and that she would go there with Philip. She agreed to meet Fox in his room the next market day following the meeting with Mortimer.

Philip, Gwenllian and their neighbours left for the meeting with Mortimer early on Tuesday morning, with the intention of reaching their destination in the early afternoon. Philip and Gwenllian took their horses and Simon drove the oxen cart. The cart would slow them down but it meant they could take more provisions with them as well as the armour and weapons.

Passing Cwm Hir Abbey brought everything about Rhys back to Philip and Gwenllian. She wished that they could have gone some other way but it was not practical. The abbey was an impressive building but Glyndŵr and his men had left their mark on the place when they occupied it a year earlier. The track passed above the abbey and they looked down on some of the monks attending to their tasks. The sun was shining on the tower giving it a red glow.

At the time Philip and Gwenllian were walking next to each other leading their horses until the dawn broke properly and the horses could be ridden without risk of them slipping on the poorly surfaced track.

Gwenllian turned to Philip and said, "I know I have said this to you many times before but I can't understand how a little boy can disappear in such a tranquil and peaceful place as this. I really hate the place now."

Philip was in a quiet mood but replied, "Hm! I suppose so". He found it too difficult to talk about. It was too hurtful.

But when he turned to look at Gwenllian, he realised that she was weeping silently for her little boy. She wanted to go in there and tear the place apart but knew that her father had done just that the previous year. Philip suggested to her that she should say a prayer for Rhys as they passed the tower. He knew that this would help her. Gwenllian said a prayer for Rhys but also vowed again that she would not forget Rhys and would find out what had become of him. She was glad to see the back of the abbey and her spirit improved as they followed the river down the long valley.

Many of the other farmers took to the tracks in a similar formation to the Cenarth band and they joined together as the morning progressed forming lines of carts, horses and walkers on the track with the lines increasing in length as they got closer to the meeting place.

There were hundreds gathered at Rhyd Ithon, people of all shapes and sizes, mingling together in a great mass. It was clear to the tenants that Sir Edward Mortimer must have had word that the rebels were active somewhere in the north otherwise such a gathering would have been very risky. If Glyndŵr were to attack now there would be mayhem with hundreds slaughtered. Clearly Mortimer was relying on the intelligence he had received.

Mortimer moved easily among his tenants. His administrators were checking which tenants were present and thus the extent of the support. The majority were meeting him for the first time. Sir Edmund was a very ordinary down-to-earth man and appeared to be a genuinely nice person whom his tenants could support. Gwenllian was excited at meeting such an important person, whose brother's children were in direct line to the throne of England and probably had a better claim to the throne than the present king.

Gwenllian made sure that she met Sir Edmund so that she could report this to Fox. She did not realise that Mortimer had noticed her anyway and would have directed his walk so as to meet her. She did stand out both because of her looks, her height and her standing. When they met she was introduced as Philip ap Rhys's wife and no mention was made of the fact that she was Glyndŵr's daughter. They spoke briefly about how lucky they were with the weather and about the journey and then he moved on. He was clearly impressed by her appearance and would remember her.

The vast majority of tenants were ambivalent about Mortimer. The Mortimers had been the lords of the area for centuries and in the main they were a hard and cruel family despite the fact that they were descended from Gladys, Llewelyn Fawr's daughter. Some of the tenants were undoubtedly sympathetic to Glyndŵr and objected to the oppressive laws against the Welsh but it was not the place to express such opinions.

After he had spoken to most of his tenants, he retraced his steps passing near where Gwenllian stood with Philip. He looked at her again and smiled pleasantly. Gwenllian realised that he was not absolutely sure of the loyalty of the Radnor men and had gathered them together to ensure that when the time came to confront Glyndŵr, they would be prepared and loyal to him and the king.

Sir Edmund proceeded to talk to the gathering, "Thank you for attending this meeting. The rebellion in Wales is causing much damage to property and the law is not being enforced properly and fairly because the courts can't meet regularly. The lawlessness is spreading and we need to bring criminals to justice. I am sure that you disapprove of this state of affairs and wish to bring it to an end as soon as possible so that you can enjoy the benefits of your own hard work. The only way that this can be achieved is to bring Glyndŵr's rebellion to an end and bring peace to our country again. I will lead you and my Hereford men against the rebels as soon as the opportunity arises or if Glyndŵr dares to bring his so-called rebel army anywhere near our area. We need to achieve a decisive victory and we need to do so soon to stop the spread of anarchy."

He paused for a moment to judge the effect of what he had said. He seemed encouraged and outlined his plan.

"I want you to organise yourselves into groups in your own localities and ensure that your archers and men at arms are well trained, equipped and ready for a battle that will inevitably take place soon. The better prepared we are the greater our victory will be. My Hereford tenants will also be preparing in the same way. It is time to bring this outlaw to account and punish these rebels who have caused such devastation to our country. I am confident that we will bring it to an end this summer. This meeting is the first step of my plan. I wish you a safe journey back to your homes to prepare for the battle ahead. God be with you."

His speech was received respectfully but not with great enthusiasm: there were no cheers but the vast majority clapped their hands, indicating their support.

Once the meeting was over the tenants started on their journey home, all of them concerned about the future. This was particularly true of Philip and Gwenllian as they discussed what action they could take. It was going to be very difficult for them because they were obliged to support Mortimer as his tenants and yet they could not easily take up arms against Glyndŵr. It seemed that the period when they were able to stay on the fence was coming to an end.

They arrived back at Cenarth safely but in a very uncertain state of mind. Gwenllian was asking herself how could she hide her true loyalties and yet support Philip and the farm. Philip did not wish to be on either side in the coming conflict.

On the following Saturday, the twenty-second day of May, Gwenllian attended the market and saw Fox at the market hall. He nodded to her in the direction of the Castle Inn and disappeared in that direction himself. Gwenllian allowed time for him to reach his room and then followed him around the back of the inn, up the stairs and into the room without knocking. Fox was waiting for her and was clearly pleased to see her.

He again sat in the chair and beckoned her to sit on the bed, which she did and he encouraged her to tell her story.

She was excited at being able to give him so much information and she told him everything she knew, describing the meeting, repeating what Mortimer had said to the tenants and she gave him her assessment of the support amongst the tenants for Mortimer.

This was very valuable information for Fox and he was obviously pleased with all the information she had given him. As an expression of his gratitude he took her hand, kissed it and thanked her saying how important this information would be for Glyndŵr.

He offered her a small jug of ale, which she took and drank quickly. They agreed that they would meet the following Saturday by the honey stall briefly unless there was something important to discuss, in which case they would meet in his room.

She left and went down the stairs silently and quickly covered the distance to the nearest corner of the inn where she almost collided with a man. She did not know him but was relieved that she was not seen coming down the stairs and that she would not be going to the room next time. She would not like to be seen coming from behind the Castle Inn too frequently.

The Cenarth family and workers like the other Mortimer tenants in the Radnor area started the preparation for the likely battle ahead. There was apprehension everywhere. Most were fearful of the deaths and injuries that would result from any military conflict. But events were now out of their hands. There was little enthusiasm for what was ahead but the swords had to come out and be sharpened.

Since these men and sometimes the women, Gwenllian being an example, were out hunting often, the archers' equipment were already in good condition as indeed were many spears. But, as decreed by Sir Edmund, the spears had to be cleaned and sharpened and the archers had to check their bows and arrows. The best tunics had to be taken out of storage and checked to see if they still fitted. Everybody at Cenarth was involved in the preparations. This was not a trip to the market: what was ahead of them would have serious consequences. The preparation had to be thorough. Unlike a hunting trip when an unfit horse or broken spear would simply mean that the quarry would get away with its life, in a battle an unfit horse could let its rider down and a damaged spear could let the carrier and a neighbour down, even resulting in death. Supplies had to be gathered and stored and the war cart prepared.

Gwenllian met with Fox again in his room the following Saturday because they both felt that the situation needed to be discussed. She sat in his chair this time. She told him everything she knew of the preparations. Replying to his questions she again gave an assessment of what the thinking was amongst the local farmers and their attitude to Glyndŵr and to Mortimer.

The two of them were now working together on a common cause. They were getting to understand each other better though Gwenllian had not revealed to him that she had the added motivation of hoping that she would discover what had happened to Rhys.

She was an inquisitive person and she now wanted to know more about Robert Fox. After they had finished the business part of their meeting. She said to him, "You seem to know a lot about me but I know hardly anything about you other than you are working for my father. Tell me something about yourself."

He told her he was not married and that he travelled about a lot in his work as an agent for Glyndŵr and that his main cover was that he was buying cattle on behalf of Hereford farmers.

Then he asked her, "Have you told Philip about our meetings yet?"

"No, I've not told him," came her definite answer.

He was very relieved and pleased when he said, "That's probably very wise."

She had often wondered to herself why she had not told Philip about her meetings with Fox but deep down she knew the reason. Philip would disapprove and would probably bring it to an end or at least try to. To continue her contact with Fox she would then have to lie to Philip and she would not want to do that. At present the wisest course of action was to say nothing and that is what she did.

"You must admire your father I should think," Fox said. "He certainly thinks highly of you."

"Do you think so?" she said, smiling nicely and taking the remark as a great compliment.

"Oh! Definitely," Fox confirmed. "He wanted me to wish you a happy birthday today."

She was immediately flattered and very pleased that her father had remembered her date of birth but she recovered her composure to ask, "Did my father tell you or was it one of the Cenarth poets?"

"Your father, of course," he said reassuringly.

Standing up and offering his hand to help her to her feet, he said, "Let me give you a birthday kiss." He then kissed her gently before releasing her to go down the stairs and across the yard.

She looked forward to these meetings with Fox for many reasons and, as risky as they were, she did like meeting him in his room.

By the end of the first week in June 1402 rumours about Glyndŵr and the rebels were circulating constantly: some were suggesting that he was going to attack Caernarfon again; others said he would attack Harlech. Some were speculating that he was going to lead a grand army to the south-west and finally sort out that area. Others were putting it around that he was going to burn Llanidloes next. Rumours were even circulating that he had been killed and that was why he had not been heard of for a while. A few were able to say with confidence that the appearance of the special star was to forewarn of his demise. The truth was much simpler. He did not campaign in the winter months. During those months the rebels were mainly at home keeping warm and enjoying merriment with the poets but keeping their weapons at the ready.

All these rumours made it very difficult for the king and his barons, such as Mortimer, to know what was going on and where and when Glyndŵr would strike next. The agents and spies were actively trying to gather information about where Glyndŵr and his family were living. It was an endless quest. If they gathered their armies too soon they would be restless and lose interest. If they gathered their forces too often on the basis of false alarm then it would be more difficult to bring them together the next time when they were really needed. They could gather them in the wrong place and find Glyndŵr attacking twenty miles away which would be over a day's march away and by the time that they would arrive at the attack scene Glyndŵr would have moved on and could be twenty miles away again or his forces might have dispersed.

This was a major difficulty for Mortimer. He had to rely on information he received from his agents and loyal tenants. His position was indeed complex because he also had the king breathing down his neck. The king held his two young nephews in prison. If Glyndŵr attacked his area and he failed to respond, the king would not be pleased with him and could well find a way of punishing him or his nephews. Information on Glyndŵr's position and plans were therefore extremely valuable to him.

Glyndŵr knew this and organised his campaign with this in mind. He ensured that false information was circulated about his whereabouts. He would send agents to talk to well-known Mortimer supporters and loyal tenants to give false information. He frequently sent small bands of armed men to cause distraction by pretending that they were investigating an area to attack. Some of these bands of men were genuinely on recognisance work; others were decoys. Glyndŵr was a master at creating this type of misinformation.

Any communication from Mortimer to his tenants was important in this battle of information handling. There was nothing in writing. Glyndŵr's men had to rely on the tenant farmer telling them accurately what Mortimer had demanded and whether the tenants would respond to the demands. Mortimer hoped for full support and Glyndŵr hoped that the tenants would have no stomach to fight for the generally unpopular Mortimer family.

People in the Radnor area knew that there was likely to be conflict in the mid Wales border area at some time or another but when and where they did not know. They could only wait and see where Glyndŵr's forces would appear next.

Gwenllian was only a small cog in this highly complex and confusing information-gathering arrangement, but a significant one, motivated as she was by the thought that she was searching for her son and was helping her father whom she wanted to impress and show that she was as much his daughter as his other daughters brought up at Sycharth.

# Chapter 8

ON THE SECOND Saturday in June, the fifteenth day of that month in 1402, the market in Llanidloes was buzzing with rumours. Glyndŵr had definitely been seen in Caersws, Newtown, Welshpool, Oswestry and Aberystwyth and there were various estimates of the number of men he had with him. Around the honey sellers he was on his own visiting a friend in Carno. In Oak Street, the view was that he was with a band of about three hundred soldiers and archers, mainly on horseback. While under the market hall he had 3,000 men with him, all on mountain ponies and surrounding Llanidloes. There was no consensus of opinion and how much of it was intentional confusion instigated by the great leader himself was impossible to judge, but almost certainly there was some truth in all the talk. Glyndŵr was in the area somewhere or had been there in recent days.

The market was doing brisk business because people were assuming that the following week's market would be cancelled and the town in ashes. So, there was more buying than usual. The chickens had all gone by early morning. The cattle market was busy with deals settled quickly between the traders and with people keen to get home early in case the terror arrived while they were in town. Some of the burgesses were talking about boarding their areas but realised that if the rebels came then boarding would not hold them back nor reduce the damage that they would inflict. Some argued that it would be better to give them a warm welcome. A few people argued that the rebels would not attack Llanidloes because the town had been quite supportive of Glyndŵr and there were no garrisons to attack. These people said there was no need to resist, it would be better to give them a good reception; surely the damage would be less.

There had been quite a panic early in the day when two monks had driven ten horses to town from Cwm Biga, to sell them in the market. Many were of a firm opinion that this was the start of the attack on Llanidloes.

People were rushing a little more than usual. The pace of their walk was quicker; they were bumping into each other more frequently and dropping the goods that they were carrying. People were in a more aggressive frame of mind than normal and their stress levels were higher. Uncertainty and concern were the predominant feelings.

By midday with the market slowing down it became the general consensus that Glyndŵr had moved his army southeast, from his strongholds of Caernarfon and Meirionydd in the north into the Meilienydd area of Radnor, which was of course Mortimer land. Mortimer would have to respond and call his tenants in Hereford and Radnor to meet in Ludlow with the intention of bringing the Welsh rebels to a pitched battle, beat them and bring the whole rebellion to an end.

While at the market in Llanidloes on that day, Gwenllian also heard the rumour that her father was active with his army south of Newtown. She met with Fox in his room and they shared the view that things were moving fast. Fox was desperate to know what Mortimer would do. He speculated that he might form an alliance with Glyndŵr against the king or would he, as he had made clear a few months earlier, do battle with Glyndŵr. Gwenllian was of the opinion that he was an honourable man and would keep to his word, gather an army around him and attack Glyndŵr at the first opportunity. Glyndŵr and his men could of course melt back north and avoid a fixed battle. These would be normal Glyndŵr tactics.

Gwenllian and Fox agreed that they would need to meet more frequently now to exchange information so that, as Fox put it, he could get the information to Glyndŵr as soon as possible. She could go to town in the middle of the week but only once. She could say that she had run out of some essential thing or another to make bread. In other words she could fake a crisis that would give her an excuse to visit town with one of the men and then lose him in town for sufficient time to have a meeting with Fox.

Fox explained that there were few options open to him also. His horse was in the town so he could go to the Cenarth area and meet Gwenllian in some secluded area off the main track, such as Tylwch woods perhaps or he could walk as far as Cenarth Mill dressed as a monk and meet Gwenllian in the woods near the mill. She was surprised and impressed by his knowledge of the area.

They agreed to meet in the woods near Tylwch on the following Wednesday morning and then arrange a further meeting for Saturday when it would be clearer as to what Glyndŵr was going to do next. The rebels might attack Llanidloes but they both thought that this was unlikely with Cenarth being so close. He would not make life difficult for his daughter.

Gwenllian was tense with the stress of the times and particularly because of her personal involvement. Fox could sense the tension in her. On one side she had her Cenarth family and their livelihood to think about and on the other her father and the rebels. She had lost her eldest son. She was meeting Fox in a clandestine manner. Fox put his arms around her and she did not resist. She needed comforting.

She needed someone to tell her what to do. She needed to be held. She lifted her head slightly to meet his gaze. Inevitably, their lips met.

She allowed him to caress and touch her but awareness of her own position and the possible consequences crept into her mind to overcome the desire to give herself to him.

Gwenllian left the room feeling much happier and strangely did not feel guilty but, convinced she now had a role to play in events and could support her father as much as her sisters and brothers. She liked Fox. Her exit from the room and into the streets of the town was swift and uneventful. By the time she was mixing with others in the streets she could not remember coming down the stairs and crossing the yard. Her heart was pounding and the adrenalin was flowing. She had to stop and think.

She went for a walk by the church and the river to calm herself because she could not meet Philip in her present state of mind. At the confluence of the Severn and the Clywedog below the church, the two rivers flowed gently and merged into a greater river. Standing there above the slow moving waters she discovered the peace she required to bring her to a more tranquil state of mind. She stayed there for a while until she was fully recovered.

Having rested her mind and soul she went to find Philip. Gwenllian went home after the market with a feeling of apprehension about her personal life but also fearful that she might let her father down by not getting the information quickly enough to save lives.

The following Tuesday, the eighteenth day of June, as expected a messenger came from Sir Edmund to give Philip his call-up notice. The war was coming to Radnor and Gwenllian was concerned: her father and Philip would be on opposite sides in the approaching conflict. She could find herself without a husband and without a father if there were a bloody battle.

She hoped that her father, when faced with Sir Edmund's strong, well-trained force, would retreat back into the mountains of north Wales. Her father's battle group was not going to be as well armed as Mortimer's men and it would be heavily outnumbered. She had witnessed herself the strength of the force that had gathered at Rhyd Ithon just a short time ago. Mortimer and his army would be a much tougher military machine than the force her father had met at Hyddgen. She felt sure that there would be no battle. Her husband would be safe as would be her father and brothers.

She concentrated on preparing for the meeting with Fox on the next day, Wednesday, to tell him of Mortimer's intention to do battle. She knew that this would be very valuable information for Glyndŵr.

Philip was unsure about what to do and went to meet with the others called to Ludlow, outside St Garmon's church. The general consensus was that they would be better off going to Ludlow: if they did not go, Mortimer would remove them from their land and destroy their living. Also, it was very possible that by the time they reached Ludlow, Glyndŵr would have returned north. It was agreed that they would go the following day, fully armed and with their men. Philip had not been enthusiastic in training his men but had spoken to the four who would accompany him and ensured that they had bows and arrows and spears and he himself had sharpened his sword.

Gwenllian was so relieved that her boys were too young to go with their father to Ludlow. She would have resisted it strongly anyway.

Early on Wednesday the nineteenth day of June, Philip prepared his horse and set off towards Ludlow with the four men, in an oxen-drawn cart which contained enough food and drink for a week and all the armour that they had to take with them on the long journey. As they progressed along the tracks they met other groups similarly armed moving in the same direction. By the time they reached Knighton there was an army of some hundreds and the tracks were full of men, horses and carts moving in the same direction in groups of various sizes. Towards late afternoon they arrived at Ludlow joining a mixed band of men on open ground. They were, to some extent, uniformly dressed in that they all wore the typical clothes of yeomen and farm workers of the time.

The predominant colours were various shades of brown and grey with people moving about like ants in a disturbed nest: some eating, some talking, some in small groups, others in large groups. It was a chaotic scene.

As soon as Philip and the men had left for Ludlow, Gwenllian told her boys and Beth that she wanted to go and get some ground corn from the mill because they had run out and that she would not be long. Beth was sure that there was a spare bag in the store but when she went to look it wasn't there. Gwenllian had already hidden it in the cart.

She had not approved of Philip going to war against her father and her brothers Gruffydd and Meredydd, who were bound to be with their father unless he had sent them on a special mission. She tried to argue against Philip going but the options were few for Philip.

She drove Cenarth's small oxen cart north along the side of Cenarth Hill towards Llanidloes. After travelling for less than 15 minutes she came across a monk as if on his way to Abbey Cwm Hir. She quickly realised that this was Fox dressed in the white habit of the Cistercian monks. He clearly trusted her and had walked there from Llanidloes that morning. There was no one about and he got up into the cart and sat behind her on the straw on the floor of the cart. She directed the oxen on to the track leading to the west towards Foel Hywel and up the valley of the Dulas. After about half a mile she turned into a wooded glade going far enough into the woods to be out of sight of the track she had just left and brought the cart to a halt.

She turned round to talk to Fox and said, "You are excellently disguised. I had difficulty in recognising you."

Fox replied, "You are looking bright and breezy this morning."

She accepted his compliment with a nod of her head but made no reply.

"Where are we?" he questioned.

"In a special room that belongs to no one: a room that is light and airy and free of charge," Gwenllian teased him.

This glade had been covered in bluebells in May and she always used to bring the boys here to play before Rhys disappeared. She knew the place well and felt it had some magic about it. The blue bells were now long dead and the plants themselves were dying back but still the place retained its magic and tranquillity. It was a special place for her; like a temple to praise and enjoy the beauty of nature.

She got out of her seat at the front, tied the oxen to a tree and gave them some straw and decided it was safer to sit and talk to Fox in the cart so she climbed in and sat opposite him on the straw on the cart floor, leaning back slightly on the bag of ground corn she had hidden there. In this way, if anyone were to stop on the road she would not be seen standing talking to anyone. She could simply climb out, untie the oxen and the onlooker would think she had stopped to enjoy a walk in the woods. Fox lying flat in the cart would not be seen under the straw. She had planned carefully.

"Philip and the other men have left for Ludlow early this morning," she said. "They will arrive this evening and will be ready to do battle, they think, in a day or two."

"Were they mentally well prepared?" Fox enquired.

Gwenllian hesitated and then replied, "I am not sure. Philip knows that I was not happy with him going to fight against my father and brothers. I could be without a father or a brother before the week is over or my husband could be dead. I wish he had not gone to Ludlow."

"Do you think they will fight for Mortimer against your father?" asked Fox.

"Unfortunately," said Gwenllian, "I think they will unless my father withdraws back to the north."

"Do you think that is likely, Gwenllian?"

"I don't know. I wish he would but my brother Gruffydd and Rhys Gethin like fighting battles, I suppose, and they have their influence on these things," said Gwenllian with concern.

"Well, for your sake, Gwenllian, since you think Mortimer is determined to fight I hope your father will return to the north," said Fox, showing that he empathised with her position.

"Thank you, Robert," she said appreciatively.

He lent forward slightly and touched her hand. She felt close to him. He listened carefully to every word and noted everything that she said. He never questioned her assessment and treated her as a person with significant opinions. He made her feel that she was an important person. She was flattered by his attention and praise.

Excited by the secrecy of the meeting, by her own deceit, by the fact that he had made such an effort to see her and by the natural wooded temple she was in, she struggled for some minutes to find reality. Her husband had just gone to war and here she was having this secret meeting, helping her father in that wonderfully romantic wood away from the rest of the world.

This time, in this special place, her desire overcame her self-awareness. She could not resist her natural feelings and she gave herself to the occasion and the circumstances that she found herself in at that moment.

# Chapter 9

THE FOLLOWING DAY, the twentieth day of June 1402, on the outskirts of Ludlow, Mortimer joined the Radnor men and organised them into groups and appointed commanders. There were a number of influential men there, many with military experience with the king's forces. The presence of these experienced soldiers gave the whole force a feeling of confidence before they set forth from Ludlow. The Hereford men were camped just south of Ludlow. Many from the Radnor area were still arriving and the day was spent in bringing the disorganised gathering into a military force capable of challenging the rebels.

The following day, the two armies were brought closer together and moved, in an orderly manner, up the river Lugg as far as Whitton where they joined the Hereford men and camped for the night. The soldiers could see the church of Pileth on the side of Bryn Glas hill in the distance. The army had been led up the valley of the Lugg with the intention of penetrating deeper into mid Wales the next day and challenging the enemy.

Early on the morning of twenty-second day of June, Mortimer's army awoke to the news that scouts had seen a small band of the enemy at the top of the Bryn Glas hill above Pileth church.

The Hereford men were in very good spirits, convinced that this action would sort out this rebellion once and for all and that they would have Glyndŵr's head before nightfall. They were laughing and talking happily about the battle ahead and what the day would bring.

The Radnor men were not so cheerful. They were unsure about what the result of this expedition would be. They had respect for Glyndŵr and his ability as a leader and they had heard of Rhys Gethin's prowess on the battlefield. They knew that Glyndŵr was generally well informed. Some of them thought that he had magical powers. Many hoped that he would not take on a force of this size and would retreat back into the northern mountains. Some, possibly many, of these men were not sure which side they supported. This was not a voluntary group of dedicated enthusiasts but a conscripted group of well-armed men.

Philip himself was quiet but could overhear some of the conversation between the men. One was saying to another that he did not wish to be involved. Philip suspected that some were there on behalf of Glyndŵr's forces to find out what the strength of the opposition was and others might be there to create insurrection at the appropriate time. He and his men dressed themselves for the battle and prepared their weapons for the fight that was to come.

They were not sure of the significance of the men sighted at the top of the hill but they could see that the numbers there were gradually increasing.

Philip could see in the distance the small church on the right-hand side of the hill with its tower facing the hill side. It was an ideal position for the rebel army to take: their commanders had an excellent view of the valley and fields below them to direct their forces. If they held that position then Mortimer's army would have to attack up the hill which could pose difficulties.

The rebels were massively outnumbered and Philip could see this himself. They had around two hundred men on Bryn Glas hill above the church. They would surely retreat and flee when they realised the numbers opposing them. It would be madness to do anything else. The message going round the ranks was "Come on let's give them a good hiding and finish them off." There were also comments like, "I bags taking Glyndŵr." There were masses of overconfident Hereford soldiers and commanders in very high spirits and their greatest concern was that the rebels would turn and run away from the battle when they realised that they were so heavily outnumbered, out-armed and with significantly less cavalry.

But luck was holding and the foolish rebel army was moving down the hillside to meet them. Philip was desperately hoping that there would be no battle. He did not wish to be a part of this fight against Glyndŵr who was fighting for his rights as a Welshman. Also, he would be fighting against Gwenllian's father and her brothers. In the confusion of the battle he could be facing Meredydd and what would he do? He would try to avoid the situation by keeping away from the centre ground somehow. He was in a very difficult dilemma and wished now he had taken Gwenllian's advice and had stayed at Cenarth.

Mortimer and his commanders arranged the army into three groups. The cavalry, which was a strong force, was moved to the left, the Hereford men took the centre and the Radnor archers went to the right. Sir Edmund had few options other than to attack the enemy on the hill. If he tried to follow the river and pass on the left of the hill to find a better position behind the rebels they could attack his army from the side as they passed. The other option was to retreat to a stronger position but that might mean that the rebels would avoid a pitched battle and disperse, which was not what Mortimer wanted. So, he decided to move his army forward towards the hill.

By now, the opposition could be seen on the hill moving and organising themselves into groups and taking positions about halfway down the hill. It did seem that the rebels were going to stand their ground and do battle though they were heavily outnumbered.

Sir Edmund consulted with his generals and decided that though it would be difficult and risky, they would charge up the hill but would weaken the enemy first with the Radnor archers. Philip was located with the archers, waiting for the order and his own men from Cenarth were nearby.

The archers fired the first flight of arrows but they fell short. However, the replying arrows fired from the hillside at the centre of Mortimer's army had the advantage of height with the result that some casualties were sustained by the Hereford men.

The rebels continued to move slowly down the hill firing their arrows at Mortimer's force. The rebels' advantageous position and their arrows were having more of a toll than the opposition archers as the two armies closed on each other. Mortimer, seeing that his men were suffering from the hail of arrows descending on them, took a crucial decision at this stage and ordered his men to charge at the rebels thinking that this would be enough to send them scrambling back up the hill for cover. It didn't. Instead they continued their very slow but menacing movement downwards while firing their effective arrows.

Seconds after Mortimer's men started the charge and past the point of no return there appeared on the summit more of Glyndŵr's men and more still appeared from the area behind the church. The ones behind the church had been hidden there but the ones appearing at the summit may have arrived just in time or was it the Glyndŵr magic? The rebels were still heavily outnumbered but it was clear to Philip that Mortimer's army was going to have to fight hard to win this battle.

At this moment Glyndŵr's standard, a golden dragon on a white background was unfurled near the summit and brought down the hill towards Mortimer's troops. This was a clear message to all present that Glyndŵr was going to face Mortimer in a pitched battle.

At the unfurling of the standard there was a loud cheer from the hill, which resounded in the valley below and could be heard above the roar of the advancing army of men and horses. It was the Glyndŵr battle cry.

Philip, like many others, was astounded by the response. The rebels were so heavily outnumbered and out armed that they were bound to be slaughtered. He wished that Glyndŵr's forces would see this and even at this late stage retreat back up the hill behind them and avoid a pitched battle. Philip realised that this was going to be disastrous for Glyndŵr, Gwenllian and himself.

Mortimer's army was now in a headlong rush towards their enemy. The rebels on the top of Bryn Glas started to move quickly down the hill to re-enforce their comrades lower down who were now preparing to charge towards the oncoming army. The rebels from behind the church also moved forward quickly to join them.

When Mortimer's men saw this development their resolve weakened fractionally but they still outnumbered the enemy by a significant factor and carried on with their charge directed by their leaders.

The Radnor men, when they heard the Glyndŵr battle cry were instantly unsettled and influenced by the situation. Many of them were feeling their Welsh blood rising and some could be heard saying "I am on the wrong side", "I can't do this" and their pace of attack visibly slowed.

The Hereford men were running up the hill and were about to engage the opposition when arrows started to strike them from the right. Some of the Radnorshire men had stopped running with their spears pointing at the enemy and were instead shooting arrows at the Hereford men and Mortimer's cavalry. Many were killed in this action. The sight of Glyndŵr's banner and the war cry had been a decisive moment for the Radnor men; they were now on Glyndŵr's side.

When Mortimer's men were approaching halfway up the hill Rhys Gethin gave the order to attack. There was a great huge roar and the Welsh force charged down at the much-slowed approaching force and broke their advance. A fierce, hand-to-hand battle took place and Mortimer and his army were pushed downhill until their ranks broke and there was a rout. Men were trying to retreat only to find they were facing Radnor-produced spears. Mortimer's men were running in all directions pursued by the opposition and many were caught and killed. The slaughter was great and ran into hundreds. Mortimer himself was captured and many of his commanders killed.

The pursuit of the enemy down the valley was without mercy. Men, who a day earlier had been at home with their wives and children, were hacked to death by Glyndŵr's men. The scenes down the slope of the hill were of men dead or dying, injured men with limbs cut off, men covered in blood nursing their wounds, blind men and men rendered insane by the chaos. The hillside was like a painting produced on a large canvas: everything was still with the church on the right and the hillside covered in bloodied bodies.

Bodies were left in the bushes and trees on the valley floor. In all about a thousand men had died in the battle, including men of standing such as Kinard de le Bere, the sheriff of Hereford Robert Whitney and Walter Devereux. These were experienced men who would have been expected to beat a rebel army. Almost equivalent to the victory in terms of success was the capture of Sir Edmund Mortimer. He was captured by Rhys Gethin himself, the second-in-command and Glyndŵr's most-feared general. From his position on the hill, helping to direct the forces he was keeping a close eye on how things were proceeding. Once he realised that Mortimer's army was in full retreat he came down the hillside with a small band of men and captured Sir Edmund.

Philip could see which way things were going and could not find it in his soul to fight Glyndŵr and his kinsmen and collected the men who had come with him. They and the other men from the St Garmon area gathered together on the right of the battlefield and became bystanders to the slaughter that took place. They had witnessed the capture of Mortimer and knew that there was nothing for them to do now other than to abandon the field of battle as soon as possible and make their way home to their own farms. No one from Cenarth had perished in the conflict; one had been slightly injured and he was taken home on the Cenarth cart.

They met many like themselves on the way and gave assistance where it was needed. They helped lift injured men on to the cart to take them back into the safety of the Radnor hills, some to recover but others to die of their wounds. They stopped for the night at Rhyd Ithon as did many others and continued their journey in the morning.

During the return journey they debated the effect of the victory on themselves and their farmsteads, the effect on Mortimer and the consequences on the country. Philip reminded them that the king had not been defeated. It was only Mortimer who had been defeated and there would be more to come. However, there was general praise for Glyndŵr, some saying he had used his magic powers, others saying that he had outwitted his enemy by choosing the battle site and by making Mortimer think that his force was much less than it actually was and hence encourage Mortimer to charge uphill.

Initially Philip had mixed feelings about the results of the battle. He had been forced by Mortimer to take sides in the rebellion and his side had lost. The end was better than the torment he had suffered at the beginning of the battle when he realised that the rebels were going to stand their ground and that he would have to fight against Gwenllian's father and brothers. He had felt a sense of relief when the Radnor men refused to fight and changed allegiance. But now he knew he had to decide whom he would have to support openly. He knew Gwenllian was supporting her father and he decided on the journey back to Cenarth that he would also support the rebels in future.

Philip and his men arrived back at Cenarth in the late afternoon and settled to tell the story of the day and to drink ale late into the night to celebrate Glyndŵr's victory and the fact that no one from Cenarth had been seriously injured. Philip and his men had set off to fight against Glyndŵr but had returned home feeling that they had been victorious. The mead helped raise the warriors' spirits and of course there were stories to be told. Exaggerations, contributed to by the mead they drank, were inevitable. It was what must have happened in many a farmstead and cottage in Radnor that night. The removal of the much-disliked Mortimer was also a cause of celebration. No one had believed it was possible to beat a Mortimer in battle because by hook or by crook – usually by crook – they always won.

No one was happier with the day's result than Gwenllian. Philip was back safely, her family was safe, her father had won a decisive battle and she felt she had played an active role in her father's victory. Fox would have informed him that the support from the Radnorshire tenants was high in numbers but very low in morale. This information was vital for Glyndŵr to have on the evening before the battle. Her joy was slightly tainted by the fear of retaliation from the king.

There was another shadow that fleetingly crossed her mind. Many would have identified it as guilt over her infidelity with Robert Fox. But, whenever this shadow threatened to appear, she could and did instantly suppress it through convincing herself that she had some feelings for Fox and, equally as powerful, a suppressing agent was her belief that the association furthered and protected her father's cause.

However, she did not forget to pray for Rhys. She knew that it was possible that Mortimer, as a supporter of Cwm Hir Abbey, might have had some part to play in Rhys's disappearance. She was glad that he had been beaten in the battle and that he had been captured. She wondered what her father would do with him now that he had him captive. Sometimes he kept the captives for ransom and surely the king would pay well for his release.

# Chapter 10

THE MORNING FOLLOWING the return of the men from Pileth, the work on the farm continued as usual. There was a slightly slow start but by late afternoon things were back to normal at Cenarth. Normality returned so soon because there was no time to brood on a past that could not be changed and the need for food for the family and the stock was an overwhelming demand on time and the mind.

The talk in Cenarth, Llanidloes and indeed the whole of Wales was that the battle of Pileth was an unexpected major victory for the rebels. It was a greater victory than Hyddgen because, not only had they beaten a large, well-led force but they had also captured Edmund Mortimer. This was a significant capture because never before had a Mortimer been captured by the Welsh in the centuries of battles between them and the Welsh princes. This could be an opportunity for that family's treachery over the years to be avenged. The speculation was that they would execute Sir Edmund, put his head on display in Dolgellau or Machynlleth or parade it through these towns.

Much to Gwenllian's relief this did not happen. She would have felt guilty of playing a part in such a barbaric act and she did not think that her father would have agreed to such behaviour. She was proud of the fact that she had played some part in the victory through giving information to Fox. She thought of him frequently and the way he looked in the monk's habit the day before the battle. Even the oxen cart looked different to her now. She wanted to visit the glade again soon to relive her meeting with Fox and absorb the magic of the place.

Philip was quieter than usual after he returned home from Pileth and so were the men who had accompanied him there. It was a strange feeling to start a battle on one side and finish on the other. Memories of the day kept returning to his mind. Some memories were disturbing and nightmarish. Immediately after the battle he and the others from Radnor feared for their lives believing that the rebels would vent their anger on them. He remembered that he and his friends had gathered together to try to make sure that the victors were aware that they were from Radnor and Glyndŵr supporters on the day. They had been surrounded and questioned by rebel soldiers who were high on their success. The fact that they could speak Welsh to them and explain their presence had been enough to save their lives. Once identified as friendly they were allowed to return home, which of course they did by the shortest route possible.

Within a few days Iolo called at the farmstead, singing one of his own songs as he came up the track from the direction of Llanidloes. He was particularly pleased with himself – probably boosted by the result at Pileth and delighted at the success of his hero. It was a little surprising that he was not there with the rebels at the battle to encourage them and later to sing their praise. It was not that he had missed an opportunity because there were no other poets there either, to wallow in the glory and write a magnificent poem that would last the ages. The speculation in Llanidloes was that the poets were not there because they did not think that Glyndŵr would win so they made sure that their own hides were safe by staying well away. The family at Cenarth, though they teased Iolo about not having been at Pileth, guessed that Glyndŵr and

Rhys Gethin would not have any of the poets there in case they gave away some of the rebels' secrets.

Iolo spoke fluently about the battle after drinking a jug of ale. He was careful not to allude to the role of the Radnor men in the battle but simply praised their action. He brought news to them about Sir Edmund Mortimer by telling them that he had heard that Mortimer had been put in prison in Leominster for a few days after the battle and then taken up north. Iolo thought he would be ransomed and that the king would pay well for his release.

Iolo's visit produced an excellent night of entertainment with the whole family involved in singing, dancing and great merriment. Early the following day he was on his horse and on his way south to entertain another family and spread his gossip.

In the weeks immediately following the battle of Pileth, Gwenllian tried to meet Fox a number of times in Llanidloes but to no avail, he seemed to have disappeared off the face of the earth. She could not go to the inn and ask if he had hired the room or whether anyone there knew where he was because it would have been far too risky. There was no one else she could talk to about him so she was left in limbo. July and most of August went by without any trace of him. She did look carefully and suspiciously at the occasional monk; if they were wearing their hoods then she would try to peer at their faces. Some monks found an attractive woman doing this very disconcerting and would gather their habits tight and move away as quickly as they could in fright.

Despite spending long periods at the market she did not see him. On two occasions, she even ventured up the stairs to their room. The first time she tried the door it was locked. The other time hearing some sounds inside, she knocked on the door, and a woman opened it. Gwenllian apologised for the intrusion immediately and turned away without giving an explanation for her presence. The woman who opened the door was scantily dressed, showing more of her frontage than was normal and had obviously been expecting a caller. There was a look of great disappointment on her face when she saw Gwenllian at the door and had merely shrugged her shoulders when Gwenllian apologised and closed the door.

After she returned to the market, she positioned herself outside the front of the Castle Inn to observe the comings and goings and wondered what type of woman was the one she had met in the room. She did not care to think nor imagine too much about her, but kept a discreet eye on the passageway leading behind the inn. She noticed that a reasonably well-dressed man went around the back not long after Gwenllian had come from there. She guessed that the room was now being put to a different use and decided to put it out of her mind.

She was very disappointed that she could not meet Fox. Her hope was that he was with Glyndŵr's army somewhere but she was worried that he had been killed at Pileth. After all, she argued, there was no reason for the army to stay in mid Wales after the victory. She felt let down that he had not sent her a message somehow to say he was well, though she could not think of how he could have done that.

In August, there was news that Glyndŵr had capitalised on his success at Pileth by attacking Glamorgan and Gwenllian assumed that Fox had gone with him to the south.

But, then, on the last market day in August she spotted him – or, to be more precise, he spotted her. They exchanged glances and they moved towards each other and

Fox told her to go to their room and that he would go there to wait for her.

She felt he was different and thought that he looked worried.

She rushed across the yard, up the stairs and into the room. Her heart was pounding fast, her legs felt longer and she was delighted to be with Fox again. She was convincing herself that it was the interest in being involved in the rebellion and being able to help her father like his other sons and daughters that was giving her this exultant feeling. In her own way she was doing as much as the others involved in the rebellion and she was proud of it.

As soon as she was in the room she asked him in a scolding manner, "Where have you been for two months?"

He motioned for her to sit in his chair while he sat on the bed. He indeed was not in a good mood and told her, rather briskly, "I have been with your father fighting in the south for the past two months and I only left them to see you and bring you a message from your father."

"What is happening to Mortimer and who is our lord at Cenarth now?"

He replied, "I don't know who the lord is now. Do not worry about it – no one other than Glyndŵr will be making demands of you and your family from now on. Mortimer is still held captive by your father and so is Lord Grey. The king intends to pay ransom for Lord Grey but is not willing, it seems, to pay any ransom for Mortimer. Most people are surprised by this, but it seems the king is happy to see Mortimer stay in prison so that he can't make any claims on the throne of England on behalf of his two young nephews."

"Well, well, how the mighty have fallen," exclaimed Gwenllian.

"I'm telling you all this so that you have the background before I ask you to do your next job for your father," said Fox.

Gwenllian was excited at the prospect of another job. "Oh! What is that?"

He asked, "When did you last see your father or brothers?"

"Oh! It's been a very long time," she said, trying to think when was it that she had seen one of them last.

"Do they know that we are meeting?" he asked, cautiously.

"No," she said. "I have not told anyone, you have my word on that."

"Have you told anyone about me?" he enquired further.

"No."

"Not even your husband?"

"No. Definitely not," she replied firmly.

"Good. Because my next task for you involves your own kith and kin and so it will be very difficult and you will see now why it is important that you do not tell a soul about our meetings or about the work you are doing for your father. It is vital that you do not share this information with anyone."

She realised that Fox was a different man from the one she had met few months earlier in his monk's garb. There was a slightly menacing tone to his voice and he made her uneasy, even a little apprehensive, if not slightly scared.

Having got this assurance, Fox went on to hint at a rift in the Glyndŵr camp. The rift was between Glyndŵr himself and her half-brother Meredydd. He said that a certain faction in the high command of the rebels, led by Meredydd, was determined to replace Glyndŵr with Meredydd as a leader.

The idea was that Meredydd would make a deal with the king and peace would return. Fox claimed that he did not know the details of the plot. Glyndŵr was aware that there was something going on and wanted Gwenllian to contact Meredydd and get him to divulge to her the details of the plot. She could then tell Fox and he could inform Glyndŵr.

It would help her father if she could find out where Meredydd was at any one time so that he could keep an eye on him and the others working with him. He told her also to make sure that she didn't alert him to the fact that his father was making enquires about him.

Gwenllian was shocked and disappointed by this request to spy on Meredydd. She felt she knew Meredydd well and found him to be the easiest of people to get on with. She was sure he was trustworthy and highly regarded by his father. She wanted to do more work for her father but not this, not spying on Meredydd.

"Look, Robert, as much as I want to help the rebels, I can't do this. I am not going to do it," she said firmly.

"You must do it. I insist," he said, calmly but definitely.

"You can insist as much as you like. I am not going to do it," she said with conviction.

"Your father and I are ordering you to do it," he insisted.

"I am not going to spy on my brother." There was a finality to this statement.

After a period of silence and some hesitation by Fox, he said that while he had been with Glyndŵr he had heard that someone in the high command structure of the rebellion had been involved in the disappearance of a young boy at Abbey Cwm Hir.

Gwenllian was stunned to the core, hurt and blushed from

some unexplained fear. The whole incident came back to her with great shock and a sinking feeling. While she had never been able to put Rhys out of her mind and there wasn't a day that went by without her thinking of Rhys and what had become of him, any hope of seeing him again had long gone. An explanation was the closest thing to her heart. She would do anything to find out what happened and to give her child a decent burial.

Fox suggested that by establishing a closer relationship with Meredydd she might be able to find out something that would lead her to the truth about what had happened to Rhys. She was faced with a difficult dilemma, but knowing about Rhys was paramount. She reluctantly agreed to spy on Meredydd and pass information to Fox about his movement if she could.

She said that as far as she knew Meredydd was always at his father's side and that wherever Glyndŵr was Meredydd would be.

"That used to be the case," said Fox getting up from the bed, "but no longer."

After a brief pause, Fox continued, "First make contact with him and invite him to Cenarth, then make some enquires."

"Are you going to stay for a cup of ale?" he asked.

He had upset and annoyed her. She did not wish to spy on her own family and what was more disturbing for her was the mention of Rhys's name. Something might have happened in the woods but not enough to make her stay now.

"Philip wants to leave early today because he has some jobs to do at home and I don't want him to come looking for me. So I had better leave," she said as though it was true.

"I will meet you by the market hall unless I have something significant to tell you," she said as she left.

She moved quickly down the stairs and across the yard and soon joined Philip who was in no hurry to go home. Gwenllian was a very troubled woman on the journey home but did not talk to Philip about any of her concerns.

# Chapter 11

O N  THE  FIRST day in September 1402, to celebrate the victory at Pileth, it was decided that the whole of Cenarth would go hunting. Gwenllian often took part in the Cenarth hunts. It was not unheard of for a woman to take to hunting but Gwenllian was part of a rare breed. She enjoyed hunting and it was an important part of her life as it was her husband's. She had her own horse and was a challenge to most of the Cenarth men when it came to following the hounds.

Iolo had promised to join them at the hunt and he tactfully turned up late but was ready to welcome them back when they returned to Cenarth. There was now a successful hunt to be celebrated as well as the Pileth victory.

There was a plentiful supply of ale and mead. People were merry, even Gwenllian had more to drink than was wise, and she enjoyed the evening. Iolo was at his best. The songs were wonderful and the storytelling was captivating. It was a memorable night with the dancing led by Gwenllian showing her superb skills and timing. The gathering was mesmerised by Gwenllian: her looks, her poise and her charm, all of which showed her to be truly a daughter of the prince of Wales.

Iolo left the following morning but three days later he was back, on his way north this time, to report that Wales had been invaded the day before on three fronts. He was not sure who led which force but a large army had entered from Chester, another from Shrewsbury and another from Hereford. He was coming to warn them to be aware that the army which entered from Shrewsbury could well be moving up the Severn Valley and could be upon them in a day or two. He couldn't stay long because he had others to warn. He was rewarded for his efforts by being given generous provisions for his journey and went on his way. Philip sent the stockman to warn the neighbours and spoke to Gwenllian as to the best course of action. They agreed that there was a possibility that Cenarth could be a target for the king's forces. This was exactly what Philip had feared since the start of the rebellion. They agreed that they would pack some provisions and be prepared to move south at short notice.

The next day a great storm hit the area and it rained continuously for days. It was impossible to move about in the storm. They did not go to the market on Saturday because of it. At Cenarth they felt safe while the storm lasted: no army could operate under such conditions. After days of heavy rain it was decided that Philip and the stockman would go to Llanidloes to check if there were any reports of the invasion and to find out if the invasion force was travelling towards Cenarth.

After a difficult journey they returned with the news that the king's army in the north had moved westwards into Gwynedd but had been stopped by the storm. The invasion force from Shrewsbury had travelled in a north westerly direction in order to pin Glyndŵr in Gwynedd. The artful Glyndŵr had avoided a pitch battle. The latest gossip was that the king was going to return to England because of the bad weather. His horses and carts were getting stuck in the mud which made them vulnerable to a Glyndŵr counter attack.

At Cenarth the storm was regarded as a great blessing and all at the farmstead were convinced that Glyndŵr had used his magic powers to produce the storm exactly at the right time. Glyndŵr's standing at Cenarth rose sharply; it was as though he had fought off the king's army by himself.

Then, a few days later, a rumour reached Cenarth that Glyndŵr was active in the Hereford area and was probably going back north past the farmstead.

The rebel army did pass north but some miles to the east of them. Gwenllian and Philip did not attend the market because of the possibility of an attack on the town by the rebels. Glyndŵr had dispatched Meredydd and a small group of armed men to visit Cenarth and give his regards to his daughter. Gwenllian could not believe her luck when, on the sixteenth day of September, Meredydd and his group arrived and dismounted outside her door.

He received a very warm welcome and he put his arms around her to hug her. She immediately gave instructions for food to be laid on the table for the visitors. Philip came into the house having heard the commotion in the yard and ordered a mug of the best mead for them.

This was the first time that they had met since the battle at Pileth when they were on opposite sides. Philip was pleased to see them and was keen to find out where they had been and where they were going. He particularly wanted to know the position of the king's invading forces. Meredydd answered some questions in a diplomatic way, giving little of their own position away. They had visited his sisters in the Hereford area and it had not been decided yet where they were going. As for the king's forces, and Meredydd enjoyed answering this last question, they had retreated back to England because of the bad weather and the harassment by native forces.

Gwenllian asked if their father and Gruffydd were near. He replied that they were only about five miles away and though they would have loved to see her they did not want to draw attention to her and Cenarth because the king had so many agents in every part of Wales. After talking to Meredydd for a while she realised that there was not much to be learnt on that day but she would like to meet him again soon. She decided to encourage him to call whenever he passed by, telling him that not only did she like to see him but that her boys were asking for him all the time, which was true.

However, before he left she thought it worth mentioning Rhys and his disappearance at Abbey Cwm Hir to him again and asked, "Do you remember the time Rhys disappeared at Abbey Cwm Hir?" Before he had time to answer, she continued, "We were told by Dafydd, though he was very young and never mentions it now, that he and Rhys went into the bell tower and Rhys went upstairs and was never seen again. But when Beth went in to look for Rhys she saw three men dressed in monks' habits coming downstairs and when she asked them if they had seen a small boy they said they hadn't. Another monk told Beth later that they had seen Rhys leaving for home with another monk."

"I remember it well – as does our father," he said.

"Well," she continued. "I wondered if there was some secret meeting going on in the belfry at the time involving our father's men."

Meredydd was firm, "I doubt very much if it was one of our men because we had no truck with the abbot or the monks there at the time. Cwm Hir is far more favourable to our cause now that we removed the abbot and some of the Ystrad Flur monks have moved there. It is our intention to install the abbot of Ystrad Fflur as the abbot of Cwm Hir soon because, as you probably know, he has been sent from Ystrad Fflur by the king. He is very supportive of our cause and is living in Cwm Hir now. I think the Avignon Pope has already agreed. Did you know that Rhys Gethin shared Mynachdy House with the old Cwm Hir abbot the night before the battle of Pileth?"

Gwenllian was disappointed by the answer – as Meredydd could see.

He considered for a moment and then said, "Gwenllian, I think it's more likely that those monks were working for Mortimer than for us."

He added, "It's possible to ask Edmund Mortimer, because he is becoming quite sympathetic to our cause and he is annoyed with the king for not paying us a ransom for him. He is also getting very friendly with Catherine, my well, our – sister. Would you like me to ask him?"

"Oh, yes please," said Gwenllian. "Not a day goes by without me thinking of Rhys."

"I understand," he said.

They continued their conversation for some time discussing the military situation but they also talked a lot about the family and in particular their sisters in the Gwenlliant area. Meredydd said eventually that he would have to leave and rejoin his father's forces since he had only been given leave of three hours to visit Cenarth.

Gwenllian thanked him for making the effort to visit Cenarth. Meredydd made two promises to Gwenllian. First that he would return to see her as soon as he could and, secondly, that he would find out if Mortimer knew anything about Rhys's disappearance.

# Chapter 12

G WENLLIAN HARDLY SLEPT at all the night following Meredydd's visit because her mind kept returning to Rhys and wondering what had happened to him and whether Meredydd would be able to find anything out from Sir Edmund Mortimer. She had too many questions in her mind and too few answers to be able to sleep. She realised that she would have to wait until Meredydd came back to her with some information from Mortimer, but she found it difficult to be patient about a thing that troubled her so much. However, her meetings with Fox were also on her mind all night and particularly the accusation that Meredydd was working against his father. Gwenllian found it very difficult to believe what Fox had suggested, but he had planted enough doubt in Gwenllian's mind to cause uncertainty.

She got up in the morning determined to talk it through again with Fox and to tell him that in her discussions with Meredydd she had found no reason to suspect him of any disloyalty. Meredydd was probably her favourite brother and this made it more difficult for her to believe anything bad about him, but she had to be certain that he was not plotting against their father. She had to know that she could trust him. As the morning progressed she could not concentrate on any of her tasks and decided that she would go to town as soon as possible to see if she could meet Fox to talk things over with him.

At first she could not think of a good reason to give Philip to go to town on her own but then she remembered that she had received a poem from Lewis, one of the local poets, asking for a bed. It was a bizarre request but in the poem he explained that his own bed had been taken from him by a woman he had taken up with in Chester. Lewis, in his poem, said that he had made a similar request to Non who lived near Tylwch. Gwenllian decided to tell Philip that she was going to visit Non to discuss Lewis's request for a bed. She would go directly to Llanidloes and to meet Fox and then call to see Non on her way back.

So she told Philip, "I think I will go and see Non to decide what to do about Lewis's request for a bed. He is such a fool as far as women are concerned. He should never have got himself involved with that woman. She was obviously out to fleece him from the moment she set eyes on him. Do you think it's alright for Non and I to arrange to give him a bed?"

Philip, who knew about the request from Lewis, replied, "Yes. I think you should give him a bed: he is a kind soul and has been loyal to us over the years and it's better to keep him on our side. It would be mean not to give him a bed as foolish as he is. If you are going, be careful because the weather did not look very promising at first light. The sky was very red and it could well be raining heavily by this afternoon. So, if you are going you had better go soon."

"I will go on my horse, rather than walk. I didn't sleep very well last night and I feel a little tired," she said.

"What was bothering you?"

"The usual and for some reason this request from Lewis," she lied.

She saddled her horse and left immediately, going down the track crossing the Dulas and then worked her way up the side of the Wenallt and down to Tylwch. She passed within half a mile of Non's farmstead and was relieved that no one saw her. Llanidloes was now a little over a mile away and she continued on her journey with haste.

She tied her horse outside the Hounds' Inn near the oak tree and a child volunteered to keep an eye on the animal. It was a Wednesday but the town was busy with quite a few people about. She walked the length of Oak Street and Long Bridge Street but did not see Fox anywhere and she felt that she had been silly to come to town with such little chance of meeting him.

Having taken the risk of lying to Philip she was determined to find Fox. She approached the inn with some trepidation and went around the back. There was no one in the yard as far as she could see but she went to the stables to check. She was shocked to come face to face with a stable lad who was on his way out. She almost collided with him but was quick witted enough to ask him if her husband was there. He replied that there was no one there and that he was on his own. She retreated out of the stable door and turned around to face the inn pretending to think of where to go to find her husband. The stable lad walked into the back of the inn and showed no interest in her.

Going directly to the stairs and climbing them as quickly as was safe and possible she knocked at the door gently. There was no reply but at that instant she could hear the back door of the inn open behind her. Making a snappy decision she tried the room door, it opened without making any noise and she went in leaving the door slightly ajar for a few moments so that she could see the inside. Apart from the furniture that she was familiar with, the room was empty. Fox was not there. She peeped out of the door into the yard. There was no one about so she opened the door a little wider to allow more light into the room. After a thorough examination of the room and the sparse furniture she concluded that it was exactly as she had left it last time. There were no signs that anyone had slept there the previous night.

The smell of the room was familiar to her and gave her a pleasant feeling but not wishing to be caught in the room she knew that she had to leave as quickly as possible. She went out of the door, closed it behind her and went down the stairs feeling disappointed but taking every step carefully knowing that it would be better to be seen coming down the steps than having to be picked up at the bottom with a twisted ankle.

To the best of her knowledge, she managed to get out of the backyard without being seen and walked in the town again with her head held high. She went to the church to pray for her family and then went down to the Cripple gate area near the river where she looked across the river at the long bridge. She knew in her heart that Fox would not be in that part of the town. She moved up the river a little distance and looked into the water at the junction of the Severn and the Clywedog. This was a favourite place of hers and she stared into the pool below the church, made a wish and threw a penny coin, which she had kept for the purpose, into the river. She went back to her horse and rewarded the child with a piece of bread.

She felt very disappointed as she made her way up from the town past Maes-y-dre up the hill towards Tylwch. Though when she thought clearly about things there was no reason for Fox to be in town. Within a short time she was at Non's farmstead and meeting her friend.

Non was pleased to see her and they had a good laugh together, especially when they discussed Lewis's request for a bed. The two women enjoyed having fun at Lewis's expense. It was not the first time for a woman to take advantage of his kind nature: he was such easy prey for any woman. They decided that they would give him a bed but that he would have to pay them a visit and explain in detail how he came to lose his lodgings.

Gwenllian returned to Cenarth, happier having met Non but very disappointed that she had not seen Fox. She arrived back in good time and without causing any suspicion.

The rest of the day she spent wondering about Fox, but in her rational moments she knew that the chances of seeing him were slim. He could be anywhere. Why would he be in Llanidloes? Yet, she remained disappointed for not having seen him. Was the disappointment entirely due to the fact that she had not been able to talk to him about her brother or was there something else? Was she more interested in Fox than she could admit? She found him intriguing and she had to admit that she found him an interesting person to be with. She was not as suspicious of him as she was at the beginning of their acquaintance and during their first meetings. She tried to get him out of her mind, knowing that she could not meet him until Saturday, but she found it very difficult.

Gwenllian went out into the yard and up between the grain shed and the stable and on to the hill. After walking about two or three hundred yards she sat on a stone and looked across towards St Garmon's church. It was September, but very mild, and the rain predicted by Philip from the early red sky had not materialised yet but the clouds now moving from the south-west indicated that it was going to rain heavily that evening.

Sitting there on the stone, she thought of Rhys first, as always, and then of Fox and the part he was playing in her life. She prayed for Rhys while looking in the direction of the church and then she prayed for guidance and forgiveness. The light was fading fast when she returned to the hall where there was a warm fire waiting for her. She drank some mead before going to bed hoping that it would help her sleep better.

On Saturday, the twenty-first day of September 1402, following her unsuccessful bid to see Fox she went to town early with Philip and this time saw Fox early in the morning under the market hall. She signalled to him that she wanted to talk to him and he glanced in the direction of their room. He left in the direction of the inn and she went the opposite way along Longbridge Street to give him ample time to reach the room. She then turned back and made towards the Castle Inn passing the market hall where Non was buying honey. Thankfully she did not notice Gwenllian gliding by swiftly.

Within seconds she was entering the yard behind the inn. There was no one there or in the stables when she popped her head through the door. She faced the steps and walked quickly towards them and went up remembering the large difficult step, third from the top. She did not knock, but glanced around, opened the door and entered. The small window seemed to be allowing more light in than she remembered – or was it that she was more prepared for the darkness? Perhaps when she had entered in the past she was more ashamed of what she was doing and the risks she was taking, but as she was getting used to going into the room she was becoming calmer and hence more observant. Indeed, she now looked forward with joy to arriving at their room and had forgotten Fox's slight change of attitude the last time they had met and put it down to his concerns about her father.

Fox was there waiting for her. She noticed his face more and found the calmness that he always displayed attractive. This much she admitted to herself. He had got up from his chair when she entered and went to sit on the bed leaving the chair for her.

She did not tell him that she had been looking for him on Wednesday. Perhaps, whatever her feelings, she did not fully trust him and also she did not want him to get the impression that she was that keen to see him. So she asked him casually if he had been in Llanidloes all week.

"No," he said. "Your father asked me to check out some things for him in Welshpool."

"Oh well! Meredydd came to see us last Tuesday and I thought you might wish to know what he had to say. I had time to talk to him about the points that you asked me to question him about."

Before she went any further, Fox intervened in panic, "You did not tell him that I or anyone else had asked you to question him?"

"Of course I didn't."

Recovering his composure quickly he said, "It's true then that Meredydd is operating without Glyndŵr's knowledge."

"How can you say that?" asked Gwenllian. "I found him very open and honest."

"Well," said Fox. "Why was he on his own? If they are as close as people think then why didn't Gruffydd and your father also come to see you?"

"He said they were too involved with leading their followers," she said but she had been thrown by the challenge to her line of thought.

"Interesting," said Fox. "But carry on with your story."

"He told me, well, he told Philip, where the rebels were on Sunday which was about five miles west of us but he was, understandably, vague about where they were going. It could be that he did not know."

"Oh he knew alright, it's just he was not going to tell you," said Fox, smiling. "He was probably going to meet with an agent of the king because I saw him in Llanidloes the following day."

After a short pause, Fox added, "He is obviously operating independently of your father and I shall report what you have said to your father. He will be very pleased and grateful to you and I have no doubt he will have the opportunity to thank you one day."

"But I came to town on that Wednesday and did not see you anywhere nor did I not see Meredydd and his men here," said Gwenllian. "We came to have some shoes repaired on Wednesday but I did not see you around the town. I wanted to report things to you as soon as possible."

Fox, without the slightest hesitation, said that he had seen them on the outskirts of Llanidloes on the Newtown road because he had gone to Newtown that day to contact Glyndŵr and receive further instructions.

Gwenllian thought that was reasonable and questioned him no further but again expressed strong disbelief in the suggestion that Meredydd was working against their father. She felt that he was completely loyal and she believed that he had left his father's army group only to come to see them at Cenarth.

She had decided not to tell Fox anything about her conversation with Meredydd about Rhys. She would wait until Meredydd reported back to her on what Mortimer had to say about Rhys's disappearance. She wondered if Mortimer would tell the truth. Gwenllian would never trust a Mortimer because they had stolen so much Welsh land and their hands were stained with too much Welsh blood.

Gwenllian had started to reflect on the possibility that

Rhys had stumbled across a meeting involving Mortimer and had overheard something said and had been killed to stop him talking about it. She had mentioned this to Philip more than once but his answer was always the same. Philip did not think it was likely because he thought they could have thrown Rhys down the stairs and pretended that he had an accident and blamed Beth and Cynwrig for not looking after him properly. She shivered every time she thought of this and dismissed the idea of her child being thrown down the stairs.

Gwenllian had thought much about it, as would be expected, but decided that the wisest thing to do was to keep that information to herself and to not involve Fox. As she had kept all aspects of her liaison with Fox to herself so she would keep some things from Fox.

She made it clear to him repeatedly that she felt that Glyndŵr had nothing to fear from Meredydd and he told her that he would report her exact words to Glyndŵr. He stressed on her how important a matter it was and for her to try to arrange another meeting with Meredydd as soon as possible and to question him more thoroughly about his relationship with his father. He reminded her that there was bound to be some jealousy between the brothers for the affection of their father. The two brothers, Gruffydd and Meredydd, were operating in close contact and some rivalry was inevitable. He reiterated that Glyndŵr was convinced of Meredydd's disloyalty.

Fox also said that Meredydd was visiting her sisters in the Hereford area without Glyndŵr's consent and one of the sisters there was reporting that Meredydd had a separate ambition to the rest of the rebels. He wanted Gwenllian to report to him as soon as possible should Meredydd mention anything to her sisters; Alice Scudamore, Janet Croft or Margaret Monnington, all living in the Gwent–Hereford border area.

Gwenllian felt that Fox wanted more contact but his demands of her were relentless and she wanted time to think things through. She hesitated before leaving but he was slow to take advantage of the delay. As she opened the door quietly she said that she would keep to their arrangement of meeting by the market hall unless there was something important to share. She left the room and went down the stairs.

The work on the farm was heavy in the autumn: preparing the stock and the supplies for the winter was important and hard work. They had to ensure that there was enough food for the family and the animals and enough wood and peat for the fire to cook and to keep the family warm.

Weeks went by and Gwenllian did not meet Fox in his room. They exchanged a few words at brief meetings by the market hall but Gwenllian had nothing to report. Meredydd did not call at Cenarth during the autumn.

# Chapter 13

O N THE TUESDAY of the first week in December 1402, Iolo came to the homestead and stayed overnight. His main news was that Sir Edmund Mortimer had married Catherine Glyndŵr on the last day of November. This was indeed astounding but excellent news for all at Cenarth and Gwenllian was particularly interested. Her sister married to Sir Edmund Mortimer. She wished she could meet Meredydd to find out if he had any news about what had happened to Rhys.

Celebrations started as soon as the work on the farm was over for the day, though Iolo had been oiling his throat from the time he had arrived. Gwenllian had been careful in the measures she had been giving him in order to have him at his peak performance in the evening and also she wanted to know where Glyndŵr and Meredydd were so she could, if possible, meet Meredydd. But, despite Gwenllian's persistence, it soon became apparent that either Iolo was not going tell her or he simply didn't know.

The boys were allowed to be present at the beginning of the merriments under Beth's supervision, but even so two of them managed to sip the occasional unattended drink and were quite merry after a while and were soon fast asleep.

Iolo started the evening with a poem he had written in praise of Philip and Gwenllian. He demanded total silence while he recited the poem, in which he gave a summary of Philip's illustrious ancestors from Glan Aeron and how he was of noble birth. Iolo could recite a long list of names going back generations. He praised Philip's strength and kindness and his generosity towards the poets and visitors.

Then he turned his attention to Gwenllian and reminded his audience how everybody admired Gwenllian's attractive physical appearance including her fine blonde hair. He described her as the most generous of hostesses and gave her high acclaim for her welcome and her kindness. He complimented her most enthusiastically for the quality of the food and drink she supplied to her guests. Every time he came to the end of a statement in his poem there were cries of support for the views he expressed about his hosts and there was a spontaneous raising of cups, which consequently had to be refilled frequently. There were jokes, there was laughter, there was harp playing by Iolo, there was singing and dancing late into the night with Gwenllian taking a leading role.

In the morning, Iolo was up and about early and, after eating a piece of bread with some milk, he was on his way to another farmstead where he would be guaranteed a similar welcome.

Gwenllian was determined to see Meredydd as soon as possible to find out if he had found anything out about her son. She felt sure now that Mortimer would tell the truth to Meredydd.

At the market on Saturday she met Fox briefly near Cripple's Gate. They had decided that it would be wiser for them to meet in a different place occasionally so that people did not become suspicious. Their meetings over the past few months had been strained with Fox showing his frustration at her inability to produce any valuable information. He went down from the direction of the church tower and she went from Long Bridge Street.

Gwenllian did not immediately report the news about

Mortimer to him because she was convinced that he would know everything and might have been told the news by her father. Perhaps he had been at the wedding wherever that was. Iolo had not been very specific about the location or the date but that was something she could ask Fox, she thought.

She told him that Meredydd had still not called at Cenarth. They exchanged pleasantries and Gwenllian caught him off guard when she asked him if he had been at Mortimer's wedding to her sister Catherine. He was taken aback and was obviously searching for an appropriate answer.

"I was unable to go," he said. "I knew he was getting married to your sister but I had been sent to south-west Wales on an urgent matter." Then, he added, "I am so pleased for them both. It will be an excellent boost to your father's position."

"Yes," she said. "Iolo brought the news last week and we celebrated the wedding that evening."

"Your hair looks lovely this morning," he said, changing the subject.

"Thank you," she said, blushing but enjoying every second.

"I hope you will get a visit from Meredydd soon, your father is very keen to get some information: it's very important to him," Fox reminded her.

"I will try my best," Gwenllian said, smiling sweetly at him.

They agreed to meet again the following week by the market hall and they then parted. She went back up towards Long Bridge Street slowly, enjoying the morning, but she noticed that he walked briskly towards the church with a far more urgent pace than her own.

She knew that they could not stay there talking for a long

time because someone who knew her might notice them but she liked his company and was disappointed that he had cut short their meeting. Their meetings filled her with excitement. As long as he kept away from the subject of a suggested rift between Glyndŵr and Meredydd she got on well with him. She looked forward to seeing him again and hopefully Meredydd would have called and she would have something to tell Fox and that something, she knew, would take the suspicion away from Meredydd. She also hoped even more that Meredydd might have drawn a confession from Mortimer. She went home from the market happier than she had felt for weeks.

In the days following her last meeting with Fox the weather became cold and wet. The fire was kept alight all day in the hall but it was necessary to go out to care for the stock, the oxen and horses. The stockman wasn't well and so Ieuan, now aged four, insisted on going out with his father to ensure that the stock was fed. It was raining with the wind blowing the rain from the west and into their clothes. They got very wet.

The following day the weather remained the same and Ieuan had a slight fever. It was one of those things that come and go in children but no one else had anything wrong with them. Ieuan insisted that he would go out again with his father to feed the stock. They went and he appeared well when he came back. They went to bed and Ieuan woke in the middle of the night crying, saying he was not well and his mother noticed he had a high fever. She woke Philip and they got him a drink but he could only sip a little of it and was violently sick shortly after. He felt better for a while again but the fever continued and he did not want any clothes on him. He kicked off the cover that was put on him and his mother could feel in the darkness that the sweat was rolling off his little face.

When the late dawn arrived, Philip and Gwenllian could see that Ieuan's face was very red and he was shivering and sweating profusely. They became seriously alarmed. They tried to keep him covered and hoped and prayed that the fever would dissipate. As the day progressed the fever continued and, if anything, it became worse. All the known remedies were applied. In the early afternoon Gwenllian went to St Garmon's church to pray and she made a wish at Curig's staff. She returned home hoping to see improvement but there was no change.

She did not look forward to facing the night. Ieuan's fever worsened as the evening progressed and he became delirious, calling for his mother without realising that she was already there, holding his little hand tightly. She wondered if Rhys had also been calling for his mother and she had not been there for him.

Ieuan's condition deteriorated during the night and just as dawn was breaking Ieuan died of his fever. His parents were distraught. His brothers could not be consoled. The whole household was in deep grief. Gwenllian felt that without warning this was the second of her boys to have slipped away from life and from her life. It was an insufferable loss.

Ieuan's funeral was held on the following Saturday. She had agreed to meet Fox but the Cenarth family did not go to the market; they went in the opposite direction towards St Garmon's church. The surrounding farmsteads always supported each other on occasions like this and Ieuan's funeral was no exception. The local families all gathered at Cenarth and followed the small coffin from Cenarth to the church. Ieuan's funeral was well attended, reflecting the status and respect the local community had for the family. The whole of Cenarth was there including the children and all who worked at the farmstead. There were villagers present also, returning the kindness that Philip and Gwenllian had shown the over the years.

They gathered at the newly opened grave near the church. Philip, Gwenllian and the three boys stood close together. Gwenllian carried the youngest, Owain, and held Meredydd's hand. Dafydd stood by his father. Beth and the other farm members were immediately behind.

The priest said some words in Latin which could be heard just above the sound of the wailing of a section of the mourners. Gwenllian was beside herself with grief but she could see that her loss of Ieuan was very different from the loss of Rhys. There was not the hope and anxiety associated with the loss of Rhys; not knowing what had happened was much more difficult to cope with.

Ieuan's small coffin was lowered into the grave at St Garmon's church three days after he first fell ill. He had gone from leading a happy life to the grave in such a short period of time. Gwenllian stood with Philip and the boys above the small grave. Gwenllian wished that there were two coffins in that grave so that she would know where Rhys was and could bring flowers to his grave. She wished that the two boys would be lying together in the grave.

She swore that while she was alive she would savour each instance of happiness that she had experienced with her two dead boys. She believed in herself with great confidence that she and her two boys would find each other again when the time came and that her God owed her that much.

She asked for forgiveness of God for, in her mind, not protecting her boys from death. She felt that they had slipped through her fingers and that she was somehow to blame. Above the grave she made an oath to Rhys to embark on a search for the truth and resolved to assume that Rhys was also represented by this grave. The grave and that moment brought some relief to her but it was only temporary and the grief seeped back as she left the grave and bade farewell to her boys through her tears.

The family returned to Cenarth but not before, at Gwenllian's insistence, leaving three small, flat, round cakes, as was the tradition in the north, on a stone near the grave. This was to recompense the birds and beasts for burying the body.

When they returned to Cenarth, Iolo was there waiting for them, pacing about in the yard outside the hall. He had learnt of the tragedy and had come to see the family. His visit this time was in a very different tone. He joined the family for food and drink. There was a very sober mood and the family was joined for a while by their workers.

Iolo took charge and said that he had written an elegy for the two dead Cenarth boys. This was the first open acceptance that Rhys was also dead and a great silence and sadness fell over Cenarth. Iolo had the skills to make people happy but he could also deal very effectively with a sad occasion and say the appropriate things.

He reminded them that it was only a short while earlier that he had written a poem of praise for the boys of Cenarth but here he was now grieving for two of those fine boys. His elegy began by naming the boys and went on to say how there were now two empty shirts at Cenarth. The two young boys had been stolen by the grave and swallowed by the earth. He described how sad Cenarth was after the loss of these boys and that Glyndŵr, their grandfather, had lost two young hawks. With their family background the two would have grown to be two eagles for Cenarth and their country. The family needed to cry to themselves and to God in heaven for the loss of these two seeds of Cenarth. The bodies of two of Gwenllian's lions had now gone from their court to the church, but their spirits were now in heaven.

Everyone in the hall was in tears – drawn by the power of Iolo's words. Gwenllian and Philip were crying openly which they had not been able to do after Rhys's disappearance. They appreciated Iolo's words.

People stood around for a while talking about the boys and gradually the conversation moved to other things. They could not afford to dwell on the deaths too long: the stock needed looking after and feeding. There was something that needed doing all the time and gradually the house emptied. Eventually, Philip went out to find comfort in work. Iolo stayed with Gwenllian, Beth and the boys, giving them comfort.

Christmas 1402 and the New Year were celebrated at Cenarth for the sake of the others boys. Gwenllian, when she was not praying, was crying. It was the attention required by her three other boys that after weeks of grieving eventually brought the family back slowly from the brink of despair.

She was a woman acquainted with much sorrow and grief through the tragic loss of her two boys and leant more on her God in the long months which followed Ieuan's funeral, but Philip retreated more into himself. He became quieter and concentrated on the farm and the stock.

# Chapter 14

G WENLLIAN'S RECOVERY AFER the death of Ieuan was unperceptively slow and a year went by without her meeting Fox or doing anything much other than grieving for her sons. Gradually, for the sake initially of her other children and later herself, she started to be more interested in the housework and the animals.

Her friends helped her. Non called to see her once a week and encouraged her to go out. Non had also lost a young girl three years earlier and was in a good position to encourage and support Gwenllian. The death of a child was a grievous loss but common. However, that did not make the loss easier to bear for Gwenllian and she also had the disappearance of Rhys to contend with, which was worse than anything. She knew where Ieuan was and she knew how much he had suffered with his illness but she had no idea how much Rhys had been made to suffer. The worst thing was she did not know what had been done with her precious child's body.

It was in those winter months at the beginning of 1403 that some aspects of Gwenllian's behaviour were perceived to be strange. She had become more dependent on her own concept of a God. Whenever there was a thunderstorm she would get out of the house and go to the small shed attached to the stable on the furthest side from the house and she would stay there for the duration of the storm. She explained that she felt safer in the shed. Others, including Philip, could not understand her reasoning, particularly since the shed was smaller and the thunder sounded much louder in the shed than in the hall. It became her pattern of behaviour and after a while no one questioned it. The truth was that she felt that God was nearer to her when the thunderstorm was about and more likely to hear her desperate prayer.

She did not wish to explain this to anyone and she never did but she kept the habit for the rest of her life. She went to the shed during the storms initially to pray, asking for information about Rhys, and to pray for Ieuan. With the passage of time her prayers lengthened to cover all her loved ones.

The farmstead was a quieter place that winter. The three brothers were anxious having lost Rhys and having seen Ieuan die so suddenly. Gwenllian consoled them by saying that God would look after them. They never asked why he had not looked after Ieuan because they knew that would hurt their mother. They also suspected that they knew their mother's answer would be that God works in mysterious ways. They talked about it amongst themselves but the eldest would always turn the subject and support his mother's view. They asked their father and he was more honest in his answer by saying that he did not know why Ieuan had died.

Gwenllian gradually accustomed herself to the trauma of Ieuan's death as far as it was possible for any mother and started to be a little more involved with her life at Cenarth.

She began visiting Non and that helped her. Non's daughter's clothes were now worn by her sister who had been born a year after her sister's death. Rhys's spare shirts had not been worn by his siblings. His spare garments were too important to Gwenllian and were kept folded tidily at the bottom of a coffer.

Month by month Gwenllian gradually improved. Religious belief played its part in the recovery. Another influence was the realisation that others had suffered worse losses. There were homes where the Black Death had visited and taken most of the children. Iolo had told them of a family in north Wales that had lost six of their seven children to the plague. Gwenllian had three boys and she had to be strong for them.

In March Meredydd called briefly with two other men. He had brought the condolences of Glyndŵr and the rest of the family for the death of Ieuan. He was on a mission on behalf of his father to Hereford to see his sisters. Gwenllian was only interested in what Mortimer had told him about Rhys's disappearance and about any meeting at Cwm Hir Abbey at the time. Meredydd had spoken to Mortimer about the event but he had categorically denied any knowledge of the boy's disappearance or of any meeting held at the abbey. Clearly, Meredydd now thought very highly of Edmund Mortimer and considered him honourable and truthful.

Gwenllian was very disappointed that he had not been able to give some clue that would help explain the disappearance and now that Mortimer was married to her sister Catherine she had to believe that what he said was true.

What Glyndŵr and his men had done over the winter months had barely interested her. There had been a lull in the fighting and there were times when it seemed that peace had arrived and the country was settling down to normal behaviour. She was totally disinterested in Fox and his work.

Then, the military storm broke again at the beginning of the summer in 1403 when, in May, Glyndŵr attacked Llandovery and Llandeilo. The town of Llandovery suffered a vicious revenge for the killing of Llewelyn ap Gruffydd Fychan. Glyndŵr also attacked Dryslwyn Castle and Newcastle Emlyn, causing panic in the south-west. This brought the king out again in a rage and he attacked Glyndŵr's homes at Sycharth and Glyndyfrdwy and burnt them down. If this was intended to silence Glyndŵr, it failed spectacularly because Glyndŵr replied by attacking other areas of south-west Wales.

The autumn months of 1403 passed Gwenllian by without her deriving her usual pleasures from seeing the trees changing colours, the fern on the hillsides turning red, then orange and finally brown. Unusually for her, she barely noticed the autumn colours and soon she had to endure the dark, winter months which she loathed – and, of course, the anniversary of Ieuan's death.

Iolo called just after Christmas and stayed to celebrate the coming of the New Year. He enlivened the atmosphere, particularly for the boys and he helped to slowly return Cenarth to the bright place it once had been. Iolo spoke to Gwenllian at length and encouraged her to try to lift her spirits in the New Year. She listened to his wise words but did not think that it would be possible for her to ever feel really happy again.

The early months of 1404 were very successful months for the rebellion and saw Glyndŵr capture Criccieth, Harlech and Aberystwyth. He held his first parliament at Machynlleth and was officially crowned prince of Wales by John Trefor, the bishop of St Asaph. This news reached the Cenarth family through visits by Iolo. He was delighted and all this good news helped raise Gwenllian's spirits and take her mind off the loss of two of her boys.

However, they were shocked and disappointed to be told that a Dafydd Gam had tried to assassinate Glyndŵr, but they were relieved to hear that he was unsuccessful and was imprisoned at Dolbadarn Castle. Many wondered why Glyndŵr had not executed him but Gwenllian was pleased that her father had not done anything so brutal.

Gwenllian had not met Robert Fox for well over a year

and did not meet him in the winter months or the early springtime of 1404. Her recovery was progressing slowly and she concentrated on her chores at Cenarth during the early months of the New Year. She did visit the market but not regularly and she was always with Philip and never strayed much from him. During her first visits she was glad when they returned home early. However, her spirit and enthusiasm for life improved as the days grew longer.

In May 1404, Glyndŵr's parliament met at Dolgellau and he established Harlech as his headquarters. His profile was higher than ever and as a result Cenarth became more exposed to the attention of the community and agents working to capture him and other leaders of the rebellion.

One day towards the end of May, by chance, Meredydd and Iolo called at Cenarth on the same day. Meredydd was recruiting in the area and also going south to see his sisters. Gwenllian had lost interest in Fox and she did not believe that Meredydd was doing anything knowingly that was detrimental to Glyndŵr. She was so sure of it that she decided to talk to Meredydd about Robert Fox as soon as she could get the opportunity to be alone with him.

Meredydd explained to Philip and Gwenllian that Glyndŵr was now holding parliaments and all Wales conferences where the main issues facing the country were discussed and ruled on. He stated that it was the first time that these types of meetings had ever taken place in Wales. They were making excellent progress and would produce a list of demands, such as wanting Wales to have an independent parliament, church and university. These were issues that would bring benefits to the whole of Wales and things that the Welsh had been requesting for years.

He stated clearly, in front of Iolo, that Glyndŵr's side was winning on all fronts and he had no doubt that their lives would soon be made easier. He suggested that it would be to their benefit to side with the rebellion now, so that they would gain the rewards that would follow the final victory. There would be additional land to distribute and Glyndŵr's supporters would do well. He went so far as to say that God supported Glyndŵr and the star that had appeared two years earlier had definitely been a signal of the success that was to come. To Meredydd it was obvious that God was protecting his father because whatever trap had been set for him he had managed to avoid it or escape from it.

Meredydd also suggested that Mortimer was very helpful in bringing strong allies in England to their side. He was careful not to be too specific in case idle talk reached the king's ear. He trusted everyone at Cenarth but he was no fool and he had learnt to be careful. He named no one. Gwenllian was all ears and wondered how her father could think that her brother was disloyal. Meredydd's visit reminded Gwenllian of her meetings with Fox and she was surprised that she could even think of them; she was convinced that it was all a sign that she was returning to her normal self.

He made a good case for Cenarth to join the rebellion and explained exactly what he was asking of them. It was the same request as was made a few years earlier: he wanted them to keep their eyes and ears open for anything that was unusual happening in their area. If there were any unknown men asking questions about the rebels then he would like to know about them. There was a war on and the control of accurate information was vital in winning that war. Both sides were gathering information and both sides had agents in every town in Wales. Meredydd agreed that the request was the same as he had made previously but now information was even more important and they had many more enemies now because they were more successful.

Gwenllian could not divulge the part she was already playing in gathering information for her father but both she and Philip agreed that they would supply any information that they had and be on alert for the king's spies in the area.

She shifted the conversation and talked to Meredydd about Rhys. She wanted to know if he had been able to find out anything more since his last visit. Meredydd repeated what he had said to Gwenllian in March of the previous year, which was that he was of the opinion that Mortimer had not played any part in Rhys's disappearance. He was convinced that he was telling the truth. Mortimer had come over to their side, had married Catherine and hated the king as much as any of the rebels.

On the other matter of her involvement with Fox it was difficult to get the opportunity with Iolo about as well. She asked Meredydd to go for a walk with her and he agreed but Dafydd overheard and insisted on going with them. His insecurity since the loss of Rhys kept him close to his mother. For one reason or another she did not get an opportunity to talk to Meredydd by himself and so was unable on this occasion to mention Fox to him. But she did manage to say to him that she wanted to talk to him next time he called and hoped that would not be too long.

Gwenllian was continuing to recover steadily and though she went to the market initially every two or three weeks, gradually her visits became more regular and her interest in the stalls increased, but she avoided all places associated with Fox. She sometimes blamed her connection with Fox for the tragedies that had come her way and this made the suffering more difficult to bear. However, by mid-summer she had gained in confidence and started to feel that she could face him again but he was not around, otherwise she would surely have seen him or he would have spotted her and come to talk to her. She ventured into the Castle Inn in September but she never saw him. She even risked going up the stairs in October but there was no answer when she knocked on the door and she did not try to open it.

There were times when she would have liked to ask the landlord of the inn if he could tell her where Robert Fox was, but the risk of being questioned as to why she was looking for him was too great. She simply had to wait and be patient.

So the months went by and Christmas would be upon her soon with more dark days and the second anniversary of Ieuan's death.

On the first Saturday in December 1404, Gwenllian, partly to support her father and partly to keep her mind active, decided to make another effort to contact Robert Fox and went, in a determined frame of mind, to the market in Llanidloes with Philip as had been the re-established pattern of the past few months. She did not need to make much of an effort to find him because as she was walking around on her own she suddenly came face to face with Fox. He showed that he was pleased to see her and whispered that he would like to see her in the usual room and that he would go there immediately.

Gwenllian had assumed that he had gone away somewhere, was injured or even killed in one of the many skirmishes that had taken place over the last year. Faced with Fox and the reality of dealing with him reduced her keenness to talk to him partly because spying on Meredydd was not a task she liked doing. However, she could not resist directing her steps towards the Castle Inn. She was not sure whether it was curiosity that drew her in Fox's direction or did she genuinely wish to help her father's cause.

She did not go up the steps with great keenness as she had in earlier times; instead she took her time, taking each step carefully. She knocked very gently on the door and pushed it open. The room was the same except that it smelt unused and more unkempt than she remembered. It was also smaller and it took her a few seconds to realise that there were two chairs there which helped to make the room feel smaller but she was pleased to find that there were two chairs and she sat in one.

"Where have you been?" she asked, challengingly.

"I have been with your father all over Wales," he replied. "As you would expect I can't give you details but I was with him on the campaign in the south-west."

He commiserated very genuinely with her over the death of Ieuan. She said a little about what she had been doing since Ieuan's death and she told him that she had taken some time to recover. She told him that Meredydd had visited her the previous May but she did not mention any of the conversation they had about Rhys.

Fox took up the same line as he had a year earlier that Meredydd was definitely plotting against his father and that the situation was getting critical. He had not contacted her recently because Glyndŵr wanted her to have time to recover but he had sent Fox now to ask for her help to find out Meredydd's whereabouts and his plans. He was convinced that the fact that Meredydd was visiting Gwenllian on his own meant that he was operating separately from his father. Gwenllian disagreed because she felt she knew Meredydd and found him loyal and trustworthy and did not believe he would ever work against his father.

They agreed to disagree. She found him convincing

as to the appeal from her father and agreed that when the occasion arose she would question Meredydd to see if there was anything she could find out. Fox wanted her to visit the rebel's camp in the north but Gwenllian dismissed that idea out of hand and said that Meredydd was bound to call and see her soon.

This was not good enough for Fox because he wanted more results and he wanted them urgently. He was a desperate man for some reason. Gwenllian couldn't understand the change in his attitude and manner.

He was adamant that she should do something more substantial to gain information. They began to argue and he became increasingly nasty, threatening to tell Philip about their meetings if she did not cooperate with him.

"Tell him what?" asked Gwenllian in annoyance.

"Tell him that you have been coming here to my room."

"I will tell him myself," said Gwenllian angrily.

"Will you tell him what we have been doing here?"

"But we have been talking about my father's rebellion and Philip would approve of that," she said.

"He would not approve of what I would tell him we have done," said Fox. "No, you will need to do as I ask Gwenllian or I can make things very difficult for you."

Gwenllian was furious with him. She was also furious with herself and got up from the chair and left the room running down the stairs and towards the corner of the inn. But her pace slowed down as she reflected on what Fox had said and she realised that he held the upper hand and she stopped her dash. Slowly, she retraced her steps towards the stairs and back up to the room.

She entered to hear Fox saying, "I thought you would be back."

It was clear that he was going to blackmail her. She would have to do as he asked or he would tell Philip of their association. She would have to agree now to all his requests, to give herself time to think and decide what to do.

So she agreed if Meredydd did not call and see her soon in the new year then she would somehow visit him at the rebels headquarters in Harlech or wherever she could find him. She had no idea how she could achieve the latter. She also decided that she would be careful not to alert Meredydd to the fact that Fox existed because that would bring greater problems to Glyndŵr and herself. Finally, she agreed to meet Fox on market days either by the market hall or in his room, depending on what they had to talk about.

She went home that day in very low spirits indeed and regretted having gone to Fox's room, and thought that it would have been preferable to have spoken to him in the street.

She could not understand why he could not go to Meredydd himself and find out what his plans were. She had no idea where to go and look for Meredydd or how she could possibly go as far as Harlech without letting Philip know. It was impossible. Perhaps she could say she was going to see her family in Meirioneth because she had not seen them for a long time. But the rebels could be anywhere in Wales and very few people knew where they were at any one time. Fox was under the impression that she knew more than she did – he probably thought that she was in frequent contact with the rebels.

She was at a loss as to what to do but it kept her mind off her grief.

During the lead up to Christmas 1404, Gwenllian's interest in life improved and she was a regular visitor to the market at

Llanidloes. She did not visit Fox in his room during December but she did meet him regularly by the market hall though she had no information to give him that was of any importance. Christmas 1404 was celebrated with more enthusiasm than the previous Christmas as time had helped to heal the wounds at Cenarth.

# Chapter 15

ON A SATURDAY in the middle of January 1405, Gwenllian met Fox by the market hall and he demanded that she go with him to his room. Gwenllian refused, saying that she could tell him all she knew without going to the room.

Fox was clearly furious with her and threatened her again with informing Philip about their meetings and that the landlord of the inn would support him and confirm that Gwenllian had been meeting Fox in his room. This shook her and she told him that she would get him some information by the following Saturday. She had a worrying journey home that Saturday. She would have to get some information for Fox but what information would satisfy him?

The following Saturday Fox was waiting for her by the market hall and she lied to him, saying that she had been talking to Meredydd during his visit to Cenarth the previous week but that there was no indication that he was working against his father. Gwenllian made it all up and played for time to find a solution to her predicament.

Fox was interested but pushed her for more information, particularly about Meredydd's safe houses and other hiding places. She had a distinct feeling that Fox was getting more desperate and that someone was pushing him for results. Was it her father who was putting pressure on him? He was blackmailing her and she did not believe that her father would wish him to do that under any circumstances.

Later that day, after she had returned home, she went for a walk by herself to try to clarify things in her mind. She knew that she was playing a dangerous game with Fox. What would he do if he found that she was lying? He might already know that Meredydd had not visited Cenarth the previous week. He might ask a trick question to catch her out. He would surely tell Philip if he caught her lying to him and Fox would add to the tale to make matters worse. She could not bear to think of Philip finding out. If only she could talk directly to her father.

During these difficult days she often walked on her own around Cenarth Hill. She would take her time and allow her mind to drift over the events. On these walks she often wished she had spoken to Philip after her first meeting with Fox. She sometimes went into St Garmon's church and would sit there in silence thinking things out and thinking of Rhys and Ieuan: what they would be doing now and how smart and strong they would have been.

Gwenllian decided that the best and safest course of action was to continue to lie to Fox and hope that he would not find out. If Meredydd was going to betray his father in any way he would have done so by now and the thought grew stronger in her that Fox was using Meredydd as a ploy to get other information. She tried to puzzle out what he was after but there were no easy answers.

Meredydd and Gruffydd were always at their father's side wherever they were on the campaign and the three were never far from each other. Was Fox trying to find out Glyndŵr's safe places by asking for information on Meredydd? She did not believe that her father would expect him to blackmail her and also would Glyndŵr not have simply asked Gruffydd to find out if Meredydd was disloyal? At last, she realised that it did not make sense. Fox must be using her to gather information about the rebels and in particular her father's hiding places.

She had not been able to see this clearly and logically for some years she thought to herself. Her thoughts had been consumed by grief.

If it were the case that he wanted information about her father then he did not know his hiding places and had not been with the rebels during the past two or three years. She concluded that Fox was probably working for someone other than her father, but who that was she had no idea.

She was amazed that this had not occurred to her a long time ago.

Mortimer was on Glyndŵr's side and had married her half sister. Meredydd seemed to think quite highly of him. So, if he was not working for Mortimer whom was he working for? Who was most desperate to find Glyndŵr? There was only one obvious answer: it had to be the king and his agents. The stakes were now much higher. There was talk of the French becoming involved and so the king would be desperate to catch Glyndŵr and hang him, she thought. It was clear to her now that Fox was an agent of the king and was being put under pressure to find Glyndŵr.

The chances of Meredydd calling at Cenarth were slim and so she decided to tell Fox that he had visited and, to make it more believable, she would say that Gruffydd was with him and she would also say that they were heading south for Gwenlliant with a plan to attack the castles there. She would simply make up the tales to tell him.

By the middle of February 1405, Gwenllian was disappointed that Meredydd had not called at Cenarth but Iolo did and he was full of stories. First he had heard that a Lady Dispenser had managed in February to abduct the two Mortimer heirs to the throne from their long captivity

in London and attempted to take them to Caerphilly castle
and eventually to Edmund Mortimer and Glyndŵr. Since
these boys had a better claim to the throne than Henry they
would have presented a strong challenge to him. It would
have been a major success for Glyndŵr but unfortunately
Lady Dispenser and the boys were caught and taken back to
London. As always happened when nobility was involved
the lady was punished by the loss of her estate but the
blacksmith who had copied the keys for her had his hands
cut off and then his head.

Iolo also informed the house that Glyndŵr had signed
a tripartite indenture with Edmund Mortimer and the earl
of Northumberland. The agreement divided the kingdom
into three parts. It was signed in Aberdaron, in the house
owned by the dean of Bangor. Iolo was convinced that
Glyndŵr was going to succeed in all his aims.

Gwenllian hung on every word of Iolo's so that she
could repeat it to Fox, knowing that it must be common
knowledge anyway if Iolo was saying it. She could mix it
up with the lies she planned to tell Fox and present the
mixture of truth and lies to him as facts.

Gwenllian went to meet Fox on the first Saturday after
Iolo's visit. They met first by the market hall and then
in the room at the top of the stairs. Gwenllian told Fox
about the Lady Dispenser plot. Fox was interested but not
enthusiastic. She guessed that it was not news to him. He
pressurised her to tell him where Meredydd was now and
where he was planning to go in the next few weeks. She
was getting annoyed by this pressure and instead of lying
to him decided to challenge him.

"Come on, Gwenllian, you must know where your
brother's safe houses are. Even if you do not know them all

you must know some," said Fox, smiling that slimy smile she had grown to hate in recent months.

"I don't know," said Gwenllian, but she then gathered courage and said "I don't think you want to know where Meredydd is – I think you want to know where my father is so that you can inform the king."

"So, you have worked it out at last. It does not improve your position. You find out where your father is or you'll learn that I will tell everything to your dear husband," said Fox. "In fact, I believe you know exactly where the rebels are likely to attack next so you had better tell me now. Where are they going to attack?" he growled at her, grabbing her wrists.

Gwenllian felt powerless in his physical and mental grip. She thought quickly, fearing that he would torture her or even kill her. She couldn't scream and shout because she could not explain why she was in that room. She had to give him some information, so she had to make up a story.

Crying convincingly, she said, "They are going to attack areas of Gwenlliant and that is all I know."

She had no idea where they were going to attack; she didn't even know if they were going to attack anywhere. She took a chance and hoped that if her father's men were going to attack anywhere it would not be Gwenlliant. She also thought of Gwenlliant because three of her half sisters lived in the area and her father was unlikely to cause too many problems for them as he had protected her as well as he could.

Fox released her wrists and moved back to decide if she was telling the truth. She had delivered a convincing performance and he had believed her.

"Good. At last," he said. "You had better come back here

exactly four weeks from today and tell me more of what you know."

Gwenllian pulled herself together and silently moved towards the door but not before she heard him repeat the order that she was to return to the room in four weeks with even more information.

In the days that followed, Gwenllian could not keep Fox and his demands out of her mind and on one of her now daily walks by herself on Cenarth Hill she realised that she had to take some action. She would not be able to lie to him for weeks on end because he would surely catch her out. She dreaded the thought that she had to meet him in less than four weeks' time. Every day that went by meant the date of their meeting was getting closer.

Then, in the middle of March, Meredydd called at Cenarth with a group of his men on his way north. It was plain to all that he was in a bad state of mind. The usual smile was not there, neither was the happy greeting. Without saying a word he hugged his sister. He was on his way from a battle in Gwenlliant with very grim news. He told them that a few days earlier, on the twelfth day of March, there had been a battle fought at Pwll Melyn, near Usk. The king's forces were somehow aware that an attack was planned and had set up their forces so as to trap the rebels.

Glyndŵr's men had been convincingly beaten.

Meredydd was very upset because he thought that his brother Gruffydd had probably been captured or killed. He thought that if Gruffydd had been captured alive that he might have been executed immediately or the king would use him as a bargaining tool against the rebels. Meredydd was not with his brother when it had happened because Gruffydd had led the attack and Meredydd had been in charge of the supplies and so was not near when his brother was captured. A friend had described what had happened and he thought that Gruffydd had been alive when captured. Meredydd had stayed in the area for some time after the battle to see if his brother had escaped but he had not appeared nor turned up at an agreed place after the battle.

Meredydd also told them that his father's brother Tudur had been killed. Many of their best soldiers had been killed or captured. It was the worst time ever for the rebellion and it raised many questions, not least who had supplied the information to the king that they were going to attack in the Usk area. He told her that the rebels had a number of double agents in the Usk area and it was difficult to understand why they had not picked up information and warned Glyndŵr that there was a trap waiting for them.

Meredydd told Gwenllian they would have to rethink their strategy and their intelligence gathering from then on. The loss of his brother was a blow to him and Gwenllian was pleased that she was able to console him but there were deep and dark guilty worries in her heart, and she wondered if she had played a part in the disaster.

Meredydd stayed for two nights but he and his men kept out of sight and then left in the evening of the third day to go north to Harlech. He and Gwenllian had grown closer during those days but she had not been able to mention her meetings with Fox because of the risk of implicating herself in the disaster at Usk.

Gwenllian, when she heard about the battle and the consequences, was convinced that it all had something to do with her and Fox. She had let her father down, caused her brother to be captured and caused the death of many of her father's men. She tried to console herself by saying to herself that she had not done it intentionally. But, she had to admit to herself that she said what she did to save her own skin. She comforted herself by remembering that she had not told Fox where in Gwenlliant they were going to attack; she had said Gwenlliant and Gwenlliant was a very large area. If only she had said to Fox that they were going to attack the south-west.

# Chapter 16

THE NEXT ARRANGED meeting with Fox fell on the last Saturday in March 1405. It weighed heavily on Gwenllian's mind but she had no choice but to meet him. He had carefully laid a trap for her, she had walked into it and was now firmly in his grip. She went over the events of the last few weeks many times in her mind and each time returned to the same conclusion that she was implicated in the capture of her brother Gruffydd. She was mortified that she had given information that had probably led to the defeat near Usk and was afraid of doing the same thing again while meeting Fox. Though the information she had given Fox was intended to mislead, it had by chance, she believed, led the king's men to Usk to set the trap that resulted in her brother's capture. It worried her that she had to be so very careful when dealing with Fox and she was determined to be better prepared for the next meeting.

As devastated as she was by the capture of her brother she could not share her guilt with anyone. She thought that he had probably been hanged by now though she had not received any information about him, which was probably a good thing. She could not bear to think about it.

To cope with the whole series of horrendous events that had befallen her she went on long walks by herself on Cenarth land, using the time to put things in perspective and prepare her mind for her next meeting with Fox. Her normal path would take her up from the farmstead on to the top of Cenarth Hill, where she could view the land around. She rested her eyes on the horizon and dreamed of better times ahead. It also helped her to remember the good times in the past. Her childhood, though lonely, had been happy and she had been loved. The time before the rebellion was also a content time for her when she became a mother for the first time. She then thought about Rhys, his loss and the soul-destroying realisation that she did not know what had happened to him or more heart wrenching where was his little body now.

She would look to the east where she knew Cwm Hir and St Garmon's church were and memories of Rhys and Ieuan would come flooding back, sometimes making her cry, at other times just remembering the thrill of their birth and the happiness that they had given her. In the early spring her spirits were raised by the brightness of the yellow- and orange-coloured Welsh poppies dotted here and there in the stone walls. These brightly coloured flowers, growing healthily in the most impossible of places gave her inspiration to continue to face life.

From the top of Cenarth Hill she could see the other hills across the valley and above the lime-washed farmsteads towards England. She could see the hill above Prysgduon and imagined again the well of cold water where Llywelyn's men had washed their hands and the words of the dark, ghostly horseman who had appeared at the well to admonish the hard men of the north. She frequently thought of the Prysgduon story these days because her own father was now a prince of Wales and she feared that his destiny would be the same as Llywelyn's. To Gwenllian, the horseman's message was clear: people's destiny was not foretold, it was in their own hands. She tried to relate this to her own predicament and kept concluding that she would have to find her own way to come to terms with her problems and find solutions. Hope alone would not be enough to solve her difficulties.

On these walks she would remind herself that she was Glyndŵr's daughter and that she should show determination. She was a woman but she was of high rank and had a strong will and a mind of her own. She needed to take hold of her destiny and her family's future.

On the specified Saturday, she attended the market and circulated the streets observing and taking in what was on display. She saw Fox watching her and saw his signal, which was no more than a slight tilt of his head in the direction of the Castle Inn. This was his way of telling her that he would meet her in his room. Once he knew that she had seen and responded to his signal, he left in the direction of the inn to wait for her.

She was very uncertain about meeting him and far more concerned than usual about being seen going to the room but she had no choice. She had to go and meet him. If she didn't she feared for her relationship with Philip. He had been a good husband to her; he was caring of their children and he had given her a good living. She had done well in marrying Philip. She loved him and would have to defend their marriage and their life together. They had been a great support to each other over the loss of two of their boys. She resolved to face up to the web of deceit she had allowed herself to get tangled in.

To allow him time to reach the room she stayed near the market hall a little while pretending to study the produce for sale but it was an anxious time for her before she began her short walk from the market hall to the inn. She was more nervous walking that street than she could remember ever being before. She took the final steps towards the inn, carefully checking who was in the area and studying faces to see if there was anyone looking at her and watching for anyone she recognised near the inn.

Deciding that it was all clear, Gwenllian slipped around the corner of the inn and went towards the yard. So far so good, she thought. But as more of the yard came to view she realised that it was not empty. There were two men talking near the middle but they took no notice of her. However, she could not be seen climbing the stairs to the room so she turned on her heels quickly and went back to the street, pretending to be looking in her basket for something she had forgotten. No sooner was she about ten yards from the inn than one of the men in the yard came walking around the front of the inn and entered by the front doorway. She was at a loss for a moment whether to continue with her walk away from the inn or whether to turn back and try again. The other man would have moved off, probably into the stables.

She decided to take a chance and go back immediately. She went round the corner of the inn again. This time the yard was empty but she could see the back of a man's head over a low part of the old castle wall, where she assumed he had probably gone to urinate. She realised that he could not see the stairs from behind the wall so she moved swiftly and went up the stairs with her woven shallow basket firmly in her hand. Nervously she reached the top and entered the room quickly, disappearing into the darkness before closing the door behind her.

Once her eyes were accustomed to the gloom she could see that Fox was sitting in one of the chairs, leaning back with pleasure all over his face. He had won: he had her brother captured and her father's brother killed – all of which, she believed, she had caused.

He welcomed her with a slight smile. He stood up from his chair with practised courtesy and beckoned her to sit on the other chair.

She knew that this was the moment of opportunity, which she had prepared herself for.

Her hand came out of the basket holding the knife firmly and pushed the blade hard with all her strength under his ribs and then upwards. She withdrew the dagger slowly. Her hatred for him dissipated in that first well-practised strike. But she had some left in her and while he was slumping down she plunged it into him again, this time into his neck, quickly withdrawing it. He collapsed on the floor.

She took the top linen from the basket and wiped the dagger once on that cloth and placed the dagger back in her basket underneath another clean cloth and left the blood-stained cloth to cover his neck wound which was bleeding profusely and spreading to form a dark, menacing red pool.

The sounds he was making as he died distracted her from her mission momentarily, but it was over quickly and he lay perfectly still, obviously dead. She sat in the chair exhausted and yet relieved that it was over and done with. Seconds later, the urgency of the situation came back to her and she stood up and took a pair of female braies from her basket and threw them on the bed.

She searched the body to take any money he had on him and found a small purse containing some coins. She placed it in her basket and quietly toppled one chair on to the floor. She did not need to check to see if he had died: she was confident that he had.

Standing by the door, she looked around the room to check that everything was as she had planned. It was perfect and obvious that he had been killed and robbed, probably by a woman of ill repute. He deserved to die, she thought – if anything, his death had been too quick. He was lucky.

She opened the door and peeped out. There was no one in the yard, so she went out and closed the door quietly behind her. She stood on the top of the steps too long, but she had to breathe. She had to accustom herself to the light. She looked around the yard again. There were some noises coming from the stables but at this crucial moment the yard was empty. She moved quickly down the stairs and within seconds was round the corner of the inn. She looked at her hands: they were clean but she went to the well to wash them anyway. There was no blood on them but she washed them thoroughly rubbing them together several times in the water as if they were soaked in blood. She then checked her clothes and they also had no trace of blood on them.

Minutes later she was herself again and walking up Oak Street searching for her husband.

Home at Cenarth she returned the dagger to Philip's sword cupboard and the small bag of coins she placed with her personal belongings in her cupboard.

Gwenllian felt a great sense of relief for some hours after the killing. She considered it an act of revenge for the killings at Usk. She was glad to get that man out of her life.

She did not wish to keep the money and decided that she would place the coins in the charity box at the church in Llanidloes, one or two at a time over a period of weeks so as not to draw attention. She wondered how many weeks it would take and untied the purse and emptied the contents into her hand. There were only four pennies and the greatest contribution to the weight of the purse was made by a silver broach. She studied the brooch and was shocked that she recognised it as the brooch that Rhys had been wearing on the day that he had disappeared. She could not believe what she saw in the palm of her hand.

It had been a gift from her father to Rhys, her eldest son. Glyndŵr had acquired the brooch when in Scotland, fighting on behalf of the king many years earlier. He had given her the brooch in person when he had visited Cenarth to see his grandson shortly after he had been born. He gave it to Gwenllian for her to give to Rhys when he got older. Memories came flooding back to her followed by pangs of grief for her lost child.

"How did Fox get this?" she asked aloud before realising that others could hear her. Her legs were almost giving way under her as she realised that had she known that he had the brooch before she had killed him she would not have killed him. She now deeply regretted killing Fox. She wanted to tell Philip about the brooch but she couldn't.

She went out of the house and walked up Cenarth Hill, gripping the brooch firmly in her hand. On reaching the top of the hill, she stopped and had another look at it, studying the fine details and carvings. Yes, she thought, this was Rhys's brooch. It was unique: it resembled the flower of a thistle plant. She smelt it hoping to smell her son on it but she could only smell the leather of the purse. She broke down sobbing. All her emotions came out: the strain of the killing in the morning and then the discovery of this link to ·Rhys. She slumped on her knees and cried without restraint. Fox's dead body was now punishing her and having its own revenge on her. He had haunted her in her dreams and nightmares in the past and he was now, she believed, going to punish her for the rest of her life for taking his life.

She would now never find out why Fox had the brooch in his purse.

It took her some time to recover and when she did she found herself lying flat on the damp ground. She struggled to stand up. Her clothes were damp and sticky. She walked slowly downhill towards her home. Her mind was clearing a little and the thought came to her again that the brooch was not the one that Rhys had worn but a similar one. This assumption would be easier to live with than the belief that it had been worn by Rhys when he disappeared and that she had killed the only person who could explain how the brooch had come to be in his possession.

But the brooch was so like the one that Rhys had worn that she felt sure it was the same brooch. She wanted to tell Philip of the discovery but there would be too many questions that she could not answer truthfully. One lie would lead to another and she would be forced to tell the whole truth and killing Fox would have achieved nothing. She felt better keeping the truth to herself – she had become used to keeping things to herself. She washed the tears from her eyes with water from the stream before she returned to the hall. She had to constantly convince herself that it had been necessary for her to kill Fox.

Quietly to herself she listed everything she knew about Fox and concluded that he was almost certainly an agent working for the king. She thought he had the task of gathering information about the rebels and he wanted to know where they were so that he could inform the king, who could then capture or kill as many of the rebels as possible. She was targeted by Fox because she was Glyndŵr's daughter and so was likely to know where he would be at any one time. All his daughters were vulnerable to the king's agents but she felt that she had been the weak one who had betrayed the rebels and caused the disastrous defeat at Usk.

She reminded herself that he was blackmailing her and that he was a ruthless man, who did not mind how many men his information killed. There was one question that she kept returning to: did he intend to use the brooch as further means of blackmailing her? He would have guessed that after the defeat at Usk she would have been far more reluctant to give any more information so perhaps he intended to use Rhys's brooch as some kind of a bargaining tool.

Had he thought of giving her the brooch as a gift if she gave him more information? She did not feel that this was strong enough a lever for him to use on her. It had to be that he would tell her what had happened to Rhys if she informed on Glyndŵr and the brooch was proof that he knew what had happened. She knew that she would have done a lot of things to find out what had happened to Rhys.

She had to conclude that Fox probably knew what had become of Rhys and that she now had no hope of finding out and she would have to live with that knowledge.

# Chapter 17

G WENLLIAN DID NOT visit the market in Llanidloes in April but she did on the first Saturday in May. She had worked out that she would have to face it at some time or another and decided that she would go there, act normally but be very alert. She had decided that she would not go anywhere near the Castle Inn.

In May in the year 1405, the bluebells on the tree-shaded slopes of Cenarth were in full bloom and it was remarked that no one could remember a better display. The smell of the wild flowers was intoxicating and with the sun shining it was a perfect day. She enjoyed her journey to town though she was a little nervous. It was an uneventful visit much to her relief but she was pleased to return to Cenarth. Thereafter she attended the market weekly.

Iolo arrived early at Cenarth on the fifteenth day of June with information that Gruffydd, her brother, had been taken to the tower of London. Gwenllian took this as good news because it meant that he was alive. He also told them that John Hanmer, Glyndŵr's brother-in-law had been captured and a reward of £26 was given to the agent who took him prisoner. This caused alarm in Gwenllian and made her wonder how many people like Fox were around Llanidloes and other towns.

A few days later, Meredydd called at Cenarth on his way to Gwenlliant. He wanted to remind them, as he was going to remind his other sisters, of the dangers posed to them by the king's agents operating throughout Wales. He reminded them of what had happened to John Hanmer and admitted that the capture had been a significant blow to the cause. He told them that it was necessary to be careful before trusting anybody.

Meredydd indicated that there were troubled times ahead with the French soldiers arriving to join the rebels and he hoped that a decisive battle would take place soon. He hoped that the coming battle would bring the war to a head and result in a victory for his father.

Gwenllian was able to talk to Meredydd on his own when they went for a walk in the morning before he left for Gwent. He was missing his brother and told her that his brother's capture and the great losses at Usk had taken a heavy toll on his father. Gwenllian did not want to hear anything about Usk – she had made every effort to blank the whole episode out of her mind.

However, the brooch she had found in Fox's purse was on her mind frequently. It was like a ray of hope for her. Hope that she might one day find out what had happened to Rhys. Aware that she could not produce a convincing story about how she had found the brooch she had to keep its discovery a secret from Meredydd and Philip. It pained her not to be able to tell the truth but it was wiser for her to say nothing than to start on a series of lies that could eventually lead her into deeper difficulties.

"Meredydd, if Mortimer knows nothing about Rhys's disappearance, have you any idea who might know something?" Gwenllian asked.

Meredydd turned to her and saw the despair on her face and the appealing look in her eyes. He considered for a moment and said, "On my way south tomorrow I intend to call at Pileth to have a look at the old battlefield and that is very close to Mynachdy where we sent the old abbot after we attacked the abbey the summer after Rhys disappeared. I can call at Mynachdy and question the old abbot again."

"Yes, but you and dad questioned him at the time and he said he didn't know anything then. So, what is different now?" Gwenllian asked him.

"Now Mortimer is on our side and any loyalties the abbot had may have changed as a consequence. Also, he is older and frailer than he was and will not appreciate being threatened with a move to Dolbadarn Castle. He has a reputation for taking care of his own skin."

"Do you think?" she said, unconvinced by the suggestion.

"It's worth a try, Gwenllian. We have nothing to lose."

"You are right. Please call and see him tomorrow and please call back here on your way back north."

Meredydd's determination to question the old abbot again raised Gwenllian's hopes of finding some clues about Rhys's disappearance.

Philip was supportive of the idea of challenging the old abbot and while he did not think it would lead to anything he agreed that it was worth a try.

Meredydd left the following morning and as he was parting Gwenllian wished him a safe journey and hoped that he would be successful with the old abbot. She also asked him to give her regards to her sisters in Gwent.

As promised, Meredydd called to see the previous abbot of Cwm Hir at his retreat in Mynachdy and did not have to use any force to get information from him. The abbot had aged considerably in the past few years and his old loyalties had weakened; he was more interested than ever in ensuring that he had as gentle an ending to his life as possible.

Though Meredydd reminded the old abbot of the details of the incident in the bell tower of Cwm Hir Abbey a few years earlier, it was not necessary because the abbot had a very good recollection of the event. The old man had known immediately when he saw Meredydd who he was and had guessed what he wanted and knew instinctively that he had to cooperate this time. He had lied on numerous occasions in the past to ensure that he kept his benefactors on his side so he could continue to rely on their support and protection.

He knew that the same protection was not available anymore.

The old abbot confessed to Meredydd that he was present when Rhys was abducted by two agents of the king. He confirmed that Mortimer was unaware of the abduction and had nothing to do with it. He said that two agents were involved and he named them as Robert Fox and his operator, whose code name was "Wolf" but his real name was William ap Bleddyn. They were there because the king did not trust Edmund Mortimer to gather information about Glyndŵr and the rebellion and blamed Mortimer for the lack of success in capturing Glyndŵr.

The abbot also claimed that the king had a paranoid fear of Mortimer's young nephews' claim to the throne.

The old abbot told Meredydd in some detail what had happened. He related how there had been a meeting at the abbey tower about a fortnight before Rhys had disappeared and that Gwenllian and her family connections had been discussed. It was known that she was Glyndŵr's daughter and it was thought that she could be used to get information about her father's whereabouts. The abbot said that they were ruthless men, particularly William, and were determined to kidnap one of Gwenllian's boys in order to blackmail her to divulge the locations of her father's safe houses.

At first, said the old man, Fox was so confident of his way with women to argue that it would not be necessary to kidnap the boy because he believed he could charm her to divulge information but William, a harder man, was adamant that one of Gwenllian's boys should be kidnapped as soon as possible.

The abbot was unclear on some details but he knew that by some means Robert Fox and William ap Bleddyn were aware that some of the Cenarth boys would be visiting the abbey on the day in question. The two men, he said had arrived there very early that morning, as they had for the previous meeting, dressed as Cistercian monks. They met in the tower away from the prying eyes of the other monks who lived at the abbey because the whole project was to be kept very secret. He, the abbot at the time, claimed that he had been forced to attend the meeting and to be part of the kidnapping plot.

Meredydd felt sure that the abbot had been a strong supporter of the king and was up to his neck in the plot. Further, he was of the opinion that the king had probably used the abbot to spy on the Mortimer family from his ideal position in the middle of the Mortimer estates.

Their plan, said the old man, was to abduct one of the boys when they were playing in the gardens but their task, he said, was made much easier when Rhys separated from his adult guardian and his brother and climbed the stairs in the tower. He described how Robert Fox and William ap Bleddyn made light work of grabbing Rhys and bundling him into a sack. Then, according to the old man, once the Cenarth sevants had left with the other boy, Rhys was taken

away by Robert Fox and his boss in a cart on the t
towards Hereford.

The abbot claimed that the abbey had nothing more to uo
with the kidnapping and that he knew no more about what
had happened to Rhys. Meredydd, despite threatening the
abbot, could get no more information from him.

Meredydd left the abbot on fairly good terms but still felt
a little suspicious that he might not have shared everything he
knew of the incident. He was very pleased, however, about
what he had learnt about Rhys's disappearance and knew that
his sister would welcome the news.

He continued his journey to the Hereford area to visit his
other sisters but a week later, towards the end of June, he was
on his way back north and called at Cenarth and reported to
Philip and Gwenllian what he had learnt from the old abbot,
including the naming of Robert Fox and William ap Bleddyn
as the king's agents who had kidnapped Rhys.

Gwenllian was shocked; elated that there was some hope
that Rhys was still alive but also apprehensive about the
future. More than ever she deeply regretted killing Robert
Fox because she thought that while Fox was alive, Rhys
would be kept alive so that she could be blackmailed. She
believed that she had probably contributed to her son's death,
but could not divulge her knowledge of Fox to Philip nor
Meredydd.

Her brother continued with his tale and Gwenllian forced
herself to concentrate on the immediate situation.

Meredydd said, "I don't know of a Robert Fox but I do
know of a William ap Bleddyn, who is also known as Wolf.
There was a report that he had been found dead inside a
burnt-out house with his face badly disfigured. We were
blamed for killing him in revenge for our losses at Usk but

my father was adamant that our agents had not killed him and he thought that Wolf had faked his own death to get our agents off his tracks."

"Did our father think that it was Wolf who set the trap at Usk?" Gwenllian asked anxiously.

"Well, that was the opinion at the time," replied Meredydd. "Wolf is still alive and well and is again acting on behalf of the king, probably in Gwent. He changed his name to goodness knows what for a while but once he was recognised and the attempt to fake his own death was exposed he reverted to calling himself by his old name of William ap Bleddyn."

"We still refer to him as Wolf, a name that befits his character and his appearance. He may well be keeping a close eye on our three sisters in the Hereford area. Remember all three are married to Englishmen and, as you know, it's been illegal since 1401 for Englishmen to marry Welsh women. I am convinced that the king knows about their illegal marriages but is keeping that information to use at some time of his own choosing and holding it over their heads like the sword of Damocles," continued Meredydd.

"Do you think if Wolf is alive he would know where Rhys is?" asked Gwenllian.

"That is a big leap you've made. There is no guarantee that they will have kept Rhys alive all this time," Philip reminded her pessimistically.

"Wolf would doubtless know what has happened to Rhys," said Meredydd.

This was the most startling and exciting news that Gwenllian and Philip had received about Rhys since his disappearance and after Meredydd left that day, his words were weighed and raked over carefully late into the night by Philip and Gwenllian.

Gwenllian took some time to recover from the shockir. news brought by Meredydd. She had to go on her walks up Cenarth Hill on her own frequently: she needed time and space to think things out for herself. She needed a plan.

# Chapter 18

THE FOLLOWING SATURDAY, a beautiful July day, Gwenllian went to the market in Llanidloes with Philip. She gave Dafydd a job to help the stockman with the cattle so that she could have time to talk to Philip on his own about what Meredydd had told them. She had failed to come to a conclusion as to what to do and what action to take. The journey to town provided her with an excellent opportunity to talk to Philip on his own. However, Philip was equally as uncertain what to do.

After entering the town, they went their separate ways as usual. She went quite briskly towards the old market hall, avoiding the Castle Inn. She almost wished to go to the room in the inn to see if Fox or his ghost was there and he might be able to give her a clue about Rhys. She wanted to know whether the room had changed or was there a clue in there that she had overlooked on the day she had killed Fox, but wisely she kept clear of the inn and the room.

There were a number of women circulating and trading underneath the roof of the market hall and in the area around it. Gwenllian ambled along Short Bridge Street away from the hall, viewing the goods for sale but before reaching the footbridge she began to retrace her steps, moving slowly towards the hall when she came face to face with a man who said to her through thin lips, "I believe you knew my friend Robert Fox."

He had grey hair and a narrow face and for some reason she took a dislike to him immediately. He apologised to her profusely for surprising her. He was trying to be charming but was false in every move from the smile to the offer of a hand to help her steady herself.

She was shocked and it showed on her face. Struggling to recover and get the right words out she eventually managed, "Yes. I know Robert Fox."

"I have been looking for you," he said. "I would like to meet you to talk some things over with you."

She kept the pretence up and said that she would only meet with Robert Fox because she trusted him.

"Allow me to introduce myself," he said "My name is William ap Bleddyn. I have a small cottage on the other side of the river and I would like to meet you there. Unfortunately, Robert couldn't be here today but he wishes you to speak to me. Please don't make things difficult for yourself. I am perfectly trustworthy and I know everything that Robert knows. Please follow about twenty yards behind me. All will be well and it will be very much to your advantage."

She noticed that he was also pretending that Fox was alive.

She was very fearful of this man but her quest for information about Rhys drove her to follow him. This William ap Bleddyn was the chief agent mentioned by Meredydd and he might be the link who would explain Rhys's fate. She had killed one source of information; she would have to be more careful this time.

As she followed William some distance behind him along Long Bridge Street towards the crossing of the river and the Frankwell area she was overjoyed in some way and yet very apprehensive. She was being given a second chance but she knew that this man was dangerous – he had taken her son from her. She was driven and determined. Her mind kept alerting her to danger but she ignored all the warnings: there was too much at stake. This man could lead her to a cottage where he could kill her in revenge for the killing of his friend Fox.

Gwenllian observed the man carefully as he walked ahead of her and realised that not only did his face remind her of a wolf but also his walk was like that of a wolf. He moved stealthily on spindly legs with his head bent slightly forward, occasionally looking over his shoulders to check that she was there and other times glancing into every nook and cranny between the wooden-framed houses for possible danger or for his next victim.

She followed him across the river over the narrow wooden footbridge and noticed that he turned left towards a small, shabby-looking cottage across the river from the church. It was made of wattle and gaud, with a poor attempt made to lime wash it at one time, but little of it showed and the thatch was old and worn. It had one low, small wooden-barred window and a low doorway.

He opened the door and went in and she followed him in seconds later. As she took that fateful step from the daylight into the dark and dank cottage she again stepped from the simple world of Cenarth into the black world of espionage but she had to take that leap for Rhys.

It took her a few seconds to absorb the interior of the house since it was so dark. There was no fire at that time of year and very little light came in through the window. She could see that there was a table and a couple of rickety chairs.

To attempt to unsettle the wolf, she immediately insisted, "I want to meet Robert Fox and I will only talk to him."

Even in the dark room she could see the flash of anger coming across his face, soon replaced by a false smile while he responded, "It won't be possible to meet Robert I'm afraid because one of his weaknesses has led him to be killed by a prostitute. But don't worry she has been caught and dealt with appropriately."

Gwenllian was relieved that her deception had worked but felt sorry for the poor woman whoever she was, if Wolf was telling the truth. She had to remember that this man was a practiced liar and a kidnapper as she asked him showing none of the fear she felt inside, "What do you want with me?"

He told her blatantly, "I want information about Glyndŵr your father and Meredydd your brother. I want to know where they are now and you are going to tell me."

Then, as if to try to soften the situation, he bizarrely offered her a drink of mead which he placed on the table in front of her. She realised that he was more calculating than Robert Fox, had a nasty manner and was not so subject to the charms of an attractive woman. He drank the mead that he had poured for himself.

He seemed to sense that she would not cooperate readily and so said to her again in his blunt way, "I have your son in prison in Ludlow and will have him killed if you do not give me information about the rebels and their French allies. It's simple. Do you understand?"

Coolly, because she was not sure that she could believe that he had kept Rhys alive all this time, Gwenllian asked, "Can you give me proof that Rhys is alive?"

Giving her one of those awful smiles where she could see his rotten, sharp teeth he replied, "Robert Fox had a brooch on him, which belonged to your son but the whore who killed him stole it and God knows where it is now. But you do not need to see it because I can describe it to you. It was silver, genuine silver and shaped like the head of a thistle plant."

Gwenllian gave the appearance of being shocked but she felt very sceptical: she had convinced herself for some time that Rhys was dead and not continuing to suffer. It was the only way she had been able to live with his loss.

The emotional strain on Gwenllian was now enormous. This horrible man was telling her that her son Rhys was alive and she wanted to run out of the door and shout it for all the world to hear. What restrained her was the fact that Rhys was in prison, and this evil man who stood in front of her was threatening to kill him if she did not give him information that would lead to the certain death of her father and brother.

The plan that she had spent so much time trying to devise on her lonely walks was beginning to formulate in her mind. First, she had to outwit Wolf and his helpers whoever they were.

While she was digesting this information and thinking of a response, Wolf said to her, "My friend Robert was far too soft with you. I want to know where and how Glyndŵr and Meredydd can be captured, dead or alive, and I want detailed information about the agreements with the French. Do you understand me?"

While digesting what he had said and thinking of ways around the blackmail, Gwenllian meekly replied, "Yes."

"Good. I will meet you here again at the same time next week and you had better have some valuable information for me or else your son will be fed to the crows," he said, drawing his hand across his throat in a gesture imitating a throat being cut.

"Another thing! You had better not tell anything of this to that husband of yours. I don't want him coming here swinging his sword or it will be the end of you know who," he said as he made the same frightening gesture.

As she got up to leave he said, "I see you have not drunk the mead I gave you." Adding, as he downed it himself, "Never mind, perhaps next time."

She left the cottage and the odious Wolf, promising him that she would be back in a week's time. Though shaken by her experience she was delighted with herself and the world as she walked along Long Bridge Street towards the market hall: Rhys was alive. But was Wolf telling the truth or just using it as part of the ploy to blackmail her?

Gwenllian went home with Philip and this time told him about how she had been approached in the town by Wolf and about her meeting with him in the cottage. Philip was incandescent with rage that she had taken the risk of going with Wolf to his cottage. But he knew her as a very self-willed woman and that he would not wish to change her. He stopped the cart to talk things through with her and while she gave him the full details of her meeting with Wolf, she was careful not to mention any of the meetings she had with Robert Fox.

Philip's first reaction was to go back and face Wolf immediately. Gwenllian calmed him by saying she would also like to act immediately but argued that it was necessary to take things slowly and think things through carefully in order to secure Rhys's safe release from captivity.

They continued the journey home and mulled over the problems facing them. They had three things to do: first Gwenllian had to convince Wolf that she would work for him, then they had to find out if Rhys was alive somewhere in Ludlow and if he was alive then they would somehow have to rescue him. The plan was developing nicely in her mind.

To convince Wolf they were cooperating with him they felt that they would have to give him information that was reliable and yet not detrimental to individual rebels.

They decided to play for time. Gwenllian would meet Wolf as agreed on the coming Saturday and tell him that she was going to see her family in Meirionydd to find out about Glyndŵr's plans. There would be some means of contacting the rebels there, especially her brother Meredydd. She would also ask Wolf to give her proof that Rhys was alive. After all, they could have killed Rhys and kept the brooch.

Gwenllian also knew that the plan would have to ensure that Philip and Wolf would not meet because she did not wish Philip to become aware of her clandestine meetings with Robert Fox.

# Chapter 19

ON THE SECOND Saturday in July, Philip and Gwenllian went to the market together, but they went their separate ways once in town. After walking around the old market hall a few times she directed her footsteps along Long Bridge Street, crossed the river and went towards the cottage.

Gwenllian rarely came to this area of the town and had not noticed the cottage before even when she had gone to the church to pray. She had no idea who lived in the Frankwell part of the town. It was one of three cottages situated across the river from the church and a few yards from the river.

She tapped very gently on the door of the cottage not wishing to draw attention to herself. The door was opened by a man of about her own age but with a very weak chin and sloping shoulders. She was taken aback and thought she had gone to the wrong cottage. She stepped back from the doorway to view the cottage better and its exact location relative to the river and the church and decided that it was indeed the right cottage.

"Please enter," said the man nervously.

He was not as confident a man as Wolf and was of a very nervous disposition. But for all he knew Gwenllian could have arrived with Philip or one of her brothers to torture him to get him to reveal what he knew before possibly killing him. Perhaps he thought that Glyndŵr's men could be waiting for him outside and so he stepped out of the cottage door and looked around.

Gwenllian noticed his concern and said, "I am on my own."

He was relieved to hear her statement.

Gwenllian was equally concerned and asked, "Where is William ap Bleddyn?"

"He is not here and has asked me to meet you," he replied. "I am Lambert ap Madog."

Gwenllian thought that Wolf was in Llanidloes somewhere, but kept himself safe ensuring that his subordinate was taking all the risks. She knew she had to make the most of the situation and so she had to keep calm and think things out. While she preferred to deal with this man than with Wolf she realised that Lambert was a passenger and not the cart driver.

"Please come in and take a chair. William wanted me to give you a drink of mead."

Gwenllian was more relaxed during this second visit to the cottage and was able to take in more of her surroundings. She noticed again that the house was very small and the wattle walls were in no better state of repair on the inside. There was a fireplace of a kind in the middle of the room but the roof hole must have been closed and hence the room was exceptionally dark. The table and two chairs were of better quality than one would expect in such a dwelling. The straw on the floor was fresh and gave off a dry smell and the typical sound of dry straw as she walked on it. There was a straw bed of a kind in the corner but not of such good quality as the table and chairs.

Lambert was unsure of himself, aware that he was in the presence of an important person and was afraid of making a mess of the task allocated to him.

She sat in the chair nearest the door and he sat opposite.

She was now disappointed that she was not facing Wolf so that she could judge his reactions when she spoke to him.

Lambert waited for her to speak.

She asked him again, hoping for the truth this time, "Where is William ap Bleddyn?"

His reply was brief but polite and repeated what she expected Wolf had told him to say, "He is sorry, but he could not be here to meet you today."

She sensed that he was again lying and that the real reason was that Wolf did not trust her and had half expected her to arrive with some strong men to capture and torture him to a confession.

She said, "I have no information about Glyndŵr, my brother or the French. But getting Rhys back is the most important thing in my life and I will do anything to get him back. I will visit my family in Meirionydd and through them I will make contact with my father and I will probably be able to get the information William wants."

Lambert was pleased to hear this and said, "William is a very angry man and is desperate to obtain information for the king who is putting great pressure on him to achieve success in Wales and is particularly concerned about the French involvement."

"I understand," said Gwenllian, sympathetically.

Lambert was satisfied that Gwenllian was going to get the needed information but Gwenllian sensed that he would have to check with Wolf that he was also satisfied. He was about to open his mouth to say that he would have to speak with Wolf when Gwenllian asked him, "How can you assure me that my son is alive?"

Before poor Lambert had time to think of an answer she challenged him with, "Yes, the brooch belonged to Rhys but it could have been taken off him after he was killed. If Rhys is dead I will not cooperate."

Lambert was clearly very disappointed. He was on the point of success and, without thinking, he blurted out, "I know that he is alive and is kept confined in a house near the castle in Ludlow. Please believe me and do as my friend William tells you if you want your son back alive."

Gwenllian was delighted with this news but, hardened by life's disappointments, showed no emotion and replied immediately, "That means I have to believe your word. For all I know you have never been to Ludlow. What type of prison is he kept in? Is he well? Is he looked after properly? Is he not kept in the castle? I need proof that he is alive," she said.

She was a much quicker thinker than Lambert; she took advantage of it.

"I was in Ludlow last week with Wolf and I know that there is a young boy kept in a house which has a small garden where he used to play, but he now works cutting logs which are sold to pay for his upkeep," said Lambert.

"It could be anybody's boy and not necessarily my Rhys," she pressurised him.

"I am sure he is your son because he has blond hair and looks like you, particularly around his eyes," he said without hesitation.

Gwenllian thought if this slow thinker is able to say that without hesitation it must be true or he has been trained to say it. She regarded the latter as unlikely.

"Where did you say this house was?" she asked.

Lambert, realising that he had probably said too much, replied, "I can't say anymore." He asked her as firmly as he could, "Are you going to cooperate and get the information for us?"

"Yes. I will cooperate with you and William," she agreed.

He then said that he wanted to go outside for a few minutes to discuss things with someone and that he would be back in no time. He went out and locked her in the cottage.

However uncomfortable she was about being locked in, at that moment she was overwhelmed by pleasure and excitement by the fact that Lambert had said that the boy held at Ludlow looked like her. People used to remark how much he looked like her when he was at Cenarth.

Lambert was true to his word and returned within minutes and was asked instantly by Gwenllian, "Been to check with William, have you?"

"I can't tell you," he said. "But I can tell you that I am very glad that you are going to cooperate."

Gwenllian just stared at him.

"William prefers to be called by his nickname, Wolf. He wants to meet you back here two weeks from today." Lambert hesitated a moment before adding, "You had better be here with information or your son will be killed."

"Did you go out to talk to Wolf?" she asked again. "Was he satisfied with my assurances?"

He got very flustered and said "Yes, I did check with Wolf. Please don't tell anyone about what I told you about your son being kept at a house in Ludlow," he pleaded.

She could detect his weakness in every word he uttered and she decided to take advantage of him.

She stood looking at him level with his eyes and asked, "Now that you have told me so much you can tell me more and I will reward you generously."

She saw the hesitation on his face and asked, "Why are you working for Wolf? Do you like working for him?"

The series of questions confused Lambert and she thought that she detected some anger on his face but continued her interrogation "Does he pay you? How much does he pay you?"

This was too much for the innocent and mild Lambert. He burst out with "No. I don't like working for him. I'm always doing his dirty and dangerous work."

She became milder in her manner and asked him gently "Where are you from?"

This was a simple question that he could answer without any risk to himself he believed and replied, "I am from Meifod and I was with the rebels until the king's soldiers captured me while we were attacking Welshpool. I was handed over to the constable of the castle and after a short time in prison I was given as a servant to Wolf. That is what I have done for the past year or so. I have not seen my parents or my sisters since I was captured and I miss them."

"Of course you do," said Gwenllian, sympathetically.

Then, she asked, "Why don't you leave him and go back to your parents?"

Another question for him to answer and this one made him uneasy. Gwenllian had decided that what Lambert needed was to be told what to do and how to deal with his captivity. "Run away from him," she said. "Go back to the rebels. Go to Dolgellau and join them there and call in and see your family on the way. Wolf can't follow you to Dolgellau: he won't dare go there."

Lambert's face lit up at the idea of freedom from Wolf but it did not last long.

He became concerned again and seemed to change his mind, "I like Wolf and I have been with him for a long time now. I am concerned that he will become suspicious that we are plotting against him because we are taking such a long time to say goodbey. I would like you to leave immediately please. I will see you in two weeks' time."

Gwenllian recognised that there was no more to be gained by staying any longer and as she was leaving, still concealed in the darkness of the inside of the dwelling place, she put her hand in her basket. She pulled out what she found quickly under the covering cloth. It was the purse she had taken from Fox and, telling Lambert to hold his hand out, she emptied its contents and placed the empty purse back in her basket and told him to use the money to get to Dolgellau the next day.

She left the cottage saying goodbye in a loud and friendly way. As she walked away she was sure that she was being watched by a man standing near the church tower on the opposite bank of the river. As she was crossing the bridge she wondered what would have happened to her if she had not cooperated with them. She suspected that Wolf would have returned to the cottage and with Lambert's help they would have forced her in some way to work with them or perhaps they would have killed her because she knew too much about them.

She met Philip at the agreed spot in Oak Street. He had been worried about her but had not moved from the agreed place. They went home and Gwenllian told him the full details of the encounter in the cottage. They both felt very encouraged and hopeful having completed the first stage of the plan but both feared the consequences of dealing with a man like Wolf.

On Monday, following the meeting with Lambert, having prepared well on Sunday, Philip and Gwenllian set off at

4 o'clock in the morning, as dawn was breaking, for Ludlow. They were mounted on a horse each and had one packhorse attached to Gwenllian's horse. This arrangement gave Philip greater flexibility if it became necessary to defend them during the course of the journey. Philip was also well armed with his bow and arrows, his sword and the dagger used by Gwenllian to kill Fox.

The journey was long but they were determined to do it in a day. They were soon passing the abbey in Cwm Hir where their trials had all began five years earlier. It was a strange moment. It was there that Rhys was last seen. It was an unsettling time for them both. Hope was near the surface of their minds and swelling larger than it had since that fateful day. Would they see Rhys alive again? If he was alive would he recognise them? Would they recognise him? There were so many unknowns that they could only progress with their plan by putting the imponderables out of their minds for a while. Philip offered to stop outside the abbey but Gwenllian insisted that they move on. She had prayed all night; it was time now to be practical.

Knighton was quiet as they passed through with no one taking any particular notice of them. Ludlow was quite busy and they stopped near the castle and absorbed the feel and the look of the area. The remainder of the day they spent looking around the castle area at the houses and seeing which ones had gardens and looked secure. Most of the cottages were made of wattle and so they did not appear secure enough to hold any prisoners. Rhys was now ten and would be quite capable of kicking his way through such a wall if determined to do so. It might be that he was held in irons when not supervised. Perhaps he had forgotten his parents, forgotten Cenarth and his brothers – after all, he had been very young when he was abducted and so might think that his present captive state was normal for a child.

They thought that the cottage holding Rhys would be stone built with strong doors and windows. There were only three such cottages in the vicinity of the castle and they decided to keep an eye on these cottages. Philip sat on a wall near the horses and opposite the cottages while Gwenllian walked about near the cottages offering wild flowers for sale to people walking past her.

They observed nothing during what remained of the first day and slept on straw in the stables of a local inn after Philip had paid the stable lad with a coin. They were up early the next day to keep an eye on the stone cottages.

There were a number of comings and goings during the early morning but nothing that helped them rule out any of the houses. Then, a man came out of one with a young boy aged about ten. The two of them were relaxed and looked like father and son. Gwenllian went towards them and passed close to the man and the boy and then went straight to Philip who was sitting on the wall. She had a look of total shock on her face with tears clouding her vision.

Through the tears she said, "I am almost sure that the boy with that man is Rhys. I so want him to be Rhys that I can't think clearly. Do you think it was our Rhys?"

Without waiting for an answer, she said, "I wanted to grab him in my arms and never let him go again. I was trying to think, does he look like me?" She posed for a moment and then said, "I don't know what to think," she said. "This is unbearable."

Philip was still considering the situation. The man and the boy had now gone out of sight. Then he asked her, "Are you sure it was Rhys? He was too far away for me to see him properly but what struck me was how similar to Cynwrig the man looked."

Gwenllian turned and looked at her husband with her mouth wide open for a few seconds and then blurted out, "My God you are right." Then, after a short pause, "Do you think he recognised me?"

"No. I am sure he didn't otherwise he would have reacted by going back into the cottage or if he is innocent he would have said something to you."

They both remained in a state of shock for a minute or two, neither of them saying anything until Gwenllian broke the silence and said, "That boy is Rhys, isn't he?"

"What do we do?" she asked, her normal calmness and dignity understandably having left her. Her desire to run and grab her lost son was great and Philip also had difficulty in restraining himself but they both knew that they had to be careful and keep to their plan.

They had discussed this possibility the previous day. It seemed a dream then but here they were in this amazing position where they had seen their son again. Philip's anger was building. Normally a very calm person, he was getting angrier by the second and was now all for attacking and killing Cynwrig immediately and taking Rhys away with them. But this time, it was Gwenllian's calm argument that prevailed and they agreed that they had to deal with Wolf first. They had to follow the plan.

Gwenllian wanted to make sure that it was Rhys. She could not believe, having thought for many years that he was dead, that he was here alive and apparently well. The presence of Cynwrig confirmed that the boy was Rhys.

They had decided that if they were to see Rhys they would not even try to release him, even if it was easy, until they had dealt with Wolf. If they were to take him now then Wolf would work out that it was their work and that would put all their family at risk. Cynwrig's presence with the boy in Ludlow was puzzling and a complicating factor. They stayed in the area until Cynwrig and the boy returned a while later, by which time Philip had positioned himself so that they had to walk past him but as they approached he partly covered his face with a cloth pretending to wipe his brow.

He returned to Gwenllian and confirmed that the man was Cynwrig and the boy indeed had similar features to hers.

They were both now certain that the boy was Rhys and decided that they should start for home as soon as possible, as difficult as it would be to leave their newly found son behind. But it was best to keep to the plan. They were so glad that they had not said anything about their plan to anyone at Cenarth or the reason for their journey other than they were going to Ceredigion to see Philip's family. They decided again in Ludlow that they were not going to tell anyone, not even Beth, about their discovery of their lost son.

The return journey to Cenarth was a happy one: they had seen that their son was alive and well. Their task now was to secure his safe release from captivity. So, as soon as they arrived home, they started the preparation for the journey to Dolgellau.

Gwenllian and Philip went to see her family in Dolgellau, again mounted on a horse each with a packhorse tied to Gwenllian's horse. One purpose of their visit was to mislead Wolf and his co-workers and to make him think that they were there to find out what Glyndŵr's plans were. The king was bound to have had some spies in Dolgellau. She wanted to be seen there so that one of the king's agents would be able to report to Wolf that they were actively trying to get information for him. They also wanted to visit a distant relative of hers.

The journey over the mountains was uneventful and they spent time at the top after passing Glaslyn lake looking west and absorbing the wonderful landscape stretching out towards Cadair Idris and the high mountains of the far north. They also took time to add details to their plan.

Dolgellau was a busy town with dark stonewalls, giving it a very dark grey appearance. Some of the stone walls had been lime washed but the general appearance was slightly menacing. Even Glyndŵr's parliament house was mainly dark and grey but the wattle and gaud recently lime washed upper part brightened the whole building and made it stand out.

While at Dolgellau, Gwenllian visited some of her relatives there. She had a number of cousins living in the area and she received their warm hospitality. They had always been pleasant and kind to her but since her grandfather had died she had not been there often, there being no close relatives left. She had kept more in contact with her father's family, particularly with Meredydd. She did not expect to meet her father or brother there and indeed she did not see them.

They received a warm welcome in the farmstead above Arthog, farmed by her cousin. They went to see her old home but she did not wish to stay long as things had changed as they do with time.

They visited some of her distant relatives high on the sides of Cadair Idris and then returned to Cenarth by the route that they had taken three days earlier, confident that they had been seen and that their presence in Dolgellau would be reported to Wolf.

# Chapter 20

B ACK AT CENARTH they worked on the plan to deal with Wolf and abduct Rhys from Ludlow.

On the fourth Saturday in July 1405, Gwenllian attended the market as agreed with Lambert and went to the cottage. This time Philip was leaning on one of the wooden posts of the narrow Long Bridge, supposedly idly watching the river flow beneath him and the animals and carts passing through the shallow crossing.

She knocked gently on the door. She did not expect to see Wolf there but was going to insist that she spoke to Wolf directly and on his own. She was going to send Lambert out to guard the house and Philip would deal with him if there was a problem. However, the door was opened by Wolf and she entered. After scanning the gloomy single-roomed cottage she realised that Lambert was not there. She had two weapons in her basket: the dagger she had used before and a small jug of poison. He offered her a cup of mead, which this time she accepted. He did not sit in the chair but drank the mead quickly, which was a great disappointment to her.

Gwenllian nervously asked, "Where is Lambert?"

"Don't worry," he said. "He's not hiding in here to jump out of the gloom at you. Then added, "Not that Lambert is likely to jump at anything much. I wanted to meet you face to face to judge whether you are truthful."

"Look," she said. "If I am going to make an agreement with you I need to know who I am dealing with. The last time I was here I was talking to Lambert. I need to know where he is and I need to know which one of you is in charge of this operation?"

As she intended, Wolf took it as an insult that she should even think that there was a possibility that Lambert was ordering him about. Wolf's face reddened visibly and he said, "I should never have used him with you last time. I have no doubt that you managed through your female charm to get more information out of him than he was supposed to give. He has been moved out of the Welsh area to Ireland where he can do less harm. Now are you satisfied? Do you want to see your son again?"

Though she could believe his comments about Lambert, she found Wolf an offensive person with no charm whatsoever and she found it very difficult to relate to him. Facing her as he did then with his angry face and long grey sideburns he really did look like a wolf. His very appearance and manner intimidated her.

"Oh, I do want my son back and I can assure you that this is not a trivial matter for me," she said, wishing to get him to trust her.

"Well? What have you got to tell me?" he asked.

She told him what she and Philip had agreed on. "Glyndŵr is planning an attack on Chester by going into England past the Hanmer estate and attacking from the English side where an attack would be least expected. The aim is to get grain and cattle back into the north-west to feed the troops so they can be kept in readiness for action during the winter months."

"That is too audacious, even for Glyndŵr," said Wolf.

"They are desperate for wheat," she said, convincingly.

While he was considering her statement he poured

himself another cup of mead and drank some. He stood up and then asked her, "Who told you this? How reliable is this information?"

He bent to look through the narrow slits in the window and she poured all the poison from her jug into her own drink. He did not notice the slight movement of her hand.

He came back to the table and again took a sip of his mead. He was deep in thought and wondering if he could believe this woman. He was under pressure because the king did not want the French involved in the rebellion and was desperate to capture or kill Glyndŵr. Five years of work and patience had gone into his plot. This was the moment he had waited for. She was desperate to get her child back but she could still be lying.

He went to the window again but did not bend to look out this time. She took a chance, switched the cups and lifted his up to her lips. He returned to the table and she was afraid that when he came to drink from his cup he would notice that it had more mead in it.

To encourage him to drink more from his cup Gwenllian sipped away at her cup. He lifted his cup but put it down again. He was obviously deep in thought. She sipped a little more of the mead and he lifted his cup again, this time to his lips. Straining to see his Adam's apple she was relieved to see that he was swallowing it – the mead and the poison. The poison, which she had got from the old lady on the side of Cadair Idris, above Dolgellau, was made from a mixture of deadly plants including the root of deadly nightshade. The old lady made large quantities of it and used it to kill vermin by putting it out for them to drink. She wouldn't give Gwenllian the exact details of the contents but she warned her that a sizable dose of it would kill a large man in a very short time. Gwenllian wondered how she knew of its effect on humans, but she did not doubt her knowledge because she could remember that the old lady's husband had been a very large man and he had died suddenly in strange circumstances. Gwenllian, jokingly, asked her how much was needed to kill a strong man, intimating that her own husband was big and strong. The old lady told her she would give her enough for two men in case she would have problems with her second husband.

It should kill him soon, she hoped. He was drinking from his cup and she had enough to kill two people in it. Also, she had Philip's dagger in her basket and if the poison did not work she would have to use it and she would, without any hesitation, on such a vile man.

Wolf, seemingly in full health asked her what was happening with the French.

"I don't know," she said, again as agreed with Philip and adding, "Nobody knows. Probably not even the French know."

He smiled at this as she assumed he would, guessing that he hated the French as much as he hated her father. This was a calculated attempt to get him on her side and to give the poison time to take effect.

Before the poison did its work she asked, "When will you bring Rhys to me? Have you got him with you in Llanidloes?"

His cruel nature came to the fore and he said, "You will have him back safe and sound when Glyndŵr attacks Chester and we capture him. Until then your precious Rhys will be kept in my safe custody."

Gwenllian kept him talking for a while to ensure that he

had emptied the cup. He poured himself some more mead and he drank that as well and she thought the more he drank the easier it would be to use the dagger on him.

She was trying her best to check if his eyes were dilated but it was impossible to see in the gloom of the cottage. She was sure that he was slurring his words. If only he would get up from his chair again so that she could see if he could stand but she did not wish to make a move to leave until she was sure that he had taken enough of the poison to kill him. She continued to talk to him about Glyndŵr and how she wished all the difficulties would be over soon. Then, without warning, he stood up quickly as if aware that there was something wrong. He stood there for a second or two staring at her. She was petrified for those few seconds but noticed that his hands were gripping the table tightly. She did not speak; she just sat there, staring up at him. He made a slight movement away from the table and stood perfectly still but he was too rigid to be normal. Seconds later, he slumped down on the straw-covered floor. She was not sure if he had tried to walk away from the table or had simply fallen.

She stood up and moved around the table. He was lying face down on the floor, moaning as if in a delirious state. Rhys's face kept returning to her mind and she became more determined as her hand felt for the dagger in her basket. However, the delirious state and moaning sound gave way to slight convulsions before his whole body started to shake violently. She turned him over with great difficulty and noticed froth coming from his mouth. This continued for what seemed a very long time for Gwenllian who wanted to get out of the cottage as soon as she could but had to make sure that he was dead before she left. Slowly, his body acquired a calmness and then a stillness that confirmed to her that the poison had done its work. She moved him with her foot, almost kicking him. There was no response other than some more froth coming from his mouth. She quickly searched his body, as she had done with Fox, and found the key to the door, which she had hoped he would have on him.

She waited for a while to make sure that the body did not move. She felt no guilt: she was glad that she had killed him. It was this man's life or her family's and also he had made her suffer for years. It took her a while to be satisfied that he was dead and she wished he had suffered more than he had. It had been too quick an end for such a cruel man who had taken her child. She was a very determined person and she knew where that determination came from. Her father had shown great determination for years. If she had seen any signs of recovery she would have used the dagger.

She spilled some of his own mead on his face and also poured a quantity from the small flagon she had brought with her in her basket. She then went out, locking the door behind her and throwing the key back in through the window.

She and Philip had thought of setting the cottage on fire so as to hide any traces of the crime but they thought that a fire would result in Wolf's body being discovered almost immediately. But leaving the body in the locked cottage would give them a few days grace before discovery; whoever found the body would think Wolf had died of natural causes, aided by the mead he had drunk.

When Philip saw her approaching Long Bridge he walked away towards the town centre and she soon joined him at the top end of town by the oak tree. They immediately returned to Cenarth to prepare for their second journey to Ludlow.

The next day, having now removed the threat Wolf posed, they started early and, as before, they were mounted on a horse each and they had an extra horse with an empty saddle on it which to all intents and purposes looked like a packhorse. They passed Cwm Hir Abbey with even greater hope this time and arrived at the castle in Ludlow in the early afternoon and began observing the cottage.

It had been decided between them that if Rhys appeared and he could be abducted without putting him in harm's way, Gwenllian would take him away and Philip would deal with Cynwrig. The idea was to capture Cynwrig alive and take him to Meredydd for questioning.

There was no movement to or from the cottage that evening but Gwenllian, when standing close to the cottage could hear the noise of logs being split for fire wood. When night came they slept in the same stable as they had during their first visit and they were back at their positions outside the cottage before dawn. After a little over an hour's wait, Cynwrig came out of the cottage door by himself and turned to lock it carefully and walked towards the castle. This was not what Gwenllian and Philip had expected.

As soon as Cynwrig was out of sight, Gwenllian went to the window and called into the small dwelling, "Rhys, are you in there?"

"Who's asking?" came the inquisitive reply and Rhys's face appeared in the window.

"Rhys, I am your mother. I have come from Cenarth to take you home," explained Gwenllian.

"Do you remember me?"

"Yes," came the very hesitant reply. "You have left me here for a long time," the boy continued from inside the cottage as he moved a little distance from the window.

"Rhys, your father and I did not know where you were," said Gwenllian, with her voice full of desperation.

Again, with great hesitation, he replied, "Cynwrig said you did not want me and that's why you did not come to get me."

Desperately, but firmly, Gwenllian said, "He is lying to you. They took you away and we did not know where they had hidden you."

Rhys now came back to the window to talk to her. He was in tears and this caused Gwenllian to become emotional and she also started to cry.

She knew that she had to control her emotions to get her son out of the cottage. She drew on her inner strength and said to Rhys, "Your father and I are going to take you home."

"Is dad here?" he asked. The sight of his mother's tears was the turning point. He wanted to go to her. Gwenllian knew that she would have work to do to help this boy to overcome the trauma he had suffered but the determination was growing in her. She would kill for him again now.

"Why did you not go out with Cynwrig this morning?" she asked.

"Sometimes Cynwrig does not let me out of the house," said Rhys. "It depends on his mood. He says that he does not like wasting his time guarding me. But the nasty man who calls every few weeks tells him it's very important work," said Rhys.

Gwenllian knew immediately that the nasty man was Wolf and had the satisfaction of knowing that she had rid the world of him. "I am moving from the window now and going back to your father to decide how we are going to get you out," she said.

She returned to Philip, who was standing with the horses about forty yards away and before she had time to talk to

Philip she could see that Cynwrig was returning from the castle. They stood behind the horses while Cynwrig went into the cottage.

They decided to move immediately and led the horses up to the front of the door and Philip knocked on it. Cynwrig opened the door and looked puzzled, but only for a fraction of a second because Philip had the point of his sword up against his throat and was pushing him backwards into the cottage. Rhys was wide eyed but Gwenllian came in behind Philip and Rhys ran to her. She took him into her arms and held his head on her chest.

Philip asked Cynwrig, "Why have you done this to us?"

Cynwrig knew that all was up and said that he had been placed at Cenarth by Wolf to spy on the family and on Gwenllian in particular, knowing that there was bound to be contact between Gwenllian and other members of the Glyndŵr family and that she would know their hiding places.

He also admitted that he had helped the planning of Rhys's abduction at Cwm Hir Abbey. The others involved were the abbot, Robert Fox and Wolf, all agents of the king. Wolf had decided that it was unlikely that Cynwrig would get good information from his position at Cenarth because he believed at the time that Philip was against the revolt and so there was little contact with Gwenllian's family. The agents had therefore decided to kidnap Rhys in order to blackmail Gwenllian and get information. Cynwrig claimed that he did not know the detail of the abduction; his task had been to keep Rhys secure and healthy after he had been kidnapped.

Cynwrig was full of remorse and was in tears, saying that he had been forced to do it by Wolf. He claimed that he had not been guarding Rhys all the time, he had done a stint at the beginning and had been with him again since Fox had died in tragic circumstances. Gwenllian was so relieved to get Rhys back that she was not thinking clearly but was vaguely aware that Cynwrig could now divulge the whole story about her and Robert Fox.

She called to Philip angrily, "He is not worth speaking to. He is a horrible liar and took our child away from us."

Philip turned to look at Gwenllian whose eyes were full of tears of happiness and he moved slightly towards her to hug her and his boy. This gave Cynwrig a chance to take to his heels, which he did at great speed.

Once he realised that Cynwrig was out of the door his first thought was to let him go but after a second's consideration he said to Gwenllian, "My God that man can come back and make our lives difficult yet again." He went after him as fast as he could.

Cynwrig had a good start of about twenty yards. He was fast and had desperation and youth on his side and he was soon round the side of a house attached to the back of the castle wall and out of Philip's sight.

When Philip reached the corner there was no sign of the fugitive. Cynwrig could have gone into the house, along the town wall behind a row of small houses or he could have gone under the archway on the left and down to the river. Philip thought that the river was the best bet and went in that direction. He reached the point where he could see the river a long way below him but there was no sign of Cynwrig. Philip knew instinctively that Cynwrig had managed to escape. He was afraid that Cynwrig would double back to the cottage and recapture Rhys, so he decided to hurry back to Gwenllian and Rhys.

All was well, but they did not wish to draw attention to

themselves, so aware that the least fuss they made in Ludlow the better, they decided to call off the search and leave the town as soon as possible.

Rhys mounted the horse with the spare saddle and they left Ludlow immediately. They moved speedily along the tracks to start with but they were able to relax a little the further from Ludlow they went. On the way back they broke the news to Rhys that Ieuan had died and his mother hugged him but Rhys had been through too much to react normally that day. They were greatly relieved to arrive back safely at Cenarth. They had decided not to tell everybody immediately that Rhys was back but to release the story slowly that he had simply returned.

Philip was a little concerned that Cynwrig had got away and he wished he had pushed the point of his sword deep into his throat. Gwenllian was of the opinion that they had seen the last of Cynwrig because he would be too afraid to come anywhere near Llanidloes in the future.

In September 1405, gossip circulated at the Llanidloes market that the king was angry again and it quickly became generally known that Prince Henry had again invaded Wales with a large army, this time from Hereford. The Cenarth family did not feel so threatened by this invasion and took no additional steps to safeguard themselves as the king's target was clearly the south of the country.

Iolo was soon at Cenarth to confirm the news and to show delight at Rhys's safe return with a new poem just for Rhys.

In the October following Rhys's return, Meredydd visited them. He was delighted to see and talk to Rhys. Gwenllian was more than a little sensitive to any talk of recruiting Rhys to the rebellion and said so openly.

Meredydd told them that at the beginning of the month

Glyndŵr had held his parliament at Harlech, his headquarters, and there was a great deal of despondency and no clear direction emerging. He was disappointed that the French troops who had arrived from Brest had not brought the whole rebellion to a head. He felt that it was a great shame that the large Welsh and French force that had marched as far as Worcester did not find the conditions right to do battle with the king's forces. A great opportunity was lost to achieve the rebellion's aims when the two armies stared at each other for days and then simply went their different ways.

He was convinced that if Gruffydd, his brother, had been with them at Worcester there would have been a decisive battle. He felt certain that it would have been worth a try. However, he had to concede that a defeat would have ended the rebellion and the king's battlefield position was a well-defended one. The history of both England and Wales hung in the balance for those few days while the commanders on both sides were deciding whether to do battle or not.

By December, life had returned to normal at Cenarth and the heavy shadow that had hung over this wonderful hall had been lifted and hope had become reality at last.

# Chapter 21

THE CHRISTMAS CELEBRATIONS and the welcoming in of 1406 at Cenarth were happier than they had been for years. Iolo and the other poets who called at the farmstead were supplied with the best of food and drink in the area and a joyful atmosphere prevailed.

However, after Rhys's return home to his family there was a constant niggling worry in Gwenllian's mind that Cynwrig would come back with a band of the king's men and take Rhys or Dafydd or one of the other two boys away with them. Philip kept reassuring her that they were safe at Cenarth and that no one would think that Wolf had died of anything other than natural causes accelerated by drinking too much mead. There was nothing to link them to his death.

The greatest concern was Cynwrig, who had shown himself to be particularly deceitful and capable of any treachery. But as time went by and there were no indications that they were to be a target for any reprisal, Gwenllian's confidence that they were safe at Cenarth grew. The boys were getting stronger and more able to defend themselves. Philip assured her that they were becoming adept at using their swords and could fire an arrow accurately.

From the day Rhys came back safely to Cenarth, Philip became a strong supporter of Glyndŵr's cause. He wanted revenge for what he regarded as the cruelty shown his family by the abduction of Rhys and he endeavoured to support Glyndŵr at every opportunity. Thus, he promised Meredydd that he would fight on the rebel's side whenever and wherever it would be necessary. While his services were not called for frequently, he was involved in a few skirmishes in mid Wales but there were no significant battles. Philip probably realised that the cause was past its peak but he would fight on valiantly for as long as it was needed.

The Penal letter written at Cefn Caer Farm was a significant statement of aims for an emerging country but Philip doubted if the military power needed to enforce it would be available to Glyndŵr. Though the demands for a separate Welsh church, two universities and a separate parliament were reasonable he doubted that they would be achieved. It was a laudable dream and one that should be achievable. Philip did not take part in the writing of the letter nor was he at Penal but he and Gwenllian were explained the essential contents of the letter by Meredydd. Iolo's version was also not far from the truth.

By November 1406, the king was sufficiently confident that he had subdued the rebellion in Wales that he established a royal commission at Beaumaris for granting pardons for those who had supported Glyndŵr. This was grim news for the rebels and worse was to follow when it was realised that many of the rebels were now requesting pardons and the future Henry V had laid siege to Aberystwyth and Harlech.

In the winter of 1407, there was severe weather and this limited military activity by both sides but Henry's sieges at Aberystwyth and Harlech continued. Following the foul weather there was a virulent illness that spread throughout Wales and many people died but it did not reach Cenarth to the great relief of Gwenllian and everyone else at the farmstead.

Gwenllian was leading an ordinary life now, enjoying giving attention to her boys, who were growing up fast and taking an increasing role on the farm. She did think of Cynwrig from time to time with concern and she sometimes wondered what had become of Lambert. She almost felt sorry for Lambert, thinking him a weak person who was easily led and influenced. Her encounters with Fox and Wolf were becoming a distant memory. She had few regrets and was overjoyed at having Rhys back. She spent much time with him to compensate for his dreadful experience. He was becoming a young man and he loved working with the animals. She noticed that he was more insular than his brothers and liked to be in his own company for long periods. However, this did not worry her as she herself liked to spend time on her own.

Gwenllian was disappointed that the rebellion had lost momentum and people were leaving the cause. The news she was receiving from Iolo and Meredydd when they called at Cenarth was depressing overall but there was the occasional uplifting incident and they made the most of it over a cup of mead.

The year 1408 brought more bad news when the earl of Northumberland, an ally of Glyndŵr, was defeated at the battle of Bramham Moor and Aberystwyth castle was captured by the king's forces.

The siege of Harlech castle was a horrific experience and there had been many heroes, not least Sir Edmund Mortimer himself who had insisted that his wife and children had the food allocated to him. Gwenllian, informed of the siege through Iolo, felt desperate to help them in some way. She wished that she could somehow take food to them but knew that there was no hope of getting anything into the castle. She also, like the captives inside the castle, clung to the hope that it could be relieved at any time.

Then came the devastating news that Sir Edmund Mortimer had died from starvation at the besieged castle. After his death, those trapped inside the castle lived on hope only with very little food to nourish them. The following year, it became apparent to most observers that the end of the rebellion was near when Harlech castle fell. Glyndŵr's wife Margaret, his daughter Catherine and three of his granddaughters were captured and taken to the Tower of London. It was generally believed that it was now only a matter of time before Glyndŵr himself would be captured, placed on trial and executed. Gwenllian was very upset and deeply worried for her father. She could see that to all intents and purposes the rebellion was over and it was now a matter of managing the defeat. Iolo now only rarely mentioned Glyndŵr on his visits to Cenarth and had reverted to writing poems about hunting and good ale again.

The years 1410 to 1415 passed with only a few minor incidents in Wales and it was clear that Glyndŵr and a few rebels had not given up on their mission. Gruffydd, his son, captured at the battle of Pwll Melyn, died in the Tower of London. Meredydd stood by his father throughout these years as did Philip and Gwenllian. If there was a rebel to be hidden, nursed back to health or needing a bed for the night then the Cenarth family did all they could to help and did so with enthusiasm. But it had to be said that life at Cenarth had returned to its happy and tranquil state with the weekly visits to market, hunting and revelry with the poets.

There were many sightings of Glyndŵr during this period. Many claimed that they knew where he was hiding but, in truth, nobody knew except for a small band of about half a dozen people. These were members of his family and his closest advisers; by 1415, probably the only person who knew where he would be at any one time was Meredydd. He moved from place to place: sometimes at Cenarth, sometimes with his daughter Alice at Kentchurch and occasionally he would call with a trusted friend here and there. Other times he would spend periods in the wild mountains of the north but there were always agents of the king looking for him and others willing to inform on him. He attempted to contact various supporters with the hope of regaining the glory days but there was no hope.

Glyndŵr and Meredydd had to be alert all the time and constantly on the move, sometimes they would be dressed as shepherds, other times as monks. It was a difficult time: one slip and they would be caught.

Gwenllian noticed that her father was ageing fast and she was getting more worried about him as time passed. By wearing a monk's habit he was not easily recognised and the fact that his beard was severely trimmed also helped him to avoid capture. It was getting more difficult for him to walk everywhere but there were no alternatives and she wondered for how long his luck would last.

By 1415, there were offers of a pardon made to both Glyndŵr and Meredydd but neither accepted. Gwenllian was pleased about this, though she knew that a pardon would resolve the difficult time. If Glyndŵr accepted a pardon it would not be right by those rebels whom he had led and who had lost their lives. To keep his image he would have to struggle on. Also, he, himself, was convinced that things would favour him again. Whenever he was at Cenarth he would mention that he regretted the fact that he and his army had not been at Shrewsbury to help Hotspur in the battle against King Henry IV instead of being near Carmarthen. If only they, with the French, had fought the king at Worcester, but it was now all in the past.

As the summer of 1415 approached life for Glyndŵr and Meredydd was becoming increasingly difficult with fewer safe places available for them to stay. The king was preparing for an expedition to France and Glyndŵr's daughters' homes were under constant observation by his agents. Father and son called frequently at Cenarth and were always made welcome there at Gwenllian's beautiful and isolated farmstead, though they never stayed for long, any more than they stayed anywhere else for long.

Their visits were never planned; they would just arrive, usually in the late evening as the light was fading and though not expected they were always welcomed. Gwenllian and Philip did offer them, on more than one occasion, a permanent place for them to stay at Cenarth but they both felt it was too risky for the family and themselves.

One day in the early autumn of 1415, Meredydd arrived on his own at Cenarth just after dawn. The leaves were beginning to lose their green colour, mist was covering the surface of the pool below Cenarth and the crows were signalling in their high trees that dawn had broken. Cenarth was awake but in the process of energising itself for the day ahead.

Meredydd, dressed as a Franciscan monk, had a concerned and sad look on his face as he entered the house calling Gwenllian's name. Philip and Gwenllian were the only people in the house, with the boys having already gone to see to their tasks and Beth had finished her first round of duties and had gone to help with the stock.

At first they were both pleased to see Meredydd but they were shocked at his early arrival which suggested that he had spent the night nearby, or that he had travelled during the hours of darkness, which was unlikely unless there was something very pressing on his mind. When they saw the distress he was in they quickly realised that there was a cause for concern.

Meredydd, as was his way, quickly came to the point and said, "My father has died near Nanerth late last night," he announced. "We were on our way to see the family in Gwent and Hereford and I was going to come as far as here with him and hoped that Rhys or Dafydd would go with him some of the way south. As we were coming down the hill near Nanerth his foot slipped, he lost his balance, fell and hit his head on a rock. He never regained consciousness and died about an hour later."

His tale was met by a stunned silence. He then added, "I came straight here. Thank God we were so close to you. I am at a loss as to what to do."

Gwenllian and Philip were visibly shocked and Gwenllian started to cry. Philip, while comforting her, asked Meredydd, "Are you sure that he has passed away?"

"Yes, I have seen too many dead people of all ages not to be sure. I was hopeful for a long while but there is no doubt."

While the two men were wondering what to do next, Gwenllian was firm, "The first thing is to get him here and off the mountain."

Meredydd swallowed a mouthful of warm mead given him by Gwenllian and said, "I have dragged him off the track and placed him behind a rocky outcrop. No one can see him from the track. I agree with Gwenllian – if we can bring him here it would give us time to think."

Philip, who by now also had a cup of warm mead in his hand said, "Of course he comes here, but we need to keep it between us for a while to give us time to plan what to do after he's here. We need the oxen and the cart made ready with some straw in it. I will go and see to it and I won't tell the boys yet. I will go with Meredydd to bring him here.

Gwenllian, you can tell the boys and prepare them. Beth is trustworthy but it might be best not to tell her anything for a while. Tell her it's a monk who has died and we are helping with the body."

Gwenllian agreed and said, "While you are away I will prepare the outhouse to receive him... No! He shall come into the hall. I will prepare a place for him. I will let everyone think, except the boys, that it's a monk who has died on the mountain and that you have gone to fetch the body here."

"Take another drink of mead before you go," she told them both but they were too keen to get away and within a short time Philip and Meredydd were on their way to collect Owain Glyndŵr's body.

They returned in the afternoon and placed Glyndŵr's body in a place in the hall prepared by Gwenllian. She had arranged for the boys to take their turn, two at a time, to stand guard over the body in a way that a prince's body should be honoured. Rhys and Dafydd took the first duty. The two boys stood tall either side of their grandfather's body with their hands resting on the hilt of their drawn swords with the pointed ends resting on the floor by their feet. They were relieved in time by their younger brothers, Meredydd and Owain, who took up identical positions.

Philip, Gwenllian and Meredydd gathered on their own, at the other end of the hall, to discuss what to do next. They had to decide who to inform and where to bury Glyndŵr's body.

They would have to get a message to their sister Alice, whose husband, John Scudamore, was now in France with Henry V fighting the French. There was talk amongst the poets that there was going to be a big battle in France soon.

Their other sisters Janet Monnington and Margaret at Croft Castle would need to be told as soon as possible. Apart from these people, most of Glyndŵr's family were dead. Margaret his wife, Catherine his daughter and her children had died in the Tower of London as had his son Gruffydd.

Meredydd said he had thought of a burial on the mountain and placing a stone on the grave but Gwenllian was adamant that her father should have a proper burial and in consecrated ground. The men were not sure how this could be achieved and were more inclined to find somewhere on the Cenarth estate or perhaps in the churchyard of St Garmon's church. They argued that there was no greater hero in Welsh history than Garmon and it would be fitting to bury a prince of Wales in a church dedicated to him.

Gwenllian made it clear that she wanted her father to be buried with the appropriate ceremony, but Meredydd was very uncertain, knowing that the support for his father had waned and that there were too many enemies and spies in the country to allow any formal ceremony.

"Assuming that we could have him buried in one of the cathedral churches, his enemies would have him dug up soon enough and have his head on London Bridge just as they did with Llywelyn. No, Gwenllian, we must do this in secret, the fewer who know the better. You can't trust many these days," said Meredydd.

Gwenllian persisted, "He was a prince and should be buried in consecrated ground."

Philip was keen on his own original suggestion and asked, "What about the church in St Garmon?"

"He was more important a person than to be buried in an ordinary church, even if it is dedicated to St Garmon," said Gwenllian. "I believe he should be buried in one of our main religious houses with an appropriate memorial over his grave."

Meredydd, who was only too well aware of the impossibility of having a memorial above Glyndŵr's grave argued that such an idea was impractical under the circumstances in Wales now and that the burial would have to be in secret otherwise he would be dug up. Meredydd also pointed out that the situation had been a concern for him for a while, ever since he had seen the revolt waning and his father becoming frail.

Gwenllian claimed, "Look at how the English bury their kings and all of our other great princes have had decent burial in consecrated grounds. Think of Owain Gwynedd in the cathedral at Bangor, Llywelyn Fawr at Aberconwy, Rhys the prince of Dyfed at Ystrad Fflur. We must have him buried in an appropriate place befitting his status."

"But how, Gwenllian? We need to be practical," appealed Philip.

"Yes," said Meredydd, adding, "The cooperation of the religious authorities would be essential and we will have difficulties in achieving that."

Gwenllian persisted, "Ideally he should be buried at the cathedral in St Asaph or even the abbey of Valle Crucis where his great-grandfather was buried with a similarly decorated coffin lid."

Meredydd explained, "Well, that can't happen, Gwenllian, because the bishop of St Asaph is Robert of Lancaster and he lives at Valle Crucis Abbey. The king replaced Bishop John Trefor, if you recall, because he was so supportive of my father. Robert of Lancaster is not to be trusted and is against our cause. Also, the king has a group of men at arms in Bala and it would be difficult to get to our homeland without going through or near Bala. With so many spies about and the way people talk we could be caught on the long journey which would put all our lives at risk and I can tell you dad's head would be on a pole in London within days."

Philip added, "Ystrad Fflur is out of the question because there are English men at arms stationed there and the monks who supported your father have been sent from there."

"What about Abbey Cwm Hir?" asked Gwenllian. "After all Llywelyn's body is buried there. Why did I not think of that earlier? I should have thought of it first. I see Pistill y Geiniog Hill above Prysgduon everyday, where Llywelyn's men stopped to wash his blood off their hands after they had buried him at Cwm Hir. Surely, if Llywelyn is at Cwm Hir why not Glyndŵr?" She sounded triumphant. She was delighted that she had found an answer that would satisfy all her wishes.

Philip thought for a second and said, "It certainly has the advantage of being very near."

"I am sorry to have brought this on you but I didn't know where else to go," said Meredydd.

Gwenllian replied immediately, "If he had died anywhere in mid Wales from Cadair Idris, Plumlymon down to Meilienydd and Brecon Beacons under the circumstances you would surely have come here. Where else could you go?"

Philip was of the same opinion, "Yes, Beth told me yesterday that when she came back from seeing her mother in Hay that there is talk that the border area is being watched and particularly Scudamore's place and Croft Castle."

"Also, Alice, Janet and Margaret have been very welcoming and helpful to dad in the past but their marriages are in effect illegal in the eyes of the king and so all three are vulnerable," Meredydd added. "At the moment the king's main ambition is to beat the French and so he is willing to turn a blind eye to their marriages in order to get their support for his French adventures."

"With Sir John Scudamore away in France since August they must feel very vulnerable I should imagine and would not wish to be involved," said Gwenllian, strengthening her case.

Meredydd went some way to agreeing with her, "Sir John, though probably the most vulnerable in the southern border area, is the one who has been most supportive to dad and the cause. As I said, you can't trust anyone north of Cadair Idris and Welshpool between the spies and the fact that the people are poor and are now easily bought by Henry's agents. The west is even worse with so many of Henry's men stationed in Ystrad Fflur. You and Philip are the only ones I could count on between Bala and Brecon."

"What about Cwm Hir, then – is it possible?" asked Gwenllian.

After a few moments of silence Philip summed up the position, "The abbot of Ystrad Fflur has, I understand, gone to Cwm Hir after being kicked out of Ystrad Fflur. Also, some of the monks sympathetic to your father who were also removed from Ystrad Fflur went first to Cymer Abbey but there were – and still are – some of King Henry's men at Cymer and the Welsh monks had no option other than to come to Cwm Hir. Since Mortimer's death there has been little interest shown in Cwm Hir Abbey and the place has declined. I would think that cooperation with Cwm Hir, in one way or other, is a possibility."

Gwenllian was encouraged and Philip continued, "If you wish I will go to the abbey tomorrow and sound them out. Do you think we should just say that a monk was found dead on the mountain and ask if he can he be buried in the abbey or do we say who it is?"

Meredydd asked, "Does the abbot know who you are, Gwenllian?"

Gwenllian replied, "Yes, I think so."

"I will of course give them a good supply of the best mead in the area. We had a very good yield last year and our mead is now far better than theirs and they know it," added Philip.

Meredydd was unsure and asked, "If the abbot knows who you are, they may work out who we are burying and if not immediately then soon afterwards. The story could get out quickly and there is always the danger that agents could force their way into the abbey and take the body away. They have no respect for anything."

Gwenllian was getting keen on the idea and said, "If we disguise dad as a monk, how can we bury his sword and shield with him like befits a true prince?"

Philip asked with some concern, "Do we have to bury the sword and shield with him? Llywelyn was not buried with his sword and shield."

"How do you know?" asked Gwenllian.

Meredydd replied to her question, "I think Philip is right. The main thing is to get a decent burial in consecrated ground. We could put a wooden cross with him in the grave: I've heard that is what they did with Llywelyn. That would have the advantage of fitting well with the burial of a monk."

Gwenllian was enthusiastic now and asked, "Are we all agreed that we try Cwm Hir then and, if so, it has to be at dusk so that the disguise will be more effective?"

They were all agreed to try Cwm Hir. Gwenllian was still keen on having his sword and shield buried with him but kept her counsel and was thinking she would perhaps be able to somehow involve her boys.

Philip asked, "Is it not a little ironic that Owain Glyndŵr would be buried in an abbey that he had attacked and severely damaged? Also, it is a place that brought us at Cenarth a great deal of sorrow."

"I can only talk about my father's view of Cwm Hir," said Meredydd. "I was there at the time. My father was furious with Mortimer then because of his continuous deceitful behaviour. We never thought then that Mortimer would be such a good ally to our cause. At the time Sir Edmund Mortimer was against us and also the majority of the monks at Cwm Hir were English spies who were informing Mortimer and the king about dad's movements in Powys. The damage was not as extensive as was reported. It was made more of by Mortimer and his agents for effect and to try to balance against the damage done at Ystrad Fflur and Cymer by the king's forces earlier. We left the place having made our presence felt, but nothing more. I've heard that the monks have since allowed parts of the old abbey go to a poor state because they are too fond of their mead."

Gwenllian expressed her views regarding what had happened to Rhys there by saying, "The men who kidnapped Rhys are all dead, including the old abbot who, according to Beth died, only a few days ago. So, I have no problem with Cwm Hir being my father's last resting place. In any case, I don't think we have many options."

Meredydd commented, "Dad knew that his burial would be a difficulty for his children and did not wish his head paraded anywhere and that's why we had the false burial in Llanrhaeadr-ym-Mochnant a while back. It took some of the pressure off him because some were fooled. I hear that Adam of Usk has swallowed the story and is already unknowingly spreading false information which will be useful in distracting attention from mid Wales. It would also be worthwhile involving the Hereford families but we shouldn't let them know exactly where he has been buried but we should ask them to let it be known that he died in, say Kentchurch, and buried locally there. It would help to create confusion over where he is buried and draw attention away from you here at Cenarth and Cwm Hir. The Hereford families would not want dad's head paraded and they will say what is needed to their local poets."

The next task then was for Philip and Gwenllian to go to the abbey in the morning and talk to the abbot. They felt that the abbey owed them a favour after what had happened to Rhys.

# Chapter 22

P HILIP AND GWENLLIAN left early in the morning to meet
the abbot. The journey gave them time to put details
on what they were going to tell him. Philip was taken into
the abbot's room but Gwenllian stayed outside and had a
good look around the outside of the building. She found
it difficult to believe the part this place had played in her
life. How could such a tranquil place have caused her such
grief? Of course it was not the abbey, it was not the belfry,
it was not the gardens that had caused her to suffer – it was
the individuals and not least the corrupt abbot who had
died recently and was supposedly buried inside the abbey.
However, looking around she thought this was an excellent
place to bury her father and a prince of his country.

Philip had taken gifts for the abbot, which included
the best produce of Cenarth. He told the abbot that a
Franciscan monk had died on the mountain track linking
Ystrad Fflur to Cwm Hir and that the body had been found
by a Cenarth shepherd. He speculated that the dead monk
must have lost his way in the mist, gone too far north and
a combination of a fall, lack of food and the cold had killed
him. He further told the abbot that, by the looks of him,
the dead monk was in his sixties and had not been in a good
state of health.

The abbot was more interested in the gifts from Philip
than he was in the dead monk. Though of Welsh extraction,
he was neutral on the revolt and so had kept his position
at the abbey safe over the past few years. The abbot agreed
to the burial over a cup of Philip's mead but stated that the

abbey did not have the means of bringing the body to the abbey. Philip told him that he would arrange the transport of the body and the abbot agreed that he would see to it that a grave was prepared immediately for the monk in the abbey's unknown person's section. Philip was quietly delighted with this and bid the abbot well and left, saying that he would be back later in the day with the body.

Gwenllian and Philip returned to Cenarth and immediately set things in motion for another visit to the abbey with Glyndŵr's body.

The funeral cortege left Cenarth without fuss late in the afternoon with the intention of arriving at the abbey as it was getting dark. A mist had settled in the valley just before they started on the journey which suited them well. Glyndŵr had been dressed in military style and Gwenllian had insisted that his sword and shield, which he was never without, were included with him in the makeshift wooden coffin. The coffin was placed in a cart driven by Philip and with Gwenllian, dressed in the Franciscan habit worn by her father, sitting in the cart with her father's coffin. Meredydd and the four boys followed on their own horses at a discreet distance. Both parts of the cortege progressed slowly and carefully to Cwm Hir Abbey.

The first part of the cortege arrived at the abbey as daylight was fading and was met by a monk with the hood of his habit covering his head leaving much of his face in darkness. He was a person of few words but introduced himself as Brother Gregory and said that the abbot had been taken ill but had given him instructions on what was necessary for the burial of the dead monk. Gregory had a large beard, which made him look venerable and Gwenllian felt he suited the occasion. In fact, she preferred the ceremony to be conducted by this monk rather than the abbot, who was more likely to be drunk on their mead than ill. To explain Gwenllian's presence in the Franciscan habit, Philip explained that they had picked up a mute Franciscan monk on the way who would like to attend the funeral. The boys and Meredydd arrived in time to help with the coffin. Philip claimed that they were there to help because he could not lift any weight since he had injured his shoulder.

They unloaded the coffin and with Meredydd taking the head and Glyndŵr's four grandsons, two supporting either side, they moved into the abbey grounds. Gwenllian was tearful under the hood of her habit. Brother Gregory told them that the abbey monks had opened the grave ready for the internment just outside the cloister but that they would have a brief service in the abbey first since the deceased was obviously a religious man. Gwenllian was relatively happy with the location and felt that the setting was suitable from what she remembered from her earlier visit that day. Brother Gregory, who was in charge of the funeral, led them into the abbey church, where another monk carrying a heavy cross upright in front of his face joined them. Brother Gregory prepared himself to say a few words in Latin over the coffin in the abbey church.

Gwenllian kept close to the coffin throughout but when it came to Gregory saying the benediction in Latin she moved back a little to observe the ceremony and take in the magnitude of the occasion. Once Gregory had completed what he had to say they adjusted their positions with the intention of moving in a procession towards the door to take the coffin to the grave. Gwenllian was clearly pleased with the influence she had on the funeral arrangements but she was not relaxed and kept a close eye on the proceedings.

Brother Gregory indicated that they would move out to the grave for the internment.

As they were moving past Gwenllian, she suddenly and without prior warning to anyone present grabbed the heavy cross from the attending monk, heaved it from his hands and promptly hit Brother Gregory on his hooded head with great fury and force, causing him to fall down like a sack of turnips. Everybody was dumbstruck, assuming that Gwenllian had lost her senses.

But Gwenllian was shouting, pointing at the monk whose cross she had used on Brother Gregory's head, "Get that man – he is Lambert and this one I have hit is Cynwrig."

The coffin was put down by the bearers but by then Philip was at Lambert's throat pushing him to the ground with immense strength and anger causing him to strike his head on the hard slab floor. There was a sharp cracking noise and everyone there knew that it was not the slab cracking. Lambert's skull was split. His convulsions lasted for a minute or two and then there was perfect stillness.

Philip turned to Brother Gregory on the floor. His hood had flopped off his head and more of his face could be seen. Dafydd supported his mother immediately as young boys do and stated that Gregory was in fact Cynwrig though he was too young to remember him at Cenarth. It was clear that Philip was uncertain in the dim light of the abbey as to the identity of the corpse. However, Rhys knew Cynwrig best and had no hesitation in identifying the prostrate body as that of Cynwrig and said in a matter of fact way, "That is Cynwrig. Mam, you have killed him."

There was finality about the two statements. They had found Cynwrig at last. Philip and Gwenllian were delighted. Gwenllian wondered what he and Lambert were doing in

Cwm Hir Abbey and concluded correctly that they had probably been there for some time keeping an eye on what was happening at Cenarth. The king would have liked to have settled the Glyndŵr issue before embarking on his war in France and would no doubt be paying agents to check what was going on at Cenarth. He might have suspected that Glyndŵr was living there at times during the past few years and who better to do the job than Cynwrig who knew more about them than anyone.

There was no time to dwell long on anything: there was a funeral to be completed. Rhys and Dafydd dragged the two dead agents into a dark corner of the church. Glyndŵr's coffin was taken to the open grave and lowered with the ropes provided. It was a surprisingly deep grave so they intended presumably to bury more monks in the same grave. This did not please Gwenllian but she said nothing.

Meredydd and Gwenllian, as the leading mourners, turned to Philip and asked him if he could say a few words above the coffin in the grave. Philip nodded to indicate that he would.

Philip bowed his head and clasped his hands together in front of his body, interlocking his fingers and said in a clear voice, "This was a brave and courageous soldier of noble birth, this was a leader of determination, this was a statesman of foresight. He led his country against all odds. He established a parliament for his country, he told us that we needed an independent church and a university where our children could learn to do great things. He gave us hope. What he could do for us, he did."

"We will be eternally grateful to this great man."

Gwenllian and Meredydd together and instinctively said, "Amen."

The ropes were then withdrawn and they threw some

soil on to the coffin until its lid was just covered. The initial intention was to leave the closing of the grave to the monks but in view of what had happened it was agreed that they had better finish filling in the grave themselves and not leave it for the monks to do. Philip picked up a spade full of soil to start the heavy work, when Gwenllian said, "I do not want anyone to know where my father's grave is in this abbey. I do not trust them not to tell anyone. I want him to rest in peace."

Meredydd said, "When we were in the church I saw that the old abbot's coffin had been interned on the south side and I could see that the main slab had only recently been closed on it. What about taking the slabs off the old abbot's coffin and putting my father in there and the old abbot in the grave intended for my father?"

There was general agreement that this was an excellent idea.

Philip had some doubts and queried, "Have we got enough time to do it?"

Gwenllian said that she could do her part, and her boys, of course, were all immediately supportive of the idea, saying that there would be no need for her to do anything – they could do it all.

Meredydd went to help Rhys and Dafydd open the old abbot's resting place. The slabs were loose because they had only recently been installed and they were removed quietly and quickly. Meredydd, seeing that the inside job was completed, went outside to check on progress there.

Outside, the two young lads had been in the grave lifting the coffin high enough to get the ropes under it so that it could be lifted out of the grave. Philip and Meredydd took the strain and the two lads got their hands under it and lifted it high enough to get the ropes back under it. The coffin was out quickly and taken into the church. It was placed in the space that had just been vacated by the old abbot's coffin and the slabs replaced by Rhys and Dafydd.

The old abbot's coffin was taken to the outside grave by Meredydd, Philip and his two younger sons and lowered with little ceremony into the grave.

They were about to start filling it in when young Owain asked, "What are we going to do with the other two monks?"

Philip went back inside to check on progress there. All the slabs were back in place over Glyndŵr's coffin and the two dead agents were lying just out of sight.

Philip came out and said, "They are all finished in there but Owain is right. We must think what to do with those two dead monks."

Gwenllian had a ready answer. "Put them in with the old abbot, they are all of a kind," she said.

No sooner said than done and the soil was quickly thrown in on top of them using the spades.

Philip was confident that Cynwrig and Lambert would never be found and would not be missed at the abbey. If they were, the monks would be too lazy to go and look for them.

They returned to Glyndŵr's new grave and stood near it for a few seconds and Gwenllian said, "If we are successful no one will ever know where this true prince of Wales is buried. I don't like the thought of that because people will forget what he achieved."

"Don't worry, Gwenllian," said Meredydd. "No one knows where Arthur is buried either but he has not been forgotten."

The men turned away from the grave and walked towards the door quietly but Gwenllian stayed a few seconds. She was pleased that her father, Owain Glyndŵr, had been buried in the presence of his family. As she was turning to leave her father's grave, she said quietly, "Rest in peace and may your grave, like King Arthur's, never be found."

They all returned to Cenarth safely. Gwenllian, her family and Cenarth flourished. She visited the abbey at Cwm Hir occasionally on the pretext of buying or selling produce. She was a good mother to her boys, a good wife to Philip and was a loyal daughter to her father. She was also a woman of great spirit and determination.

Meredydd stayed the night and left for Llanidloes and the north at dawn. After a little over an hour he was through Llanidloes and up into the hills again. Soon he would be able to see Cadair Idris in the distance, leaving his father, Owain Glyndŵr, buried at Cwm Hir Abbey at dusk in the dark season of the autumn of 1415.

*Glyndŵr's Daughter* is just one of a whole range of publications from Y Lolfa. For a full list of books currently in print, send now for your free copy of our new full-colour catalogue. Or simply surf into our website

## www.ylolfa.com

for secure on-line ordering.

TALYBONT CEREDIGION CYMRU SY24 5HE
*e-mail* ylolfa@ylolfa.com
*website* www.ylolfa.com
*phone* (01970) 832 304
*fax* 832 782